# SPUR DOUBLE EDITION!

## TWICE THE SHOOTIN', TWICE THE LOVIN' FOR ONE LOW PRICE!

## TEXAS TART

"Galloway, a word of warning. Your men in town tried to backshoot me the way they did the last three of four sheriffs. It didn't work. You better put the word out. If anybody tries to gun me down again, from the front or the back, I'll get a hundred men out here and blast you and your people straight to hell."

Spur turned his horse around and the posse pounded along behind him. Far behind the galloping horses, a pistol went off, but Spur didn't bother to look around.

## THE MINER'S MOLL

"Quiet, girl!" Spur said. "We're here to help you."

He holstered his weapon and quietly ran down the stairs.

"Come on!" McCoy yelled to Kincaid and the girl.

The three of them hurried down the stairs. Spur surveyed the scene as they descended into the saloon.

"Hey!" a lean cowboy shouted, staring at the trio. "They're taking away the new girl!"

Spur crashed through two sodden men. He and Kincaid rushed toward the door, fighting through the angry drunks bent on keeping the new girl at their disposal.

Suddenly, Spur saw a knife slicing through the air toward them.

# SPUR

## TEXAS TART

## THE MINER'S MOLL

### Dirk Fletcher

**LEISURE BOOKS**  **NEW YORK CITY**

A LEISURE BOOK®

February 1995

Published by

Dorchester Publishing Co., Inc.
276 Fifth Avenue
New York, NY 10001

Printed in the United States of America.

# SPUR

## TEXAS TART

# CHAPTER ONE

*June 4, 1873*

*Ulysses S. Grant began his second term as President of the United States on March 3, 1873. His vice president was Henry Wilson. Aberdeen-Angus cattle were first imported to the U.S. in that year by George Grant to his ranch at Victoria, Kansas. Celluloid was patented on January 14; this was also the year the earmuff was invented. The first post card was issued in May, and the first cable car went into service in San Francisco. Barbed wire, the beginning of the end of the old west, was invented in De Kalb, Illinois. In September of this year, a series of bank failures occurred, plunging the nation into a five year depression.*

They came out of the west, with the sun behind them so anyone in the ranch house would have to stare directly into the golden orb which was almost ready to set over the dry, windswept Texas prairie.

It had been hot all week. The two hands of the Flying R ranch sat at the kitchen table with the family having an early supper. Matt Rogers, who owned the spread, had not returned from his ride to the lower pasture to check on the steer that was down near the Clear River.

The first anyone knew of trouble came when the faint snap of a rifle shot and the scream of the big dog outside penetrated the clapboard house.

Luke tipped over his chair in his haste to get to the window. "Damn, it's Smoky! He's been shot, sure as hell!" Luke grabbed the rifle from the pegs above the kitchen fireplace and raced outside. The minute he opened and took a step into the sunshine, two rifle slugs slammed into his chest, driving him partway back into the two-story ranch house. He groaned once, tried to sit up and then fell on the steps, dead.

Jeremy, the other hand, had jumped to the window, his .44 out of leather as he stared through the wavy pane.

"Don't see no one, Miz Rogers! They killed Luke for sure. You get down on the floor—you kids, too! Them guys out there is killers and they don't care who they shoot. I heard about raw-hiders like this just after the war."

Gloria Rogers was not one to stay on the floor.

She had shoulder-length red hair and a flaming anger to match. Her first thought was of Matt. Had they found him before they came here? She had been raised on the edge of the frontier, in the early days before Texas was a state. She could use a rifle as well as the hands could, but now their only rifle was outside on the steps.

She took a six-gun from a kitchen drawer and checked the loads, then ran to the bedroom window. Through the curtain she saw a face. She aimed carefully and fired. Gloria shivered as the gun went off, but she saw the bullet shatter the glass, and tear into the side of the face there. The scream came almost at once, and three rounds blasted through the window frame. She dropped to the floor, unhurt.

It seemed to be a signal. Guns spoke from all around the house, smashing every window, forcing the people inside to seek whatever cover was available.

Upstairs in the bedroom, Vicky Sue, 13, cried softly to herself as she wormed farther under the bed, her hands over her ears. She was tall for thirteen, well developed and with her mother's dark red hair. Now she cried with a hint of hysteria. She had never seen a man killed before. First Luke was trying to protect them, then the next second he lay in a heap on the porch, dead and gone forever. Forever!

Her brother, Will, twelve years old, had gone under the bed too, but now he crawled out and peeked through the side of the window. A pistol shot barked and the slug sailed through the broken window and hit the far wall. Will ducked back. He was twelve.

"Wish I had a gun! Pa promised to teach me to shoot."

Downstairs, Jeremy saw one of the attackers run from the outhouse to the well. There was no chance for a shot. He had to save his rounds for the time they came closer. Rifle rounds pounded into the window frame and through it regularly. Jeremy couldn't spot the shooter. There had to be four, maybe five. He had heard Mrs. Rogers shoot in back. He prayed that she had reduced the odds a little.

They came in like rawhiders. Human life to them meant less than stepping on a bug in the dirt. The man at the well moved again, running for the front door. Jeremy let him come. At thirty feet, Jeremy fired twice with his .44, saw the man go down, roll and dart back to the well, holding his shoulder.

Jeremy knew the odds were poor. If the attackers couldn't shoot them out, they would burn them out. That always worked. So it probably wasn't Galloway and his Circle G Ranch riders. If he ran them off, as he had threatened to do so often, he'd want the buildings to use as a line spread.

Six more rounds blasted into the house, through the open kitchen door and the broken window; then all was quiet.

A voice rumbled at them from the well.

"You inside! We just want the other man in there. You send him out and we won't hurt the rest of you."

Jeremy answered with a round through the window. The moment his gun showed, four guns barked and one of the slugs smashed into his hand, tearing off a finger, mashing his palm before the round exited out of his wrist. He fell to the floor and couldn't stop a wail of pain and anger.

The firing outside increased to a roar, then suddenly stopped and someone stormed through the kitchen door, six-guns in both hands. He was a Mexican, and had a knife between his teeth. He saw Jeremy on the floor and shot him in the shoulder, then in his other hand.

As he fired the second time, Gloria Rogers crept around the hall and stepped into the kitchen. She shot the attacker from six feet away, blowing his right eye back into his brain, splattering blood and tissue on the wall and driving him into Hell in a half-second.

She picked up one of his dropped guns and pressed hard against the wall beside the kitchen door. Her face was a mask of determination and terror. Gloria heard someone outside, boots scraping on the dry ground. She tensed, her eyes flared wide and she shivered. Both the six-guns had triggers cocked, ready to blast.

But before she was set, a form rushed through the door, jammed it hard open against the wall and aimed a sawed-off shotgun at Gloria. Her finger tensed, then pulled. The shot went wild and the man hit her in the stomach with the barrel of the scattergun before she could fire again. She cried out softly, the revolvers dropping from her hands as she doubled over on the floor. She retched against the wall, then painfully sat up and stared at the man.

He was tall, blonde, with a jagged scar on his cheek, above a full beard, and wore a black cape resembling a poncho. Dark brown eyes checked her from behind thick brows. He made sure Jeremy had no other weapons, then touched the dead man from his band who lay against the wall.

"Two men, they said there was two men here—nothing about a gun-toting fucker like you who can shoot! Christ, you killed Jose here and bloodied old Bill. Are there just two men here?"

Gloria started to say something, but Jeremy shouted louder with his harsh, pained voice.

"Yes, you bastard. You leave my wife alone. This is between you and me. What do you want?"

"Just to know that you're Rogers, and that you're a dead man."

"Who paid you?"

"Hell, you'll never know."

"Galloway?"

The tall man with the scar glanced up quickly. "Yeah. So what? You ain't telling anybody."

Jeremy got to his feet, careful not to touch anything with his hands. He staggered, then lunged at the gunman, who stepped aside and kicked him in the crotch. Jeremy went down, keening with pain.

"You gonna try anything else?"

Jeremy bit through his lip from the pain. Blood spilled down his chin, dripped to the wooden floor. He stood again and came toward the shotgun.

The sound of the twelve-gauge going off in the room deafened Gloria at once. She feared it had shattered her eardrums. Her eyes widened as she saw Jeremy's face disintegrate in front of her, the pellets from the shotgun tore into him from four feet away. The angry hot shot stripped most of the flesh from his face and skull, tore through the bone and splattered the back kitchen wall with his brain, hair and bone fragments. Gloria couldn't turn her head, just stared as though hypnotized.

She watched Jeremy jolt backwards and fall over the supper table, scattering the dinner, dumping over the good stew she had cooked.

When the body stopped moving, she looked back at the big man. He said something but she couldn't hear. She looked up as he lifted the shotgun again. He pointed it at the hallway.

Before he could fire, an arrow made from a cut cedar shingle shot through the space and sank deep into the gunman's forearm.

Her hearing came back in bits and pieces.

"Come . . . I see you, you little . . . Don't care if you are just a kid."

Will! She jumped up and ran at the man, oblivious of his gun. He turned and pushed her

11

down, then ran across the room and pulled Will back by his short brown hair.

"Outside, woman!" he yelled at her.

She heard. She could hear everything now. From upstairs the sound of crying came. Vicky Sue. They wouldn't hurt Vicky Sue, would they? Then she saw that Vicky Sue was already outside, under the cottonwood tree, sitting in the dust. Her face was tear-streaked. The big man threw Will down beside her.

Two more men came. One had a shot-up shoulder. He was small and weasely-looking. The third man was a Mexican, with black hair and a drooping black moustache.

"Now, what the hell we gonna do here?" the tall man with the shotgun said. "Here I got me two women, one young one . . ."

"She's just a child," Gloria shouted. "Only thirteen. Leave her be. Have me, take me, do anything you want, but leave her alone!"

The big man smiled, then shrugged. "Sounds good to me. Old Herman liked little boys, and we promised him one, but you took care of that at the back window. You killed two of my boys, Mrs. Rogers. Now strip, woman!"

"Inside, on the bed."

"Sounds fair."

He followed her inside, the shotgun at her back. She was hoping there might be a way to get the deadly gun away from him and use it.

"Strip."

She glared at him. If only she could get him

12

satisfied and gone before Matt got home. She had to!

Gloria pulled off her long dress quickly, then the chemise and cotton drawers that went to her knees, and her shoes. She stood in front of him, naked.

He looked her over as if she were a side of prime beef.

"Well, now—pretty face, lots of long red hair, and two tits, not the biggest I've seen. But any tit in a storm. Tiny waist and fucking good hips. Lay down."

She did, wishing she had fought him every step, clawing out his eyes, raking his face with her nails. But she hadn't. She heard Vicky Sue scream in the yard and ran to the window. One of the men had pulled her blouse off, showing her young breasts.

"You promised!" Gloria screamed.

"Hell, *I* promised. *They* didn't." He threw her down on the bed and she began to fight. He pushed her legs apart, held both her hands with one of his and bent down to her breasts.

She lay there like a corpse, trying to pretend this wasn't happening. Until right now, Matt Rogers was the only man who had ever seen her naked, even made love to her, and he would be the only one until the day she died. For just a moment she wondered if that would be today. No, probably not today. This beast was too hungry for a woman. She would satisfy him, make him ride on, give him all of the ranch's guns and food,

13

anything so he'd spare the lives of her husband and children.

He had opened his pants and his penis sprang out. She gasped when she saw the size of it, then tried not to show her astonishment. He laughed.

"Looks like you 'preciate my tool here, woman. Like it all the more when he's rammed up hard inside your tender little pussy."

He spread her legs farther and she shrieked as he tried to plunge dry into her. He swore, spit on his hand, and a moment later she cried out again as he rammed inside her until their pelvic bones smashed together.

She lay there like a rag doll as he pumped. She was saving the lives of her children and her husband. She was sure of it. Their two ranch hands were dead, but she would save the rest of them. Matt wouldn't be back for hours yet, and by then these three outlaws would be gone. She realized she might have to service all three, perhaps twice. But she could do it. It wasn't as if they were shooting her. It didn't hurt a body. The fancy ladies did it eight or ten times a night. She didn't blush thinking about them. Right now she had a lot more respect for them. He paid little attention to her reactions.

She knew he was close, then he began grunting and yelping and snorting and his hips jolted against hers hard six times and he went limp for a moment, then rolled away and out of her. He didn't bother to button his pants, just tucked himself inside and grabbed the shotgun.

Vicky Sue screamed.

Gloria leaped off the bed and raced to the window, the man close behind her. In the yard Gloria saw her thirteen-year-old daughter naked to the waist. Gloria knew Vicky Sue had been developing, but was surprised when she saw her bare breasts. The two men were caressing her. One held her struggling hands and the other kissed and chewed on her breasts.

"Make then stop, she's only a child!" Gloria cried.

The big man snorted. "*You* go out there and make them stop. They probably gambled to see who gets her maidenhead."

Gloria ran into the kitchen, then came back for her dress. She started to pull it on, but he stopped her.

"You want to stop them, go out bare-butt naked!"

She hesitated only a second, then ran, her breasts swinging, jolting. She slowed as she went out the door, then screamed at them, "Leave her alone! Take me instead!"

Vicky Sue looked at her mother, and tears poured down her cheeks. One of the men held her hands behind her back, while the other pulled down her skirt and was unbuttoning her drawers.

Gloria ran at the man on the ground and plowed into him, knocking him into the dirt, but spilling herself into the dust and chicken droppings. She tried to roll out of the way, but the man was on top of her. He wiped the dirt off her breasts.

"Well, now, this one first, that one second." His pants were already open, his erect penis pointing at her.

A scream came from behind Gloria. She half turned and saw Will running toward them. He was three steps away and swinging a four-foot-long two-by-four. It swished over her head and whacked into the man's side. A rib snapped and he cried out in fury.

Then he was off her, pulling a six-inch bladed knife from his boot and dancing toward Will. The boy swung the two-by-four again and missed. The man dove forward, slashing Will across the chest, then on one cheek. Before the boy could turn to run, the sharp blade bit into his neck, slicing his jugular vein.

Will's face went white.

Gloria shrieked.

Will dropped to his knees, then looked at his mother, trying to tell her he was sorry he hadn't protected her and Vicky Sue. Then he fell forward, his eyes glazed by the sharp scythe of death before his face burrowed into the Texas dust.

Gloria did not mourn the death of her second born. Automatically she defended what was left. She dashed to Vicky Sue, pulled her blouse on and buttoned it, then ran with her toward the house.

The Mexican who had been holding Vicky Sue was jolted out of his fascination with the knifing death. He had climaxed inside his pants when he saw the blood flow. It was the biggest sexual

16

thrill he had ever experienced. Then he was running, stopped the woman, and dragged them back to the shade under the old cottonwood tree.

Both the men took Gloria then. One held her and one raped her, then they changed places. She was sore and felt soiled and used, but she was alive, and so was Vicky Sue. Then they tied her hands and feet and made her watch as the younger man tore off Vicky Sue's clothes, cut them off when he could and left her cringing, crying and hysterical.

He slapped her twice, then sucked her tender nipples until they were red and swollen. He turned her over, spanked her and made her lie on her stomach as he parted her legs and took her from the rear, roaring with pent-up fury and rage as he did so.

Vicky Sue fainted.

The big man with the scar on his cheek glared at the other two men. "Enough," he said. "Tie her up, then let's get anything worth saving."

The three men worked for an hour taking harness, equipment and supplies from the house and barn, loading the loot on the light wagon and hitching up one of the mules. Then they roped the four horses in the corral and tied them together behind the wagon.

Vicky Sue came back to consciousness now and then, went into screaming hysterics, then passed out again.

Gloria watched it all in a kind of strange, foggy unreality. She saw what they were doing, but it didn't register. They were looting the place, then they would burn it to the ground. She wouldn't think beyond that . . .

When she looked up, the big man was staring down at her.

"Another time, another place," he said. "It might have been different with us." Then he shot her in the forehead, killing Gloria Rogers instantly.

He walked to the girl and shook his head. She would have been a beauty. He'd hoped to take her with them, but she was out of her mind. Wouldn't be good for anything, let alone educating into a great little whore. He sighed and shot Vicky Sue twice in the back of the head where she lay in the dirt.

Ten minutes later the house, all three outbuildings and the barn were burning. They rounded up the horses and drove the herd of 500 head of range beef to the north, as if they were heading for the Western Trail that led all the way to Dodge City Kansas and the railroad.

The big man with the scar smiled. They were two men short for the drive, but with luck they could handle the cattle all right. He could sell the critters to Galloway on top of the fee and he and his two men could take off a year and live it up in Fort Worth or Houston.

Fort Worth! Now *there* was a town!

# CHAPTER TWO

Spur McCoy sat in a leather chair in an office over the Texas Republic Bank, in the community of Clearwater, Texas. He had come in response to a call from the senior senator from Texas who had talked Spur's boss into assigning him to the mission. A small man in a vested suit with a gold chain extending from vest to pocket to vest pocket was striding from one window to another in the carpeted office, talking earnestly. He wore spectacles, had a fringe of dark hair around his balding head and squinted through the glasses at the three men seated in front of him.

"Sir, I say it is time to divest Doak Galloway of his title and his power and bring him down among the rest of the ordinary citizens of Galloway County. He's lived like a king of this county long enough. We need a sheriff who can stand up to him once and for all."

The other two men listening were middle-aged, one clean-shaven in work clothes, the other wearing an inexpensive black suit, white shirt and tie, and a full, closely trimmed beard.

"Sure, Victor. We know all that. We need another sheriff. How many we had in the last year —three, or was it four? Two quit before they got killed and the other two are buried out in the graveyard. This your next candidate?" The man turned and looked at Spur.

Victor nodded. "Gentlemen, let me introduce Spur McCoy, a lawman of top reputation. He was sent to us thorugh the good offices of our senior U.S. Senator John Foland. John said he would help, and he has. We got no cause to get the militia up here or the Texas Rangers. We have here a man who should be able to handle the problem. Mr. McCoy."

Spur stood up, feeling like a bug on a pin being examined by a pair of scientists. He wore the same clothes he'd had on when he hit town on the stage two hours ago—tan pants, brown shirt, leather vest and a string tie. One of the new Colt Peacemaker .45's hung from his right hip, the holster tied down low with a leather thong.

"Afternoon, gentlemen. Looks like it's up to me to put things straight here in Galloway county. Be my pleasure."

"Behind you! Draw!" the man in working clothes shouted.

Spur drew the Colt, palmed the trigger back to

20

full cock and spun with the weapon up and ready to fire. The elapsed time from shout to ready to fire to the rear was less than half a second.

Clint Bascomb reached in the pocket of his black suit and pulled our four cigars. He grinned. "Well, gentlemen, it looks like we have a fine candidate here. He's big, he looks tough and he can use his pistol."

"That don't keep nobody from being shot in the back," the man in working clothes said. His name was Rick Yettilow and he owned the livery stable and half the other stores in town. He was also a building contractor. "Remember the last two out of three sheriffs we had here was gunshot from the back."

Spur eased to one side until his back was against the wall. He still held the six-gun.

"Is your weapon broke, son?" Yettilow asked.

"No, sir."

"Trigger guard is gone in front."

"True. I can save half, maybe a third of a second by not having to find the trigger hole. I just slam my trigger finger back along the underside of the chamber housing, and the blamed thing goes off."

"Well, I'll be," Victor said. "Heard about doing that, never seen one."

"You a gunfighter, then, with a big rep?" Bascomb asked.

"No."

"The senator was a little vague about your background, just that you had been a lawman, wasn't wanted anywhere, and that you were the best man he could offer."

"I'll thank Senator Foland the next time I see him," Spur said.

"Hell, men, why all the chatter?" Victor said. "Let's just vote Spur McCoy here as our interim sheriff in Galloway County, until the next regularly scheduled election."

"So move," Bascomb said.

"Second."

Three hands raised on the "aye" vote. Spur had been unanimously elected the new sheriff of Galloway County.

"Do I have any deputies?" he asked.

"Budget allows for one, but we ain't had one in over a year. Last one got himself gutshot." It was Bascomb who provided the history.

A half hour later, Spur had moved into the sheriff's office and jail. There were two cells that looked sturdy enough. The small front room was divided by a three foot high barrier of polished wood railing. The rolltop desk behind the railing was open, a few wanted posters on top. In the gun rack on the wall stood three rifles; a Spencer repeater, an old Sharps and one of the new Winchester .44 Carbines. In another rack he found a pair of 12 gauge, double-barreled, sawed-off shotguns.

He found a wood saw and cut twelve inches off the shotgun's wooden stock, leaving just enough room for both his hands behind the trigger guard. Then he went next door to the mercantile, borrowed a hacksaw and cut two feet off the metal barrel and the wooden stock underneath. He hefted it. Wicked. The 12 gauge would throw buckshot in a twenty-foot-wide pattern not more than ten feet from the end of the barrel. Nobody in his right mind would argue with that weapon. He carried it in one hand as he made a circuit of the little town.

Main Street in Clearwater was two blocks long. Businesses were grouped in the first block, with newer stores in the next one on both sides. There were four saloons and gambling halls—not bad for a Texas town. The blacksmith shop was the biggest and best Spur had seen for a while. Three farriers worked over the horses' hooves and two more men pounded iron red hot out of the forges.

Spur had pinned the star on and decided he wanted to get the first confrontation over as quickly as possible, then find out who he had to work on and how to satisfy the instructions of his assignment.

General Wilton D. Halleck in Washington, D.C., the number two man in the United States Secret Service, had wired Spur his orders. McCoy was based in the Secret Service office in St. Louis, and had the entire western half of the United States as his territory. The orders told him to proceed by the fastest available means to Clearwater, Texas, about 130 miles west of Fort Worth, and to reinstate law and order in Galloway County. He was to do so with a minimum loss of life, and the least possible interruption of the normal business and commerce of the county.

Spur had snorted as he read that last sentence. It sounded like Senator Foland had dictated it. McCoy would do what had to be done. He was a big man, standing six-feet-two. The average man in this year of 1873 was a little over five-feet-nine. Spur was thirty-two years old and weighed an even 200 pounds. He had brownish hair with touches of red, a full moustache and mutton chop sideburns.

He was a master with pistol and rifle, in top physical condition and an expert hand-to-hand fighter with fists, knife or staff. He had been on the job as a Secret Service Agent for six years now. The agency had been first set up in 1865 by congress with William Wood as its first chief.

Spur had grown up in New York City where his father was a well known merchant and trader. Spur went to Harvard University and graduated at the age of twenty-four. After two years with his father's business, he joined the army with a commission as a second lieutenant, and advanced in the infantry to the rank of captain before he resigned his commission. He was then called to Washington to be senior aide to New York Senator Arthur B. Walton, a long time family friend.

After the Secret Service Act was passed, Spur was appointed one of the first agents. Since the Secret Service was one of only two federal law enforcement agencies at that time, it handled a wide range of problems, most far removed from its original task of preventing currency counter-feiting.

McCoy served six months in Washington before he was transferred to the St. Louis office because he was the man who could ride best. He had also won the service marksmanship shoot each year with both pistol and rifle. His boss figured Spur would need both skills when he took on the whole Wild West.

Spur paused in each of the saloons long enough for the citizens to get a look at him, and to let them see a sawed-off shotgun the likes of which they had never seen before. In effect, it became almost as easy to handle as a long-barreled pistol. In each of the saloons he heard the talk, then continued his rounds.

At the stores he stopped in and introduced himself. The owners shook his hand and told him to be careful.

The barber was the most direct.

"Last sheriff we had lasted only three days, and the guy who shot him said the next one wouldn't last three hours. Today is the day you need to watch your back."

Spur thanked him and said he would drop around the next day for a shave and haircut.

The barber pointed at the shotgun.

"Birdshot?"

"Double-ought buck. I aim to blow somebody into bits and pieces, not just tickle his butt with birdshot."

Spur had just come around the edge of the barbershop door when he heard two shots down the street. Two men stood in the middle of the street firing into the ground, forcing a Mexican boy to dance or lose a toe.

The new sheriff stood by the barber shop and checked the situation. Two roofs to the left were ideal for backshooters. The alley was close by on the right for front protection. He figured this was the setup for him. He loosened the six gun. He had put an extra round into the sixth chamber before he came out of the office, so with the shotgun he had eight shots. He would need them.

Spur took in the whole scene, evaluating, selecting the best protective spot. The hardware store had a blank wall right on the street. The alley was far enough away to make a risky pistol shot. Both the roof locations were awkward. And he would have his back against the hardware wall. No backshooting today.

He walked up the street casually. The sound of the pistols came again. He heard the laughter, then a scream of pain, and saw the two men reloading. Both were cowboy types, with slightly bowed legs, high heeled boots, jeans and faded blue shirts. Both had yellow tags hanging out of their pockets, indicating that a sack of Bull Durham was inside. Both men glanced at Spur from time to time, but not for long.

When Spur got to his selected spot against the hardware, he held the shotgun in his left hand, muzzle down, and used his best parade ground voice to bellow at the pair of rousters.

"That's about enough of that!" Spur roared at them. The noise in the street dropped to a whisper. "I said, that's enough of the gunplay. You two in the street with your guns out—listen. Lay the weapons on the ground, then walk over here."

The men stared at him, not believing his unexpected move.

"We just funning him," one called.

"Good. Put down the irons, both of you, and walk over here."

"What if we don't want to do that?" the taller of the two said. He wore a low crowned brown hat, and his face was pale and sallow though he was dressed like a cowboy, he looked as if he was seldom outside.

"Then you'll find yourself either eating lead, or spending ten days in jail."

"Not me, sheriff." The pale man stood, legs spread. Slowly he put his pistol back in the holster. "I just need me one round for the likes of you."

"Don't try it," Spur said.

As he spoke, Spur caught a flicker of movement in the darkness of the shadowed alley fifty feet to his right and across the street. He swept his glance upward without moving his head. One man on the roof, lying in the shadows.

Odds seemed about right—three to one.

"I aim to try it, Sheriff. Just you and me. My friend here is holstering and backing out of the play."

"If you're anxious to die, give me a try," Spur

said.

"We'll walk toward each other," the gunman said.

"I like it here," Spur countered. "You come ahead."

"You loco? It ain't done that way."

"Upset you, boy? You got legs. Use them, or put your iron on the ground!"

He shrugged. "Hell, you're dead anyway. I never miss. Here I come, asshole!"

He was sixty feet away. He wouldn't fire until thirty feet at the earliest. And his buddies in ambush couldn't fire until the man on the ground did, so the sound of his shot would cover theirs.

Spur waited, the shotgun still at his side, his finger on one trigger.

Fifty feet. Nothing happened.

Spur watched the shadows; they were moving, getting ready. He guessed the man in the alley would have a six-gun but there would be a rifle on the roof.

Forty feet.

"You getting ready to die, you stupid-ass sheriff? Ain't gonna ever be a sheriff in this county again!"

Thirty-five feet.

As the young man approached Spur, his face and figure took on detailed characteristics. Spur guessed he was about twenty-four or twenty-five. Overweight, waddling a little, face puffy, unhealthy-looking. Then Spur saw the telltale facial movement a lot of gunmen use just before they draw.

Spur levered the heavy shotgun up, aimed it at the alley, and fired. At the same time he drew his six-gun and blasted two rounds into the roofline, then had the shotgun up and sent the second round from the double barrel into the shadowed roof of the saloon across the street.

The man in front of him had been so surprised by Spur's actions that he hadn't drawn. He stared at Spur.

"What the hell—a shotgun? What the hell you doing?"

The man on the roof gave a scream as the pain of the slugs was too much. He yelled again, then rolled down the roof, still holding the rifle in his hands in a death grip.

Somebody came out of the alley, dragging another body.

"Look! Nance had another backshooter over here. No wonder he always won his gunfights!"

There was a rumble of comments from the crowd.

Spur put his six-gun back in his holster.

"Now, Nance, suppose we get back to the business at hand. You called me out. So go ahead, make your play, anytime. I'm waiting."

The young man hesitated. He looked at the two dead men in the dirt. Then he screamed and pawed at his six-gun. He had it out of leather but it was still pointed at the dirt when Spur's first round slammed into his chest. He staggered and started to lift the gun as Spur put two more slugs into Nance's chest, the last slicing through his heart and lodging against his spine.

29

Nance was dead before Spur got to him. Spur pointed at two men standing nearby.

"There's another man on the hardware roof. Go up and get him and bring him here," he ordered.

The men nodded and ran away toward the back of the store.

Spur looked down at the dead man. He was more bloated at close range.

"Who was he?" Spur asked.

A short, balding man dressed in a fine black suit and gold chain came through the crowd. He looked at the body, then up at Spur.

"That man is Nance Galloway, son of Doak Galloway. Doak thinks he runs this country just because it was named after his daddy." He mopped moisture off his bald head. "Jesus, this really ties it! Now we're going to have a war. When old Doak hears about this, he's gonna come in town with about fifty of his hands and kill everybody in sight!"

# CHAPTER THREE

Spur McCoy stared at the County Commissioner who had just said they were going to have a war with the Galloway ranch.

"Galloway would come here and shoot up the town?"

"Hell, yes. The kid gave him a lot of trouble during the last ten years, but he was still a son. Nance spent so much money gambling and whoring in town that Galloway finally bought the saloon, gambling hall and bordello for the kid to play with. If they made money, fine. We got ourselves a real problem here."

"How far from town is the ranch?"

"Most of twenty miles to the main hacienda."

"So nobody can get out there and back today." Spur turned to the crowd of about fifty people who were listening.

"I need two men to earn a dollar a day. I'd prefer somebody with military experience."

Three men came forward and stood in front of him. Spur picked the two who looked the most determined, and told them what he wanted. They would act as forward scouts on the trail to the Galloway ranch.

"First sign of a large group of riders coming this way, you both hightail it for town and let us know. I want you about three or four miles out so you can see six or eight miles or more. Understand?"

Both men nodded.

"Get out there as soon as you can. Make a hidden camp and keep any fire small, shielded and out of sight. One man awake all night—stand watches. If anybody rides in, you let us know at the sheriff's office. You both have weapons?"

They nodded.

"Fine, mount up. I want you in place well before dark."

One man saluted. They both did neat about-faces, military style, and trotted away.

Spur turned to Paul Victor, the short, balding County Commissioner. "Mr. Victor, I want you to organize the able-bodied men of the town into two watches. We need fifty rifles on five minutes' call. The watches will be from twelve midnight to twelve noon, and noon to midnight. Each man to have a rifle and pistol and fifty rounds for each one. Can you do that?"

Victor frowned. "Most of these men are not professional gunfighters. . . ."

"But they don't want to be slaughtered in their sleep, either." Spur turned to the crowd, which had grown as word spread that the Galloway kid had been killed and the new sheriff was talking tough.

"What do you mean think? Can we defend this town against a bunch of cowboys? Can we put fifty guns on guard twenty-four hours a day?"

"Damn right!"

"Count me in."

"Hell, me and my three sons want to help!"

More voices were raised in support.

"If Galloway knows we have fifty rifles facing him every minute of the day, he's going to think twice before he charges in here and starts shooting off his mouth or his weapons. And I want his messenger to know about this before he leaves. So whoever is going to sneak off and tell Galloway what's going on, better have the whole story."

Victor nodded. "We'll give it a try. We might put another lookout in the church steeple. Tallest building in town." Victor nodded to himself. "Yes, we'll do that. I've got to get a tablet of paper and I'll start signing you up. Right this way."

Spur watched the town men scurrying around, talking about old Sharps, Spencers and Winchesters. There was a spirit of excitement and anger in the air. He sensed a new-found desire to put an end to Galloway's bully-boy tactics and his control of the town. Give honest men a chance to help themselves and usually they will give it their best effort.

He went back to the sheriff's office and saw someone inside. Spur went through the door with his colt .45 on full cock and aimed at the man's chest.

"Hey, I'm here to help!" the man said, eyes wide.

He was the third volunteer who had come forward to be a guard.

Spur let down the hammer slowly on the round and slapped the Colt into leather.

"What's your name?"

"Phillips, sir. Ed Phillips."

The man had braced at attention, his eyes straight ahead.

"At ease, Phillips. We're not in the army now. You want to help out in the office, be kind of a deputy? Pay is a dollar a day."

"Yes, sir!"

"Good. First find the keys to the gun cabinets and the jail cells. Should be in one of those drawers. Then get a broom and clean out this place. Light a lamp when it gets dark. You can bunk down in the jail cell if you want to. I'm going to the hotel and then get some supper. Can you write?"

"Yes, sir."

"Take down a report about any problems people come in with. Probably won't be any. I'll be back."

Spur had slept half the day on the stage, then met with the commissioners and had the big shootout. Things were moving too fast. Time for a nice quiet meal, if the hotel had a dining room. Some did, some didn't.

He picked up his battered suitcase with the double leather straps around it at the stage office, and went to the town's only hotel. Not surprisingly, it was the Hotel Galloway. He got a room in front on the second floor, and fell across the bed. It was as hard as it looked, but had a feather pillow so he decided he could stand it. He was washing up in the china bowl on the small stand, using water from the blue and white china pitcher, when he heard someone at the door. Before he could reach for his Colt on the bed, the panel pushed open and a girl's round face poked inside. Then the rest of her followed and she whirled and closed the door.

She had no weapon and she looked a little frightened.

"Please, don't be alarmed. Are you the new sheriff?" she asked.

Spur nodded.

"My name is Holly Kane. You've got to help me."

Spur finished washing his face, took the towel provided and dried it and his hands. He realized he was bare to the waist and saw her looking at his hairy chest and well-developed torso. He made no move to cover up.

"Holly—a pretty name. I'm Spur McCoy. How am I supposed to help you?" He guessed that she was eighteen, maybe nineteen.

"Well, Doak Galloway has been . . . nice to me. He's taken care of me since my Pa died on the ranch. Gave me a pretty little house to live in . . . and all."

"Sounds like Mr. Galloway is a very kind and considerate man."

"Yes." She looked at him and quick tears came, but she brushed them away. She pushed back her long brown hair, and her green eyes took on sparks. "Then he told me I had to be nice to him . . . and . . . he made me to it."

"He took advantage of you?"

"Yes, whenever he was in town. He kept me. I've had no other way to live for almost a year now."

She flipped her hair back and stared at Spur. "Now I want to be free of him. I . . . I . . . I only know how to do one thing, but I do that good." She looked away. The tears began to flow again. "What I'm saying is that I can be nice for you, if you'll protect me from Doak Galloway. He's an old man! I hate him! But I'm afraid he'll try to kill me if I refuse him. And now, since we've got a strong man to stand up to him . . . Is it too much to want to get away from him, to get free?"

She was crying then, sobbing unrestrainedly. She took a step toward the bed, then Spur moved forward and she ran to him and flung her arms around him, her face pressed against his bare chest as she cried and cried.

Spur held her. Another strike against Doak Galloway. It was one thing to make love with a grown woman who agreed, but to trap a child like this into being his mistress was a criminal offense. Statutory rape, the lawyers called it.

She looked up at him, drying her tears. "Land sakes, I must look a fright!" She eased her hold and stepped back. "I usually don't go all to pieces that way. Sorry." She shrugged, laughed nervously and then blinked rapidly as more tears welled up.

"I know what you must think of me. People in town call me a whore to my face. I guess I'm used to it—almost." She blinked but some of the wetness seeped out. Holly slashed at it with her hand. "What was I to do?"

"There was nothing you could do. I'll get you a room here in the hotel, under my name. You can stay here until this is all settled with Galloway. It won't be more than a few days."

"I heard you killed Nance, is that right?"

"True."

"Good! He was a no-good bastard. Tried to get me into his bordello. The pig!"

Spur grinned. "There won't be a big outcry about losing a leading citizen then?"

She laughed and he liked the way it brightened up her pretty face. She wore a bright red and white print dress that showed off her good figure. Spur pushed down those thoughts.

"Like I said, Nance Galloway was a no-good bastard. I'm glad he's dead. You did a public service." She looked up at him and smiled. "Look, you don't have to rent another room. I . . . I can stay here if you'd like. I mean . . . I can use a blanket and sleep on the floor. I've done it before."

"No, I want you to have your own room. Then what you do after that is strictly up to you. A lot of people in town will understand about Galloway. Or after this is all over, you might want to go to another town. Let's see what happens after a week or so." He watched her. Her mouth fell open in surprise. Before she could say anything, he pulled on a shirt and buttoned it.

"I'll go down and get another room. Do you have anything you want to get from the house? Clothes, personal things?"

She nodded.

"You go get them and come back here. I'll leave the door open. If I'm not here you can wait for me."

She stood, blinking back tears again. "I don't know how to . . ."

He shushed her and led her to the door. "Come back soon, before this town blows up."

When she was gone, he took his wallet and went down to the little desk and told them he needed a second room, the one beside him if possible.

"You the one who shot old Nance?" the clerk asked.

"Yep."

"Hell, you can have a second room for free! You done this town a real service."

Spur thanked him and went to the dining room, where he ordered two steak dinners with all the trimmings, a bottle of beer and a glass of milk sent up to his room.

As he expected, Holly got back to his room before the steaks did.

She had two suitcases filled with clothes, so he took her to the next room and told her to get unpacked. Their dinner would be up shortly.

The food was wholesome and hot, if not exceptionally tasty. When they were finished eating, they set the little cart in the hallway with the dirty dishes.

Holly sat on the room's one straight backed chair and smiled at Spur. "Mr. McCoy, did I tell you that you're the most handsome man I've ever seen?"

"No, but this is a small town. You really haven't seen many men, but I thank you for your kindness."

"Oh, my but you talk nice! Most of the men in this town are cowboys who say 'yep' and 'nope'—and then there's Doak Galloway who almost never talks at all." She frowned, then lifted her eyes and smiled. "But I don't have to worry about him anymore, do I? I hate to think how mad he's gonna be when he finds out I moved out on him!" She shivered. Tears sprang to her eyes and rolled down her cheeks as she stood and moved toward where he looked out the window.

"Mr. McCoy, would you . . . would you hold me for a minute? I feel so . . . so alone, kind of lost."

"Easy," Spur said holding open his arms. She hurried to him and nestled there, her head feeling natural and right on his chest as his arms went around her. She snuggled there, and sighed.

She took another deep breath and burrowed against him. "Yes," she said softly. "I like you, Mr. Spur McCoy. You're kind and gentle and you've come to rescue our town from the Galloways, and I want to stay with you."

She pressed closely to him, her breasts hard against him, her body tight against his all the way down, and slowly her hips began a soft pressure on his. Spur felt the heat building in her. It streamed through her clothes and his into his flesh, and when she turned her face up to his and offered her lips for his kiss, he was more than ready. Her mouth was soft and tender.

Her eyes opened and she breathed heavily.

"Oh, yes! So wonderful! I knew kissing you would be just the best ever." Her hips ground against his crotch harder now. "Again," she said. This time her lips parted as they met his, and her tongue darted into his mouth.

She moaned softly deep in her throat as the fire of the kiss enveloped them both and their tongues battled. Then Spur reached down and picked her up, and without breaking the kiss, carried her to the bed and lay her down gently. For just a moment their lips parted, then met again and he lay on top of her on the bed. She sighed voluptuously.

One of her hands moved down to his crotch and fumbled between their bodies until she pressed against the bulge in his pants. She sighed again, then broke off the kiss and opened her eyes.

"Dear Spur, I didn't mean to seduce you. But you are such a gentleman, and so nice that I knew you would not make the first move, and you are so wonderful. I am delighted that you are here and I'm just so ever grateful that you have helped me get away from Galloway. And I am a person who likes to show her appreciation." She rubbed his erection.

Spur kissed her again. He had not intended to make love to her. She already had suffered a tough life, but this was different. She really had seduced him, and he wasn't going to disappoint her.

He pushed back from her a ways and put his hand over one of her breasts. Her green eyes flashed with pleasure as she looked up at him.

"Oh, yes! That feels so good. Please, more!"

He massaged first one breast, then the second one and gently kissed both through the red print dress.

"Oh, yes, wonderful, could you . . . could you please unbutton me?"

Spur moved his hands to the buttons down the front of the dress and unfastened them quickly, then pushed aside her chemise and lifted it. His hand thrust inside and found one breast. It was hot, pulsing with desire. The nipple felt hard to his palm.

"Big Honey Bear Spur, let me sit up," she whispered.

He helped to lift her up and she shrugged out of

the top of the dress. He pulled the chemise over her head and her full breasts swung out.

"Oh, my! Beautiful!" Spur said softly. "Magnificent!" He touched the satiny flesh and she trembled.

"Yes, Honey Bear, yes!" She moaned softly. "It just makes me feel warm all over when you touch me there. Makes me want to do just anything you ask me to, want me to do. I have to touch you—can I touch you?"

He took her hands and put them at his crotch and felt her opening the buttons. Her breasts had faint pink areolas and bright pink nipples that looked as though they had never known a suckling. He bent and kissed them softly and she began to cry tears of joy.

"Just so beautiful! Nobody ever did that before. He just took me quick and fast and left. So tender! So beautiful!"

She had his buttons open now and worked the staff from his pants.

"Oh, my!" She pushed Spur away from her breasts and bent to look closer at him. "He's huge! So big and beautiful!" Both her hands went around him then and Spur went back to anointing her breasts, kissing them, then licking her standing, proud nipples until she shivered. He bit both gently, then tugged at her dress.

"Over my head," she instructed, chiding him. She stood and lifted the dress off, so she was naked to the waist. Below, a pair of soft blue drawers extended down each leg to her knee.

They were decorated with dozens of small blue ribbons and lots of lace.

She curled up on the bed, then raised herself up on her hands and knees so her breasts hung down like twin peaks.

Spur lay under her, lying on his back and sucking one after the other morsels into his mouth. As he did, his hand worked up one leg to her thigh and the tender inside where he massaged it gently through the fabric. Slowly he saw her legs spread apart, inviting him upward.

Holly sat up and took his shirt off, then jumped off the bed and pulled off his boots. Next she drew down his pants and his underpants, and stood there a minute, admiring his naked body.

"A man is the most beautiful thing I've ever seen," she said softly. "So strong! Such shoulders and arms, and such a broad chest, narrow waist and thighs like oak limbs. And of course, the good part too!" She giggled and unbuttoned, then stepped out of her drawers.

Spur caught his breath. Her hips were slender below a tiny waist, and there was a soft thatch of brown hair at her crotch. She had virtually no belly at all. She came to him and kissed his belly, then up to his lips as she lay fully on top of him, her breasts hot and hard pressing against his chest.

"I want you to make love to me, Honey Bear— I want you to fuck me at least a dozen times, right now!"

Spur growled at her, rolling over and taking her

with him. She spread her legs. He loomed over her for a moment, then found the spot and edged into her slowly.

"Oh, damn! Yes! Wonderful! Go deeper, Honey Bear, go in more!" she cried, raising her hips and arching her body against his.

Now she was trembling and moaning, her slender hips pumping up against him in a gasping spasm of rapture that shattered into a gyrating, bouncing, wailing climax that went on and on. It seemed like she would never stop. At last she came down from the heights and Spur knew he was starting to build to the explosion he could no longer prevent.

It built and built until he couldn't stand it any longer, and he erupted like a volcano, with an intensity that left him weak and drained. At last he gave a huge gasp of satiation and dropped across her, his head beside hers on the pillow.

He saw tears in her eyes.

"Just beautiful!" she said through the tears. "I always cry when I'm happy. This is the first time I've ever cried after—after doing it." She wiped the tears away.

He kissed her cheeks.

"You go right ahead and cry," he said, sucking in big lungsful of breath as he tried to resupply his starved system with oxygen.

They lay there for about ten minutes, then he eased away from her and settled down beside her. She had stopped crying, but still wanted to touch him.

"How did your father die on the ranch?" Spur asked her.

"In a stampede. It was on a trail drive up to Abilene, Kansas. He got thrown and trampled to death by the herd. At least that's what Doak told me. My mother had died just four years before in childbirth. Baby just wouldn't come out and they both died." She was quiet for a moment. "Some of the hands told me that the baby was Doak Galloway's, and that he didn't try too hard to get Ma to the doctor here in Clearwater. And some said that Pa got himself shot by Doak Galloway on that trail drive before the stampede. But them riders got send on down the trail when they said it, so who can tell what really happened out there?"

"Looks like Galloway owes you something. We'll see what we can do about it." He got up and began dressing. "As sheriff, I got to make some rounds, uphold the law, and see how our Clearwater army is shaping up." He kissed her forehead.

"You want me to go back to my room?" she asked.

Spur smiled. "Sweet Holly, you can stay in either room you want to. You're a free woman now, remember?" He grinned at her, waved and went down to the main street to check doors and get a report on his civilian army.

# CHAPTER FOUR

Spur walked the length of Main on one side, then moved across the street, which was an inch deep with the continual dust the wagon wheels and horses' hoofs churned up. On the other side were the four saloons. He tried doors as he moved up to the first one. Inside were a dozen card tables, a long bar on one side and a stairway to the cribs he was sure were upstairs. Four saloon girls worked from table to table. All four were shopworn and tired, but they were some of the best available.

As soon as Spur pushed through the batwings, the whole room quieted. Thirty pairs of eyes stared at him. Then a voice lifted from the back.

"Nice shooting, Sheriff!"

It broke the tension. Men came up to shake his hand, clap him on the back. Everyone in the place seemed glad that Nance Galloway was dead and that they had a sheriff who was smart enough to tell a set-up a mile off.

"We knowed that Nance didn't really shoot those two sheriffs," one small bearded man said, "But hell, how was we to prove it with the sheriff dead, and Nance and his side men ready to gun down anybody who even hinted it might not have been a fair fight?"

Others echoed him. Spur had a beer with them, then a man came in the saloon door and a dozen eyes turned to watch him. Spur watched too. He was a tall, thin man, wearing range clothes that had a lot of dust on them. His face was covered with sweat and dirt, but it was his expression that stopped them.

He had the look of a dead man hunting for somewhere to dig his own grave. His eyes were dull, dead gray, but as he came closer, Spur saw the fury burning in their centers. He'd seen the killing rage of men take many forms, and this was one. This man was dedicated to one action—vengeance. He would either complete the vengeance trail, or die trying.

Spur left the group at the bar, picked up a bottle of whiskey and a glass and met the tall, thin spector.

"My friend, it looks like you could use a drink," Spur said. The man nodded. Spur pointed to the nearest table and sat down, pouring a shot of bar whiskey for the man, who sat down heavily. He drank the whiskey in one shot and motioned for another one.

After the third shot, Spur began talking to the man, softly, gently.

"My name is Sheriff Spur McCoy. I'm new in town today, and I probably don't know your troubles. This is a new age in Clearwater. Today

Nance Galloway was shot to death defying the law. As I say, I don't know what your problem is, but I know you look like you have a god-awful load on your shoulders. This might be a good time to unload some of it."

The man stared at Spur for a minute and then his face twisted up and he began to sob. Gradually the rest of the sounds and the chatter in the saloon stopped until all that could be heard was the sobbing of the tall death-bringing man who sat at the table with Spur McCoy.

Spur poured him another shot of whiskey, which vanished at once. For five minutes the man sobbed his heart out, then wiped the tears from his cheeks, and started talking. He spoke softly, so Spur had to lean forward to hear.

"My name is Matt Rogers. I had a small spread about five miles out of town on a tributary to the Clear River. I had a wife and two kids and two hands and about 500 head of cattle. Now I got nothing."

He told Spur what he'd found when he came back to his small ranch.

"At least they paid. Five rode in, and three rode out. They drove my stock to the Western trail, and the tracks was wiped out there by a trail herd going north. My bet is they circled the wagon and the horses back south again and came out at the Galloway Circle G ranch. Doak has tried to scare me off for five years—claims it's his land, but it ain't. I got a registered deed. Proved up on it four years ago. Bet my wagon and some of my machinery and gear is over there. I know that my stuff there would prove that Galloway ordered it done.''

Clint Bascomb had shed his banker's suit coat and tie, and was dealing a hand of poker at the green-covered card table at the side of the room. Bascomb was a conservative banker, and a cautious poker player. He loved the game, and was learning, but he almost never bluffed, or went for an inside straight or tried to fill out a flush. If he bid, he had the cards. Which is no way to play poker.

Bascomb tried to listen to the conversation at the table between Spur and Matt Rogers. He knew what had happened. Galloway had not taken his advice and had burned the family out. With Galloway's usual finesse, the men he'd sent to do the job had probably also raped and killed everyone in sight. Damn! Things had been moving along at an even keel, then the county commissioners demanded a top lawman. Bascomb asked for cards needed and dealt them automatically. He was out of this hand. He never lost more than twenty dollars in any one night. Playing poker kept him in touch with the town, with the ordinary men, and in the saloon he could get an idea of what the population would do. Right now the people were tired of Galloway's domination—the ease with which Victor had signed up his fifty volunteer watchmen proved that.

There still had to be a way around this. At least

Nance was gone. He had been a serious threat to the whole plan from the first. Galloway had taken care of his end, and Bascomb had worked behind the scenes to keep everything in town running smoothly. Now he didn't know what Galloway's reaction would be. Bascomb had sent a rider out to the ranch an hour after the shooting with a written message warning Galloway against coming into town. Bascomb's worry was that Galloway would forget his actual position and begin to believe the town talk about his power and his strength.

Bascomb folded, watched a pair of kings take a nine-dollar pot, and passed the deal to the next man. He would just have to watch and wait and listen . . .

Spur had told the cook at the Hotel Galloway to cook up a steak dinner for Rogers, got him checked in at the hotel and told him to come by the office first thing in the morning. The food and sleep would do him good.

Spur checked in at the office. His second new deputy's name was Toby, and he reported that the only person to come in had been Mr. Victor with a copy fo the volunteer guard list.

"Mr. Victor said the first guards would go on duty tonight at midnight. He said he had the men concealed and spotted all around the outskirts of town so Galloway won't be able to sneak up on us."

Spur told Toby to go get a couple hours of sleep. "You'll have to be up all night, so grab some shut-eye now, Toby."

"Yes, sir!" Toby said and vanished into the jail. Spur sat behind his new desk and put his feet up on it, crossed them and laced his hands behind his head.

Galloway was a problem. Rooting him out would be harder than identifying him. The death of his son should get the pot boiling, but Spur was convinced now that Galloway wouldn't stage a raid on the town. He should know he was out-gunned here, and Spur was sure his contact in town would caution him against a frontal assault.

If Spur could implicate Galloway in the deaths of the Rogers woman, children and hands, he would have ample reason to bring him up on charges. But there were no witnesses to the killings, except the perpetrators. Getting one of them to testify against the other two and Gallo-way would be next to impossible.

At midnight, Spur watched as the militia gathered. They were assigned to various sections of the town, covering all four sides. Paul Victor had on work clothes and was acting as the com-mander, which was fine with Spur. Victor had named lieutenants to work each of the four areas. Victor would be in the church steeple, using it as a command post. Anyone with a message for him was to send a runner there.

Victor inspected each man before he went out to be sure his weapons worked and that he had ammunition. Then they scattered.

"Professionally smooth," Spur told Victor. The

other man smiled.

"You don't have to be tall to be smart, or good with a rifle. The six-gun became the great equalizer, remember?" Victor turned and jogged toward the church.

Spur rousted Toby from his sleep and put him in charge of the sheriff's office.

Back at the hotel, Spur used his key in the lock and was startled when he saw light under his door, then remembered—Holly. He opened the door gently, made sure she was the only one in the room, then went in, locked the door and wedged the chair under the door handle.

Holly had been lying down. She sat up, then knelt on the bed. She wore a thin nightgown that had been cut off so it barely covered her crotch.

"Good! I was hoping you would come back before I went to sleep."

She insisted on undressing him, and by the time she finished, Spur was aroused and they made love softly, gently, and went to sleep in each other's arms.

During the night they rolled apart and when morning came she slept curled almost in a ball, with one hand resting on his shoulder. Spur woke with the sunrise, got out of bed quietly and kissed her cheek. She mumbled something, smiled, and slept on.

Spur had a quick breakfast in the dining room and went up to room 212 where he found Matt Rogers already up. Briefly Spur outlined the plan he'd come up with during the night, and the tall man with the haunted eyes nodded.

"Be right glad to help you, Sheriff. I'm ready now."

"You have breakfast, I'll get some supplies and a mount and a good rifle, and meet you at the livery in an hour."

Spur left the deputy in charge of the office and the two tall men rode out shortly after seven.

The burned-out buildings were what Spur saw first as they came up to the Rogers' ranch. As they rode into what had been the yard, he saw five fresh graves near the one shade tree. The house had been two stories high, and had not burned to the ground as Spur had anticipated. One side had barely been touched. The kitchen and living room and part of the second floor were missing from the far side.

Spur asked Matt where the children would have been sent when danger came, and Matt told him up the stairs to the unburned room.

"The kids . . . they slept in here."

Spur looked around. "You said your boy was good with a pencil. Suppose he could have written anything down before they went up to get him?"

"He didn't write much, more of a picture drawer."

They looked in the small cupboard, in a box, and then Spur looked under the big double bed. Something showed far back by the wall. He pulled the bed out and reached down by the wall.

It was a pad of tablet paper with faint lines. On the outside was a name and the words, "My

Sketch Pad." Spur lifted the cover and looked at the pencil drawings. They were good. There was one of his father that no one could mistake, another of his mother and sister. Then one of a dog, and animals. At the back were three hastily drawn faces.

One showed a man with a long face that had a crescent-shaped scar on his cheek. He had high cheekbones, and hair parted on one side. His expression was one of anger.

The second was of a Mexican man, with a drooping moustache that was longer on the left than on the right. He wore a small earring in his left ear.

The third man was older with a beard and sad eyes, sparse hair on top of his head but long around the sides.

Spur showed the drawings to Matt Rogers.

"I don't know who they are, I've never seen them before," said Matt.

Spur turned back to the last picture before the three faces. It was a coyote howling at the moon.

"Yes, I've seen that one," Matt Rogers said. "Will drew that night before last. He showed it to me."

"Then he must have drawn these last three yesterday. Could they be three of the men who attacked your house? Could he have seen them in the yard from the window?"

Matt looked at the faces again. All were angry, all were vicious. "Those expressions ain't like Will usually drawed." Matt nodded. "Yes, yes,

Sheriff. I think they could be three of the men who killed my . . ." His voice broke off, choked by tears.

They went downstairs. Spur saw that Matt had not buried the two attackers who had been killed. The one in the kitchen of the house had been badly burned. Spur took down a description and found a moneybelt on the body that had a name in it, and over a hundred dollars. The Secret Service agent gave the money to Matt, then they checked the second body. Spur looked from the body to the sketch book. The man who lay with half his face shot off, was the exact image of the third drawing in the sketch book.

"It's one of them," Spur said. "Will had time to sketch three of the five who attacked your ranch. We've got all the evidence we need. Now, let's find the other two men. Normally we would head straight for the Galloway ranch and line up the hands until we found the right one. But I don't think we're going to be able to do that this time."

Matt Rogers stood, gripping his fingers into fists and relaxing them, then clenching them again. He kicked the corpse in the side, then in the head. "I aim to kill the other three, Sheriff, whoever they are and wherever they are. I'm gonna track them down and kill them as slowly as possible," he grated.

"That way you let Galloway off scott free."

"How's that? I aim to kill him too."

"Let the law take care of it. That way you will have the right to sue in civil court for damages.

He'll have to pay for the cattle, the horses, for your sheds and barns, for the house. And you can ask for a hundred thousand dollars for the wrongful death of each of the three members of your family. It won't bring back your family, but it will give you some cash to get started again, here or somewhere else."

"I'd rather kill them all."

"Think about it, Matt. Don't make up your mind so quickly. Think of the long run. You'll be punishing Galloway much more if you ruin him financially, before he gets convicted and hung for the murders. Think about it. Now, let's ride. We've got a lot of miles to cover before dark.

"Where we going?" Matt asked.

"The Galloway ranch, and we're going at night for a little midnight interviewing of ranch hands. All very quietly, of course, and without Mr. Galloway knowing anything about it."

# CHAPTER FIVE

Sheriff Spur McCoy and Matt Rogers arrived at the Clear River below the Circle G Ranch just before dark. They found a secluded spot safe from prying eyes, and had a cold supper of biscuits and fruit Spur had brought from town. Both men settled down for a quick nap as darkness fell, and by midnight were rested and ready to move.

They left their horses in the copse of cottonwoods, and taking their rifles and pistols, moved toward the ranch. Matt had been there before, and he angled them toward the bunkhouse where the hands would be sleeping.

"We're looking for either man," Spur said. "The thin-faced one with the scar on his cheek, or the Mexican with the drooping moustache and the earring."

"I know what to do with them," Matt growled.

"We get them out of the bunkhouse and take them back to town to stand trial and to testify against Galloway. Ordering someone to kill is, in the eyes of the law, exactly the same as pulling the trigger yourself. So if we can get one or both of them to testify, we have Galloway cold on the gallows."

"Sounds good to me," Matt said.

They edged closer, using a small row of trees along a tiny feeder stream for cover, then waited for a cloud to cover the moon before they crossed an open stretch a quarter of a mile from the buildings. Spur hoped they didn't have any dogs on the ranch. Some owners wouldn't keep dogs because they bedeviled the horses and cattle. Other ranchers trained dogs to help do herding work, and to stand watch at night.

They went past a big corral, then walked to the well that was in a swale a hundred yards from the buildings. After that they had only one more move from the well toward the dark shape of a building that Matt said was the bunkhouse.

It was a rough frame building thirty feet long and half that wide, with one smokestack. No smoke came out. The two windows were dark. They went halfway around it from the side opposite the ranch house but saw only one door at the front. They both came out of the darkness, walked casually to the bunkhouse and went inside. Both had packets of matches, and Spur lit one, found a small lamp and lit it but kept the wick low. They were in a typical bunk house with rough lumber bunks built two high against each wall.

Men were sleeping on rough straw mattresses, some covered with a light blanket, although the night was still warm. Most had undressed to summer underwear. Spur and Matt moved quickly down the line and found the Mexican first. Everyone still slept soundly. A little further along, they spotted the thin-faced man with the crescent scar. Spur shook the man's shoulder and eased his six-gun muzzle under the suspect's chin.

"What?" the big man with the scar mumbled. Then he was fully awake and felt the gun muzzle pressing painfully upward under the soft fleshy part of his chin.

"Yeah? What you want?" he asked softly.

"You make another sound and I'll blow your head off!" Spur hissed at him. "Get up and outside, now!"

"Wearing my long johns?" the man protested, weakly.

"Tough," Spur whispered, and pulled him by one ear out of the bed. Spur passed the big, slender man to Matt, who bent one arm behind his back and rammed him ahead through the door and outside. Spur moved back up the narrow aisle between the bunks to the Mexican. He drew his knife from his boot and pressed the sharp blade to the Mexican's throat as he shook him. He came awake at once without moving. His eyes sought Spur's and he nodded.

"Out," Spur said. The man stood; he was fully

dressed except for his boots. Spur bent one arm behind his back, kept the blade across his throat and propelled the short man outside.

Just around the corner of the bunkhouse, Spur found Matt and his prisoner. A door slammed and a cowboy left the main house and walked toward the corral, away from their position.

Spur pointed in the other direction and they marched their prisoners straight away from the bunkhouse, shielding themselves from the rest of the ranch. A quarter of a mile out into the black Texas night, they turned south toward the trees and the river where their horses were.

The big man with the scar spoke at last.

"Who are you? What's this all about?"

Matt roared and slammed his six-gun across the man's face, tearing his cheek, jolting him to the ground.

"No," Spur said softly.

"By God, yes!" Matt bellowed. "This bastard killed my family! I'm not going to let him get away with it!"

"What the hell you talking about? You half tore my face off!"

"I'm going to tear you into little pieces before I'm done, just the way you did to my family."

"I never killed nobody. I'm a cowboy. Never been off the Galloway place in six months. Got thirty witnesses."

"I bet you have," Spur said, moving in. He handed the Mexican to Matt. "You keep track of this one, and no rough stuff. We'll let the court take care of them."

"Hanging is too good," Matt said. "They got to suffer the way Gloria did, and Vicki, and Will."

The man with the scar reacted to the names, then shrugged.

"My name is Weed. I been on the Galloway ranch for the past six months," he repeated. "Didn't even go into town."

They heard shouts from the ranch buildings then. A shot was fired.

"We got to get out of here!" Spur said. "That means riding double. Come on!"

They pushed the prisoners ahead of them. Running hard, they made it to the trees, tied the prisoners' hands, and mounted up double.

Spur had the Mexican as they rode back toward town. Now and then they heard shouts and a shot or two behind them. Then their pursuers seemed to move in another direction.

When they were ten miles from the ranch, and when the Big Dipper told Spur that it was a little past three A.M., he called a halt.

"Can't kill our horses," Spur said. They tied both prisoners hand and foot, then made a small fire and Spur brewed some coffee. When he looked up, he was staring into Matt Rogers' six-gun muzzle.

"Hand me your iron, Sheriff," Matt said evenly.

"Don't, Matt. You don't want to ruin our case against Galloway. He's the boss, he's the important one. These are just the scum who work for him."

"Take it out with a thumb and finger, Sheriff."

"My way is better, Matt."

"No."

Spur had seen desperate men before. He knew that Matt was so poisoned with anger and blood lust that he was going to have his own way or die trying. Spur took out his Peacemaker .45 gingerly and handed it over.

"Now them new-fangled manacles you got, the ones that tie a man's hands together," Matt continued. Spur took them out of a back pocket and watched resignedly as Matt snapped the iron bracelets on him and pocketed the key.

"Just relax, Sheriff, and I'll give you a lesson in making a man confess. Saw some Sioux use this once up north."

Spur sat by the fire. Matt had built it up with some dry drift wood from the river until it was roaring three feet into the air. It lighted up the whole campsite. He turned to the Mexican. Matt's knife flashed in the firelight as he dragged the protesting man closer to the flames.

"What's your name?"

"Raoul."

"Did you kill my family, burn my buildings? My name is Matt Rogers, the Flying R. You were there, weren't you?"

"No. Never left the Galloway spread."

The knife flashed and Raoul screamed. Matt held out the Mexican's ear, the one with the earring, and showed it to the dazed cowboy whose eyes had gone wide with pain and surprise. His screams came again and again. Tears poured down his cheeks and his hate-filled eyes focused on Matt.

"Don't lie to me Raoul, it's a mortal sin. You have another ear, ten fingers and ten toes. I never have made it all the way to a man's eyes, but maybe you're a stubborn and tremendously strong type. Were you one of the five men who attacked the Flying R, where two cowhands, my wife and daughter and son were all killed?"

Tears still gushed from Raoul's eyes, glistening on his cheeks.

"If I say no, you will cut me again. If I say yes, you will kill me. What can I do?"

"Tell the truth, Raoul," Spur said. "We know you were there. We have proof. We want you to testify that Doak Galloway ordered you to burn the ranch and kill everyone there. You agree to do that and we'll go easy on you."

"Did you do it, Raoul?" Matt asked.

Raoul held his bound hands over his bleeding ear. He looked up at Matt. "Will you promise not to kill me, no matter what I say?"

"Did you give my wife and children and hands a choice in whether they lived or died?"

The knife darted through the air again. Matt's trained hand used it delicately, and sliced a gash four inches long down Raoul's cheek.

Raoul screamed and lunged to one side, barely missing the fire.

The terrified Mexican sat up as best he could. He felt his slashed cheek with his tied hands and glared at Matt.

"Bastard! Untie my hands and give me a fair chance with a blade against you."

"The same way you gave my son Will a fair chance?" Matt kicked Raoul under the chin, driving him backwards, rolling him in the dirt, then caught him by the hair and dragged him back to the fire. Matt took out the notebook from inside his shirt and showed Raoul the drawing.

"You rotten sonofabitch! How do you suppose we knew who to come after? Look at that picture! Can you deny that's a drawing of you? It's accurate right down to your earring. My son Will drew that as he lay upstairs frightened to death. He drew three pictures while he waited to be killed. One of them was the man you left at my ranch, dead. And one of them was you, Raoul. I should execute you right now. But I'll give you one more chance."

"Matt, open the cuffs and let me help you," Spur said. "You mustn't do this. If he dies, I'll have to charge you with murder. You don't want that to happen. I can't let you do that to yourself, Matt."

"Just shut up! You got your job, and I got mine. I owe Galloway ten dead men for every person on my ranch he killed. Galloway is going to be number three tonight after I take care of these two. Don't try to talk me out of it!"

"Will it be worth it, Matt? You'll be on the run for the rest of your life, always looking over your shoulder, always waiting for that tap on the arm by a man with a warrant. You don't want to live like that. Let the law take your revenge. I can help you. If you kill Raoul, it will make it hard. We need him for a witness against Galloway."

"I can't think any farther than today. Don't confuse me!" Matt kicked Raoul in the side and the Mexican rolled over. Then Matt turned to stare at Spur. He seemed to be thinking about it. Spur hoped he'd come to his senses. Matt squatted down and stared into the fire.

Then Raoul was standing. He had a big rock in both hands and was hopping toward Matt by the fire.

Spur shouted a warning, and Matt leaped aside just in time. Raoul swung the heavy rock at Matt's head, and now, off balance, he couldn't change his direction. He fell head first into the fire, screaming. The fire of logs and brush was white-hot. Raoul's hair burst into flame and was burned away before his head touched the glowing coals and buried his face in the shimmering heat. Matt stumbled and fell as he lunged sideways. He rolled and sat up, then saw Raoul in the fire.

"No, no! Don't cheat me that way!" Matt leaped back to the Mexican's body, grabbed his ankles and dragged him out of the flames. He beat out the burning shirt until it stopped flaming, then dumped the cup of coffee over the smoldering cloth.

When he turned Raoul over and looked at his face, Matt shivered and gasped in horror. There were only vacant, still-steaming craters where his eyeballs had been. His nose was gone, all the flesh burned off his cheeks. The whole front of his face was a charred, shapeless mass.

There was no heartbeat. No human being could have survived through such intense heat. Raoul's lungs had been seared in seconds.

Matt sat beside the body and wept, shaking his head in anger and defeat. He turned when Spur spoke.

"It was an accident, Matt. He killed himself when he tried to attack you. Now, give me the key. Open these manacles."

Matt turned as though he were a machine, reached in his pocket and found the key, then opened the restraints. Spur thanked him, took the key and put it back in his pocket along with the cuffs.

Then he checked Weed. He had loosened the ropes around his wrists. Spur put the manacles on Weed and locked them tight. The odor of burning flesh was so strong around the fire that Spur moved the camp a quarter of a mile downstream. They did not make another fire.

"Time we get some sleep. We'll be up at dawn, then move on into town. We should be there well before any of Galloway's men."

Matt Rogers nodded. He hadn't said a word since Raoul's hideous death. Some of the anger seemed to have burned out of him with the accident. It had happened so quickly, and with such finality, that it had made a tremendous impression on him. Spur watched Matt carefully for a few minutes. He had suffered another tremendous emotional shock; would he weather this one?

Spur watched the two men sleeping near him, and knew he should get some rest. He was pleased with the results of his campaign so far. He had absolute proof of Galloway's involvement in the five killings, and a witness who could probably be persuaded to swear that Galloway had ordered him to kill. Matt would get his revenge at the hands of the law, and both Galloway and his henchman would hang.

Spur nodded and went to sleep.

He woke with the dawn, got up and washed his face in the river, then made breakfast from the supplies they brought. They were on the trail by seven. At first Spur wondered why Galloway had given up the search so easily. He must know that the two witnesses could testify against him, that since these two had been taken, it could be proved that they had participated in the murders. He must have some other plan, but Spur couldn't think what it could be.

They were less than ten miles from town now.

Even though Spur and Weed rode double, they made good time. An hour away from their night camp, they stopped to change riders, putting Weed with Matt on the other horse. The tall man had got down from Spur's mount and walked a dozen feet to Rogers' horse, when two rifle shots punctuated the morning calm. Spur dropped to the ground behind his mount, away from where he thought the rounds came from. Only then did he turn to look at the other two men.

Weed lay on his back with his hands clutching his chest. In back of him, Spur heard Matt Rogers cursing. Rogers peeked over his horse and sent four quick shots into the brush and boulders to the left of the trail. There was no return fire.

Spur realized that Weed had been the target. That had been Galloway's long range plan—eliminate the remaining witness. The sheriff crawled to the downed man and checked him. Weed blinked and stared up at Spur.

"Hit bad?" Spur asked.

Weed nodded.

"You were at the Rogers' place, weren't you?"

Again the head nodded.

"Who was the fifth man there? Who else helped you burn down the ranch and kill everyone?"

For a moment Weed didn't respond. Then he nodded. Matt crawled up.

"Who was it, man? It can't hurt you now," Matt demanded.

"Zane," Weed said, and then coughed, showering a gout of blood on his chest.

"Zane?" Spur asked.

Weed nodded.

"Last name?" Matt asked. "What was his last name?"

Weed's head began to turn, then his eyes flickered and he looked back at Rogers. "Sorry," he said. The fires went out and his eyes stared at the sun without blinking. A long sigh whistled out of the dead lungs, and his bladder voided, making a dark stain on his pants.

"Zane," Spur said. "We had it wrapped up so neatly. Now we have to start all over."

# CHAPTER SIX

Matt Rogers stood looking down at the body of the man who had killed his family. He kicked the form, turned and marched away, a hundred yards or so up the bank of the Clear River, then came back. At once he got on his horse. He rode to where Spur stood looking down at the body.

"I guess we should bury him," McCoy said.

"Why? He don't care now. Do it if you want. I got to get moving."

"On into town?"

"No, back to the Circle G. I've got to find Zane."

"That's a law matter, Rogers. Stay out of it."

Matt Rogers snorted, wheeled his mount around and rode back up the trail toward the Galloway ranch.

Spur watched him go, powerless to stop him.

Matt might scare off Zane, whoever he was. Then again, Zane might be out of the state by now. Spur looked down at the dead man. He had no shovel, no way to dig a grave.

Spur mounted and rode for Clearwater, pushing the horse, knowing it would need walking out once back at the livery, but there was no time to spare.

A lookout picked him up five miles out of town and rode along a ways. He said that no one had come to town on this route from the Galloway ranch. Spur told him to hold his position.

Once in town, Spur found Victor and told him what he wanted. The word went out; within half an hour, Spur had a posse of forty mounted men, all armed with rifles and pistols and ready to ride. Victor rode at Spur's side.

Spur told Victor his plans. With a posse this size, there was no chance that Galloway would oppose them. He would not declare war on the county government because Galloway knew it was a war that he could not win.

"By now he must have heard that we have a new sheriff," Victor said. "He'll be anxious to size you up, to feel you out and see what he has to do, or what he *can* do."

"That doesn't bother me, Victor. I'm sure he was the one who sent those five men to burn out Rogers. He probably gave them free rein to do whatever they wanted to, knowing what would happen. Galloway gave them orders to kill all six, only they missed Matt. If that's true, and Galloway knows that only one of his men is left, he might do something to Zane if he knows we're coming."

"Hard to sneak forty-two men into a ranch," said Victor dryly.

"The ranch is about twenty miles, which means we need four to five hours to get there. It's about one o'clock now—it won't be dark by the time we arrive. We ride in like an army, everyone with rifle muzzles raised in the air so they're easy to see. Will Galloway have lookouts posted?"

Victor nodded. "Be surprised if he didn't have somebody at least two miles out."

"Good. Then the old man will know we're coming in force."

They stopped at three o'clock that afternoon to water the horses and let them have a blow, then pressed on.

At five-thirty they flushed a lookout. They could see the ranch house a mile distant. The lookout tore away from a small stand of trees and rode flat out for the ranch.

"We'll be expected," Spur told Victor. He stopped the posse and gave the men final instructions.

"This is not a war. We are not out here to blast this ranch into rubble. Our only mission is to arrest a man called Zane in connection with the five murders at the Rogers ranch. We ride in with our pistols holstered, and the butts of our rifles on our right thighs, muzzles pointing in the air, so they can be plainly seen. Every man's weapons will be loaded and locked and no one, I said *no one*, will fire before I give the command. We'll ride in, in formation, six wide and six long. Let's form up and ride in."

They were a quarter of a mile from the ranch buildings when Spur saw four horsemen riding toward them. The middle man was Doak Galloway, Victor told Spur. McCoy rode to within ten feet of the other men and held up his hand to halt his troops. Most stopped; a few had to back up into formation.

Galloway was not a big man. He sat his horse with a tilt to the right, favoring a shoulder. His tall Texas Stetson was white and rounded on top. The face below the hat was soft and pale, showing that he had become a gentleman rancher. He peered at Spur with anger.

"What the hell are you doing on my land?" Galloway bellowed.

"I'm Sheriff McCoy, duly authorized lawman of Galloway County, state of Texas. I have a warrant for the arrest of some of your hands. We're looking for that man, and for no other reason."

"What's the name of the hand?"

"Zane is the man's name. An unusual one. I'm sure you don't have more than one person here by that name."

"He's not here. Hasn't been for a month. I fired him for stealing. I have ten men who will swear in a court of law to that fact."

"I bet you do, Galloway. What about a man

76

named Weed and another one called Raoul, a Mexican with an earring? Did you fire them a month ago as well?"

"I've never had any hands with those names."

"Evidently you don't keep very good books, Galloway. Since I have a warrant, I'll need to make an inspection of your property. I'll start with the bunkhouse."

"You'll do no such thing! My word is as good as gold," Galloway blustered.

"I'm not much of a man to collect gold, Galloway. Now, will you stand aside, or do we ride over you?" Spur lifted his right arm in the air to give the forward signal.

Reluctantly, Galloway wheeled his mount and the three men with him did the same. When the four men were ten yards ahead, Spur motioned his posse forward at a walk.

He ordered five of the men to dismount and follow him as he took a quick survey of the bunkhouse. Only two men were inside, and both said that the man called Zane Smith had left over a month ago, heading north.

Spur checked the dining hall next to the cook house. Twenty men were bending over tin plates of food. McCoy introduced himself and asked about the three cowboys. Some of the hands grinned, others snickered when he asked about the hands. But everyone agreed that Weed and Raoul had never worked there and Zane had left a month ago.

"Just to satisfy your curiosity, Weed, Raoul

and two more hands, including Zane, raped and murdered a woman and a thirteen-year-old girl, then butchered a boy of twelve and two hands at the Flying R. Ranch. It was done on orders from Doak Galloway. To further enlighten you, Galloway had Weed shot this morning when I was taking him to jail. Raoul was also being taken to jail when he attempted to kill my deputy, but fell headfirst into a fire so hot his brains exploded before we could pull him out. That was a shame. We wanted him alive. Now, what odds would you give on Zane being alive by this time?" Spur spun around and walked out of the dining hall.

But he knew he was wasting his time. If Zane were here, he was six feet under the Texas sod somewhere and Spur would never find him. Galloway might well have shot the man who dug Zane's grave and shoved him in it too, just like the pirates of old used to do. Spur whistled for the other men. They went back to their horses and mounted up.

Galloway still sat on his dun, with his three henchmen close by. Spur rode up to him.

"Galloway, a word of warning. Your men in town tried to backshoot me the way they did the last three or four sheriffs. It didn't work. Three of them are dead. You better put the word out. If anybody tries to gun me down again, from the front or the back, I'll get a hundred men out here and blast you and your people straight to hell, burn down your buildings and scatter your stock.

"Your special privileges, your bullyboy tactics and your bullshit in this county are all through, over and done with. If you want to live respectably and peacefully here, you can—unless and until you're convicted of a crime. Then the state will feed you and do your laundry."

Spur turned his horse around and the posse pounded along behind him. Far behind the galloping horses, a pistol went off, but Spur didn't bother to look around. That would be Doak Galloway venting some of his frustrated anger.

Spur and his men had a five-hour ride back to Clearwater. Just after nine that evening, they stopped for a break and a breather for the horses. Half a dozen flasks turned up, and a pint or two, and the whiskey made the rounds.

The second half of the trip was easier and they came into town, all singing. For the record, not a single man fell off his horse during the return march to Clearwater, no weapon was discharged and there were no casualties. The fruitless ride cost the county forty-one dollars for posse members, nothing for bullets and nothing for the whiskey.

Spur checked in at the sheriff's office. Deputy Toby had fixed the small wood stove, had a pot of coffee brewing, and had a drunk in the first cell. His name was Johnson and he always came into the cell to sleep off his drunks because his wife wouldn't let him in the house when he was soused.

"Anything else happen?" Spur asked.

"No, sir. Most of the men were out of town. Quiet as a grave around here."

On the way past their advanced lookout, Spur had reduced the position to one man. He would be relieved at eight A.M. Spur and Victor decided a duty guard was not needed around town. They would keep four men in the church tower as a token precaution for the next week. Victor positioned new men there when they got back.

Spur said goodnight to Victor and headed for his hotel room. He dragged up the steps and had trouble getting the key in the lock. It opened from inside and he staggered in and saw Holly Kane clutching the short nightshirt to her, her eyes wide with worry.

"Are you hurt?" she asked. She closed the door and ran to him, trying to turn him over where he lay face down on the comforter. She couldn't budge him.

"I'm fine, just tired. Rode sixty-five miles today. Beat. Dead. Talk to me in the morning."

She grinned, straddled one of his legs and pulled one boot off. Then she took the other one off and whispered in his ear to turn over. Grudgingly he did. She unbuttoned his vest and his shirt, then his fly and tugged his pants down and off his legs. His shirt and vest went next. By the time she had them pulled from under him, she was panting. She threw off the nightgown and sat on his chest, kissing his mouth, but unable to awaken him.

At last she shrugged. Laughing softly, she

looked at the cut-off briefs he wore. She worked at them, pulling them down, rolling them, and at last drawing them off over his feet. She stared at his limp penis. She had heard it could be done. At the worst she would wake him up. With both hands she began playing with his genitals, rubbing and stroking and petting him.

It took only a few seconds before she could see his automatic response as the flaccid tool began to lengthen and harden. She giggled softly. Soon his member was stiff, hard and ready. Spur had slept through it all quietly, not even snoring, his mouth closed, one hand thrown over his chest.

The more she played with him, the more excited she became. There was something thrilling, almost wicked about it! Surely she couldn't insert him without him feeling it. If she did, would he come?

She shivered, rubbed her breasts with both hands, and felt her blood boil. One hand crept down to her crotch and she touched her nether lips—warm, wet and ready!

Carefully she knelt beside the big naked man, then eased one knee to his far hip and began letting herself down toward him. Almost at once she felt him touch her and she adjusted and then lowered more and the hard, purple head penetrated between her soft lips.

She was slipping him inside her, and he didn't even know it!

She giggled again, but then the excitement of what she was doing swept over her. Lust overpowered her and she sank down with a little cry as he was thrust deeper into her than she had ever thought possible. She was impaled with his big penis and it felt wonderful!

Slowly, gradually she lifted off him, then settled down, again, then again. One of her hands rubbed each full breast in turn as she used the other for support. Slowly she bent forward and put both hands on the bed beside him. The up-and-down motion now became one more of back-and-forth, almost like riding a horse.

Powerful emotions swept through her as she jolted back and forth faster and faster until she knew she was going to cry out.

The wildest climax she had ever known left her gasping as the tremors shook her a dozen ways. The spasms rattled Holly and jolted her. She felt as if she were going to break apart.

As she stopped the motion, the spasms trailed off, then she began the "ride" again and the rock-hard penis activated her climax again and again. She wondered how long her body could react that way.

Suddenly she was aware that the man below her was moving, his hips rising to meet her thrusts. His hands reached up to fondle her breasts, but his eyes were still closed; she was sure he was sleeping.

It was fantastic! He was so exhausted he didn't know that he was about to ejaculate!

She kept him moving and listened to his breathing speed up. He moaned and gasped deeply, and panted as his hips pounded upward. Then he let out a long sigh, his hands dropped away from her breasts, and he began to breath regularly again.

She knew he was still huge inside her. Again she rode him like a stallion, and still more climaxes vibrating through her. At last she quieted and lay full length on top of him, her breasts crushed against his chest. She relaxed. She would go to sleep there, with him still inside her! Yes, she had always dreamed about doing that . . .

It took a long time, but she at last went to sleep. The night was warm. Once he tried to move, but stopped when he felt her there. She came half awake, rolled off him and snuggled into the feather pillow. Vaguely she wondered if she should tell him when he woke up. She hadn't decided by the time she drifted back to sleep. Morning . . . She would decide in the morning.

# CHAPTER SEVEN

Doak Galloway watched the sheriff and his posse ride away, heading back to Clearwater after their ridiculous assault on his ranch and his honor. He would have the man horsewhipped!

He rode back to his ranchhouse door, dismounted painfully from his horse and gave the reins to one of his men. Galloway limped slightly as he went to the house, up the four steps to the main door and inside. The heavy stone and adobe walls of the house still held some of the previous evening's coolness. Galloway swore roundly at his infirmity, and at the criminal ineptitude of the sawbones who had set his leg wrong during the war. A thousand times he had wished that he could have just five minutes with that Yankee doctor.

He slid into the big leather chair facing the

dead fireplace. It was his thinking place, and he had planning to do. If he wanted vengeance on Sheriff McCoy, he first had to catch him alone. Galloway refused to dwell on the death of his only son. He had screamed out his grief the day before, and now he was coldly efficient in his planning. He knew about the sheriff's takeover of the town, and the mindless support the townspeople had given him. The forty-man posse was further proof of that support.

There had to be a way to get rid of Spur McCoy. All he had to do was find it. He rang the bell on the sturdy low table beside him and a dark-eyed young Mexican girl game in quickly. She carried a tray with a bottle of whiskey, a bottle of branch water and two glasses.

He watched her, a small diversion from his problems. She was new in the house, had been here only about a month. He figured she was about seventeen, no more, from the Mex village two miles down the valley. She wore the tight white blouse and blue skirt he had provided. When she put the tray down on the table, her blouse top fell open so he could see the tops of her breasts.

"Yes, is all?" she asked in her soft, young voice.

Christ, what he wouldn't give to be seventeen again! He watched her, then rubbed his crotch, and saw her glance away quickly. He motioned her to come closer, and rubbed one of her breasts gently with his hand.

"No," he said, his voice husky. "I want you to stay here with me for a while."

86

She nodded and sat in a chair near the fireplace.

"No, over here," he said indicating a footstool beside the big leather chair. She moved at once, but he knew she was trembling. "Felice, I am not a monster. I will not hurt you. Now smile pretty."

She sat below him and he stared past her. The problem. Spur McCoy. He must kill him and ruin his reputation at the same time. A rifleman could kill him with some risk, ruining his reputation would be harder.

As he thought about it he reached down and motioned for Felicidad to move closer. His hands stroked her long black hair that glistened in the soft light of the lamps she had lighted. His hands found her shoulders and the bareness of her throat.

He would kill McCoy with a woman, a prominent woman in town. Yes! The idea grew. At once he knew which woman, and he smiled as he thought of her. He would send a man to town tomorrow to get it started. The arrangements would take a few days, but that would be all.

When he had found out that both Weed and Raoul had been kidnapped from the bunk house the previous night, he had known this new sheriff would have to be dealt with. His riders had reported the death of Raoul, and then their rifles had settled the account with Weed. Before Galloway knew it, Zane Smith had bolted. He'd been told that Zane had heard the men enter the bunkhouse and haul away his two friends. Somehow they had identified them as having been involved in the massacre at the Rogers ranch.

Zane must have feared for his own life, rightly so. By the time the other hands reported the missing pair, Zane had ridden away with a meager sack of supplies.

Galloway had sent two men to track him that morning. One came back just before dark with a rifle slug in his shoulder. The other tracker was dead. Galloway sighed. He'd done what he could.

His hands moved lower, and he heard Felice gasp as he found her left breast and stroked it. She would learn in time. She was so young and unspoiled, and *unused!* He watched her face.

"Small flower," he told her. "I have no intention of hurting you. Just relax and enjoy life as it comes."

Yes, the woman in town would be easy. He shifted his weight in the chair, brushed his hand back through thin strands of brown hair. His eyes were pale blue, usually squinting. Now they shone as he stared down at the girl.

Both his hands touched her breasts now, massaged them gently, watched her eyes, and saw the touch of fear.

"Felicidad, have I ever hurt you?"

She shook her head.

"And I will not hurt you now, believe me. I have a great fondness for you. Relax, smile. Does not my touch on your big titties feel just a little bit exciting?"

She shivered, then nodded. It was true. She did thrill to his touch. No man had ever touched her there before. She was a virgin, carefully protected by her father so she might marry well in their small community and he could ask for a large dowry. But then *El Jefe* had seen her and demanded that she come work for him in his house, and her father had agreed, but had asked for a payment of three strong mares. They had been given, along with a breeding cow with calf so he could start a small herd. She would live at the big house and earn as much money as her father made as a vaquero. She was proud.

Then her mother had told her that she could refuse. They could send her back to Mexico. If she went to live in the big house, she would become Senor Galloway's mistress. She understood, but her *padre* loved the three mares so much that she would not run away.

Felicidad looked up at the face that was to her both old and ugly. She smiled, and she knew that tonight she would lose her virginity. As if to affirm her thoughts, Galloway's rough hands began unbuttoning the white blouse which was the only upper garment she wore.

"Slow and gently," Galloway said to himself. "I will treat you with tenderness, let you explore, let you help as I undress you, and then have you undress me and you will discover why your *padre* protected your sweet young pussy all these years."

But he was also thinking of how he would get his revenge on Spur McCoy. He would send a man to the bank—any rancher has to go to the bank now and then. Yes, that would be the beginning.

He would make the contact in town, offer cash for the job, and it would happen soon. Perhaps in as little as three or four days.

Galloway spread back the white blouse, and caught his breath when he looked at the soft tan breasts so richly nippled and with red aerolas. It was going to be a good night.

He stood up with a groan, and motioned for her to bring the whiskey tray, then led the way up the sweeping open stairway to the master bedroom where the large bed had been turned down.

Of course the woman would never cooperate willingly, not that prissy female, so he would have his man lure her to McCoy's room under some pretext, or even do it right in her bedroom. Yes, brilliant, that was even better! The shot could be muffled and then Spur knocked unconscious and brought on the scene, and both of them stripped naked and put in bed. Oh, yes, he might even go to town himself just to see everyone's reaction to the scandal.

It would be a brilliant way to settle two major problems at once.

He caught the girl's hand and led her into his bedroom, closed and locked the door. For a moment fear glazed her eyes. Then he smiled at her and the fear vanished, and a look replaced it that he could not understand.

"Now, Felice, don't you worry your pretty little head about a thing. I've done this before. I know what girls like and I'll go slow and gentle."

"*Si.* I hope so, Senor Galloway." She shivered

again and he gently took off her blouse and watched her breasts tremble.

"Little pussy. Any girl with big tits like you got is bound to like to be poked. Ain't never seen a woman yet that didn't like to be fucked; whether she admitted it was another thing." He laughed. "Hell, in a month or two you'll be fuckin' and suckin' like all the rest. You'll love it, be asking for more all the time."

She crossed her arms over her breasts. He slapped them away.

"Dammit, no! I like to look at tits. Don't ever try to cover up them big tits when I'm around again!"

She was trembling now. He sat on the bed. "Felice, get these damn boots off, and then undress me. I'm gonna want to have nice hot sponge bath before I get in bed. Be nice and clean for you. Put your blouse on and go bring hot water and two of them big towels. Come on, move! Get your little round bottom moving. We got a big night ahead."

As Doak Galloway lay there waiting for her to come back, he thought about the ranch. It had been a run-down joke when he took it over from his father. In twenty years he had built it into one of the biggest outfits in that part of Texas. And he could still run it, though he had a general foreman now who handled the daily operation.

They would have a cattle drive moving up the Chisholm trail soon, heading for the railhead in Kansas. New brands on the five hundred head that Weed had brought in from the Flying R would be healed by then and blend in with his stock. One step ahead. He had warned Rogers three times that he was grazing his cattle on part of the Circle G range. Just because it wasn't deeded yet didn't mean it wasn't his land. Damn the man! The final showdown had been inevitable.

Yet, first he would get rid of this new sheriff. What he would do then was put one of his own men in as sheriff. He would talk to his man in town about that, eliminate all this problem between him and the county. Hell, he owned most of the county now anyway.

After the sheriff, he would get the cattle drive set up. Then when things calmed down, he might take a trip into Fort Worth for a little holiday. Live in a fancy hotel, have his meals served in his room. Go out to a concert or a stage play even, if they had them there.

Only two things bothered him right then: Spur McCoy, and the escape of Zane Smith. Smith should have been silenced. He hoped that McCoy didn't send someone looking for him. He would handle both problems when they came up. And McCoy would be first. He would get things moving in the morning.

Felicidad came in and he smiled at her. She carried a big bowl of hot water and towels. When she put them down, he sat up on the bed and took her white blouse off, then bent and kissed her breasts. She shivered, then moaned in surprise as a climax pulsed through her slender form.

"Well, now," he said, "aren't you just full of surprises? You must be an honest-to-God virgin afterall. I may give your *padre* another horse!"

She had understood some of what he said, but not all. Her English was improving. As she climaxed she had reached out for him and caught his shoulders. As the spasms trailed off, she stared at him in wonder, then he bent and kissed her breasts again and sucked on them gently.

"Damn, I'm getting old! When I was younger I'd have fucked you twice before my bath, then twice afterwards." He took his shirt off and let her pull off his pants.

"Come on, Felice, let's get started. I got me a couple of fine killings to figure out."

# CHAPTER EIGHT

When Matt Rogers had turned his horse around and headed back to the Galloway Circle G ranch just after Weed had been gunned down, he knew he had only one chance of finding the other man who had killed his family: he had to get to the ranch before the fifth man ran for it.

Either luck had not been with him or the fifth man had been a light sleeper and had seen them roust Weed and Raoul from their bunks earlier that night. Rogers had got close enough to the ranch to hear that the man called Zane Smith had sneaked out of the bunk house as soon as the two men had left, taking a horse and stealing a sack of food from the cook shack. He'd ridden straight north, the shortest way off Circle G land.

Matt pulled back carefully from the bunkhouse and the Circle G buildings, and began crisscrossing the range a mile from the bunkhouse. On his fifth pass he found the prints of a big horse moving north fast. It had to be Zane Smith's trail. He got off and examined the tracks for a hundred yards. There were no distinguishing marks on the shoes, except that the mount had been newly shod. No chance it would lose a shoe soon.

Rogers settled down to tracking. He always had been good at it. Many times he had found a lost steer and brought it back to the herd. He was not prepared for a long trip. He had only a few provisions that Spur had put in his saddlebags the day they left Clearwater.

He would ride the grub trail wherever he could, hunt for rabbits or anything else he could find that was edible, and he would press on.

The trail he followed was a fast one, with no attempt at deception. Two miles out from the ranch, he found a new development. Two more sets of prints joined the trail, and turned to follow it.

Apparently Galloway's backshooters were moving out to eliminate the last witness against the ranch owner. For a short time Matt's target changed. The two other gunmen would have to be eliminated. Now the rifle in his boot had a new purpose. Killing a Galloway hand would be one small satisfaction. He figured they had a six hour start on him, maybe less. It's impossible to track a horse through the open country at night, so they had to wait until daylight to begin. Five hours.

Matt urged his horse to a canter to cut down their lead time. The first hour he figured he had covered five miles. Too fast. He slowed his mount to a steady walk. He could do four miles an hour that way and walk for ten hours. Forty miles a day, day after day, if there was enough water and some forage for the horse.

The first slight rise on the trail provided him with a view ahead. He strained his eyes, but could see nothing across the rolling plateau marked by a few small streams, and a green patch of trees here and there near the streams. Far off to the left he saw smoke. A cabin—a small rancher perhaps, but too far off the trail to waste time on. Later perhaps, when he ran out of what food he had.

He rode automatically now, watching the trail, turning when it turned. The three-horse trail was simple to follow. It had another horse to change off to, he could catch up with the tracking pair in a few hours, but with one mount he could not afford to let her go lame or ride her to death. The sun shone down with its broiling beams and the heat climbed along with the golden orb.

Matt had nothing on his mind but his ranch and his family. He had come into Galloway County just over five years ago, staked his claim and began proving up on his homestead. Galloway had given him a little trouble, but Matt had showed him he had a homestead certificate, and that everything was all proper and legal, and well off the Galloway property. Nothing happened for two years.

Gloria had taken to the ranch life well. He

helped her so she had not faded and become rough with the hard work as so many ranchers wives did. He pampered her, and she had flowered. He had never seen a more beautiful woman, and one who could please him so well in bed. Their life here had been so much better than their abortive attempt at ranching in Kansas. The trouble there was all behind them. He had learned his lesson. He would take all possible pains to get along with his neighbors. Never lose a neighbor over a family dog.

Then the trouble began. Galloway had waited until he saw that the newcomer knew what he was doing, and that the small ranch would make a go of it. Then he began small pressures, small raids, then threats and at last violence. Matt had four hands until one of them was wounded by an unknown rifleman; another one just up and left. Two hands stuck by him, and got themselves killed for their loyalty.

Anger surged through him again, and Matt Rogers screamed into the wilderness. He would find this last murderer, kill him and then come back for Galloway himself. After that, nothing mattered. If Galloway's men killed him or if he was caught and hanged, it would all be the same.

At last dusk came. Matt surged a hundred yards ahead at a gallop now, paused to read the trail, then moved again. There was only one place the trail could lead. It was headed toward a bluff straight ahead that blocked the way north. It wasn't big enough to show on a map, but it was too steep to climb. There was a notch, a break or a pass of some kind that he could see straight ahead.

That would be the only reasonable place for Smith to ride if he were continuing north, and every indication showed that he was. The gap was still a half day's ride away. Matt cursed the on-coming night, since there was no chance to find the pass in the dark. Then the blackness intensi-fied; stars came out, and he could see the black outline of the bluff far ahead, and the notch.

Matt rode into the darkness, slowed by the problem of safety. He didn't want to break his mount's leg. He figured he could slip up on the pair of trackers, maybe catch them around a campfire.

He rode for two hours, making nearly his four miles an hour. The notch seemed little closer, but on a small rise he spotted what could be a camp-fire ahead. He had no idea how far away it was—that depended how big the fire was.

It turned out to be a small cooking fire, and he was less than a mile from it when he saw the first twinkling light. The men had not tried to conceal it from behind. It was against a huge boulder that would shield it from the north, which was the only direction they were concerned with.

A half mile from the fire, he got off and walked. Matt left his horse two hundred yards from the fire and moved up without a sound. He carried his Winchester .44 rifle with seventeen shots in the magazine, his Starr double action .44 revolver, and a six-inch hunting knife on his belt.

He crept up silently. The fire was roaring higher now, giving them more protection from the darkness, but also offering Matt a perfect target for the rifle.

At forty yards away, he edged around a big rock next to a feeder stream and saw the first man. He sat in front of the fire, talking to the man who was stirring coffee brewing on the edge of the fire.

"Way I see it is, the old man wants Zane's mouth closed for good. Told us to bring him back. Hell, Zane gonna shoot soon as he sees us. Figure he's about ten miles ahead. If'n we knew where he was going, we could cut him off."

The other man put the top of the coffee pot and belched.

"Hell, you saw Galloway wink when he said bring back Zane. He wants him dead. Didn't figure anybody would get away over at Rogers'. They fucked up bad over there."

Matt lay there. His fury was building up inside him and he was having trouble preventing himself from shooting the men where they sat. There was no doubt that they worked for Galloway.

"Damn, those guys had a field day over there with that girl and his woman! You ever taken it away from thirteen year old? Christ, but that is sweet! I got me one once. Sure wish I could have been over at Rogers' place that day."

Matt Rogers took a deep breath. His eyes were

glazed with rage. He blinked, then sighted in on the speaker's head just over his nose, and stroked the Winchester's trigger.

The rifle shot shattered the silent Texas night and blasted one cowboy into the hereafter. The heavy .44 rifle slug bored through the cowhand's forehead and exploded out the back of his head, tearing off half the back of his skull.

The second man froze in place for a second, giving Matt time to work the lever on the Winchester, planting another round in the chamber. He fired as the second man moved, caught him in the shoulder, and then the man screamed and rolled into the blackness out of range of the fire's glow. Matt sent fifteen more shots into the darkness in the direction where the second man had scrambled, but couldn't be sure if he hit him or not.

Matt had hoped for a clean double kill, then he could have ridden in, taken a horse and continued after Zane with a backup mount. As it was, he had to wait. He could not see either of the horses in the firelight.

He reloaded the Winchester and lay silently in the cool darkness. Small sounds came to him from the campsite. The fire slowly burned down, and he heard more sounds, but he had no target.

An hour later, the fire was out. With a sudden clatter, he heard a horse being ridden away down the rocky shore of the small stream. The man on board sent five angry six-gun shots in Matt's direction in a futile attempt to kill his attacker, then he was gone.

Matt waited until daylight.

Then he rode into the camp of death. He found the dead man's horse, took his pistol and rifle and kicked the corpse in the side; then he rode. He had tied the second mount to his saddle horn and rode hard for an hour, following the trail that angled directly for the north. After an hour, he let both horses drink, then changed mounts and rode again. He would alternate the horses this way for as long as he could. With any good fortune, he could overtake the man on one horse before darkness.

But this was Texas, and a person could never tell what was going to happen in Texas, particularly out here in the west central part where ranches were few and far between, and friendly faces were often hard to find.

Matt rode on. He had a mission. There was not a chance that he was going to fail, or that he would quit. He had to kill Zane Smith!

# CHAPTER NINE

Spur woke up the morning after he had been sexually assaulted in his sleep by Holly, and didn't remember a thing about it. He was up with the sun, kissed Holly's bare breast peeking over the top sheep, and dressed. He slipped out of the room, had breakfast and was waiting at the Mercantile when it opened. He needed some trail goods.

Spur had been sitting in one of the six chairs against the wall outside the store, when a woman came down the boardwalk from the other way and unlocked the front door. As she looked at him, he saw tendrils of red hair escaping from her bonnet.

"Are you waiting to buy something?" she said, her voice lower than he expected.

The front legs of his chair hit the boards as he came down and stood.

"Yes, ma'am. There's a few things I could use."

"I'm open," she said, smiling at him. "Aren't you that new sheriff I've heard tell about?"

"Yes, ma'am."

"Come in." She smiled as she said it and he thought he saw alluring glints in her green eyes. "I'm not open for business yet, but I can always do our new lawman a favor. I'm damn glad you gunned Nance Galloway. The man was a leech, and an all around bastard." She smiled. "Sorry if my language embarrasses you. I was raised by my dad. I've been around men all my life. Pop ran this store until he died three years ago. Now it's mine to run or sell or what the hell." She grinned.

Spur smiled back at her and took off his hat as they went inside. He saw that she locked the door behind him.

"My name is Spur McCoy."

She held out her hand like a man. "Howdy, I'm Katherine. My close friends call me Katie. You I want to call me Katie."

"Thanks, and I'm not concerned with how you talk. Strong language isn't only the prerogative of men. A question: are you hiding that beautiful red hair for some reason, or would you take your sunbonnet off?"

She laughed and pulled the strings under her chin, took off the bonnet and let her dark red hair fly as she shook her head. It settled into a deep red cascade around her face and down her shoulders.

"Beautiful," Spur said. "I'm going to arrest you if I see you covering it up again."

"Well, now, I heard that you were nice. Come back here—I have something I want to show you." The Mercantile was a huge store, and they went past saddles, barbed wire rolls, tools, dishes, housewares, and horse collars. She opened a door and stepped inside. He followed her. They were in a set of rooms that could only be a residence.

"I live here most of the time," she said. "I went out for breakfast this morning. Tired of my own dull cooking." She stepped closer to him. "Mr. McCoy, would you do me a favor?"

He caught a scent of lavender from her and smiled. She was taller than he had thought at first. The simple calico dress she wore did not conceal her womanly figure.

"It would be a pleasure to do you a favor."

"I've had this little problem lately, one I think you can help me with. My lips have had this strange malady . . ." She moved closer and her arms went under his and around his back as she pressed her full body against his. "It's been too damned long since they've been kissed!"

Spur laughed with delight and bent toward her. Her face was raised to him and he touched her lips gently, then drew away; he went back, kissing her harder, then broke it and again went back, this time with his lips slightly parted. He saw that her eyes were closed and the third time, her lips opened too, and they kissed in soft, gentle motions. Her tongue darted into his mouth, probed for a moment and retreated.

His tongue followed and she sighed and pressed hard against him, moving her hips against his crotch in a sensuous little wriggle.

Spur pulled away from Katie and her eyes opened lazily and remained half hooded as she looked at him.

"So that's what I've been missing!" she said.

"Only if you want to. My guess is that you continually have to beat the local romeos off with an axe handle."

"Bunch of dirty farmers and cowboys! They aren't hard to beat off." She looked up at him. They were still holding each other tightly. "Would it be too forward of me if I ask if we could try that kissing thing again?"

"Sounds reasonable, and a lot of fun."

They kissed and her tongue devoured him, pushing his back each time he tried to get his tongue in her mouth. Then all at once the resistance ended and she sighed softly and broke the kiss, holding his hand as they moved through a doorway into her bedroom.

She sat on the bed and pulled him down beside her.

"I am a very forward person, Mr. McCoy."

"My friends call me Spur. I want you to call me Spur."

Her face broke into a marvelous smile. "Spur, I don't know what you must think of me, but I believe that men are men and women are women and they are both human beings, and both should have the right to do what they want to. Why should men get to mess around with anyone they want, and women not have the same right? So sometimes I get all amorous feeling, and when I see a beautiful, handsome man like you, and things are just right, I ask him to make love to me." She smiled. "Later on when I get *really* sexy-feeling I'll say 'fuck' and 'cock' and all those things, but I can't yet."

She smiled, lay back on the bed and pulled him down over her, then kissed him and put her hands behind his neck and kept him there for a long, hard kiss. When they broke his eyes sparkled.

"Katie, I'd be honored to make love to you. And a lot of what you say about men and women I agree with. Of course, in addition, you give up the traditional wife's right of ownership of the husband as well as his responsibility to honor and protect her forever."

"Yeah, all that bullshit!"

"True." He reached down to her breasts and petted them. She waited as he found the buttons. Then she purred in her throat and helped him unfasten the bodice when he was too slow. His hand moved under her chemise and touched her warm breasts.

"Oh, yes, wonderful! It always delights me the way my body reacts to a man's touch, his caress. The female body is so beautifully constructed to respond. Sex has a way of shattering a person's logic and ambition and control—but I guess you know that."

"And I guess *you* know what the sight of a lovely curved breast does to a man's resolve and goodwill and decorum?"

She sat up, pushed her dress down and took off the chemise over her head. Her lovely breasts swung out as she moved, and writhed beneath Spur's fascinated gaze.

"What does this do to you? How do you feel right now?" she asked.

"I feel all hot and sexy. My crotch is tight and hot and my cock is in agony, trying to get hard and straight. My heartbeat's speeded up, I can hardly breathe, and I want nothing more than to touch those delightful breasts."

She kissed him quickly. "No man has ever told me that before. Those are a lot of the same feelings I get, but for me they come slower, more gently I think. Touch me."

His hands caught her breasts and she gasped in wonder and satisfaction. Gently he massaged her, concentrating on the pink nipples which he watched enlarge and harden.

"I want to undress you!" she said.

"Please!"

He was wearing black pants, a dark shirt and soft leather vest and she had them unbuttoned and off quickly. She pulled his boots and socks off and watched him.

"One man I know gets embarrassed when I want to undress him," she confessed.

"Not me. I'm delighted."

"I can tell!"

He bent and kissed one breast, licked her nipple and then drew half of one breast into his mouth, chewing and sucking on it.

"Yes, nice, but not very sexy to me, I don't see why men get so excited about tits." She reached and caught his erect phallus. "Now *this* is sexy. Cock. That is so sexy I want to pee right here!"

Spur nodded. "What else is sexy?" He reached down and moved his hand up her leg under her skirt.

Katie gasped and looked quickly at him. "Yes, yes—that is sexy. Do it again!"

He did, pushed her down and rolled over on her, kissing her soft mouth and bringing his hand slowly up her leg. He felt her thighs part and move further apart.

"Yes, sweetheart, fine, I love that!"

He sat up and brunched her heavy skirt over her waist, exposing her soft silk underdrawers. Slowly his hand slid up one inner thigh and then the other, touching through the soft fabric, then moving to the other thigh. She was panting when he stopped.

"Oh, yes, lover, that is wonderful!"

He sat up and lifted the dress over her head, then ran his finger under the top of the silk drawers. Then he moved his hand down across them, skirting the soft mound of her pubis. She gasped.

"Do that again!"

His fingers feather-touched across her pubis, then down past the tight crotch of the silk drawers.

"Sweet heaven! That is so wonderful!"

He repeated the movement and this time the

silk was damp. Gently he rubbed harder at the damp spot and she climaxed swiftly, jolting and whimpering for a minute and a half, then she stopped abruptly.

She leaned over and whispered in his ear. "Lover, kiss me," she said. He did. She shook her head. "No, lover, sweetness lover. Kiss me . . . down there."

She helped him as he stripped the soft pink silk drawers down and off her feet, then she lay on her back, her knees raised and her thighs parted. A soft red thatch covered her crotch. He slid lower and parted the forest of red and she gasped and then whimpered. His fingers brushed the tender pinkness and she moaned in joy.

"Kiss me, darling wonderful Spur. Kiss me and then I'll eat you up!"

Spur pushed in, found the hard bud of her clitoris and twanged it as he kissed her pulsating nether lips.

Katie exploded. Her hips pumped and she shrieked, then a keening moan came from her as she shivered and shook and mewed in joy as the climax tore through her delicious body. He triggered her clit again and again, sending her into an unending roll of overlapping climaxes until she was panting, and a soft sheen of perspiration covered her body. Katie was panting and humping her hips. Her hands had found her breasts and she kneaded them, pulling them, petting them, and at last drawing his mouth upward to suck on them as her climax tapered off into a sensuous writing. She was ready for more pleasure.

She rested a moment, then sat up, pushed Spur down on his back and sat astride his chest, dangling her big breasts near his mouth. She let him chew on each a moment, then she moved down and caught his cock and squealed in delight.

She ended the squeal by kissing it from root to purple arrow tip, then licked the head until his shaft jerked in anticipation.

"Sweet Spur, I hope you have lots of staying power," she said and bent and took him in her mouth.

Today he did have a lot of staying power. But soon Spur pulled away from her, pushed her on her back and held her legs straight in the air as he aimed and then drove into her in one powerful thrust that brought tears to her eyes, and a moan of joyful approval.

"So this is what I've been missing," Katie said. "Why didn't you tell me sex games were so much fun?"

"Katie, you've played your share, and I bet you won most of them."

"Really, Spur! I'm a blushing virgin."

She was doing strange things beneath him and a sudden series of muscles gripped him and released and gripped and released and almost at once he climaxed. It was over so fast that he dropped on her in surprise.

"How did you do that?"

"What?"

"That inside hugging."

"Muscle control. Did you like it?"

"Next time I'll like it even better."

She laughed. "Next time right now, or tonight?"

"Later. Not sure where I'll be tonight. Do you have a door to the alley?"

"I'll show you, later." She put her arms around his shoulders, holding him for another five minutes, then she moved and he lifted away.

She sat up and then stood.

"Don't move," he said.

She was startled. "Why?"

"I want to remember you this way, flushed, happy, your breasts swaying free and unbound, your slender waist, fine, strong hips and that delightful red forest down below."

"Sure you're not a poet?"

"Are you sure you're not some kind of magical love goddess?"

"Wish I were. Then I could put a spell on you and hogtie you and marry you and fuck you twice a day!"

They both laughed.

He watched her as she dressed.

"Hobby of mine. Watching a woman dress is like a ballet. All grace and perfection."

"You've never seen me try to get in a whalebone corset."

"You don't need one."

"Thanks—I'll throw mine away."

He dressed and held her, kissing her softly, then asked her if she really was ready to do some business.

"I guess it's about time. Christ, but I enjoyed that! Real serendipity."

"But one that could happen again. Now, damnit, I've got to get back to work."

A half hour later, Spur had a horse at the rail in front of the Mercantile outfitted the way he needed it. He had arranged for one of the two lookouts to come with him and had his horse stocked for the trip. The man he took with him was called Oliver. He said he had been in the Union army and had been a sergeant. Now he was married and had a son but the only work he could find was as a cowboy. He needed something better. Oliver was medium height with a pinched face and close-set eyes, and he was said to be one of the best rifle shots in town.

"Sheriff, just where we heading?" Oliver asked.

"Hell, if I knew I wouldn't need you along. Understand you worked on the Circle G for a while."

"Yep. We going out there?"

"Might be in that general direction."

Spur waved to Katie, who had come to the door to see him off. She fluttered one hand to him and smiled a special smile. Spur knew he was certainly going to make time to bounce on her feather bed again before he left town.

"Let's go," Spur said, and they rode toward the Clear River.

# CHAPTER TEN

The Circle G ranch lands were roughly thirty miles long and ten miles deep fronting the Clear River. Most of that land was west of Clearwater. Spur outlined the problem to Oliver as they rode.

"I'm looking for the 500 cattle that Matt Rogers said were rustled off his ranch by the Circle G riders. Matt said he figured they had been taken onto Galloway ranges and maybe scattered in several areas. Where would the most reasonable place be to take the herd, and where might we find some of the Flying R brands, or some cattle with the Flying R branded over the Circle G?"

Oliver scratched his head for a minute, then nodded.

"Hell, if'n it was me trying to hide them, I wouldn't scatter them. Anybody might find just one that way. I'd keep them all together, rebrand and get them up the trail to Kansas soon as I damn well could. Keeping the herd together would be best, far as I can see."

"And knowing where they came from, where would you take them to hide them?"

"Some box canyon, or a finger canyon with steep sides where you could throw a quick fence across the narrow mouth to pen them in."

"Fine. Where?"

They had ridden from town toward the heart of the Galloway ranch. There were no signs, no fences, just open prairie and natural streams, swales, little hills and clusters of trees and brush around the streams. Here and there they saw cattle, all with the prominent branded circle with a "G" inside.

"It's what we call a heavy brand. The idea is so it can be used over other brands. Perfectly legal when you buy stock from another ranch and rebrand it. Then again, works just as well on stolen cattle, or those of other brands on open range."

"Where can we start looking?"

"Never got down in this section much when I worked for Galloway. But I heard about three or four small valleys where they wintered over some stock one year. They cut wild hay in one valley, put it in haystacks to use to feed if there was a bad snow storm."

They came to a small rise in the land and pulled up to look ahead. Spur motioned Oliver back at

116

once. Not a quarter of a mile away, McCoy saw six cowboys working a herd of two or three hundred head, moving them north and west.

Oliver nodded. "Looks like one of the small roundups they have this time of year. Should be taking the second drive to Kansas before long. Probably aim to take the Rogers herd along with them."

The drive had been moving north and slightly east. Spur looked at Oliver questioningly.

"Yep, they'll move them east some. One branch of the Chisholm Trail goes right through the ranch. It angles northeast up to the Red River Station a hundred miles or so due north of Fort Worth. All the Chisholm Trail branches feed into the Red River Station, then follow the same route to Kansas."

"So we look around here anywhere?"

"Seems reasonable. No sense in driving 500 head thirty miles west, and then two weeks later drive them thirty miles east again."

They followed the small herd, hanging back three or four miles, staying out of sight, shadowing the herd and staying away from the outriders that were looking for strays.

"Blackberry Canyon," Oliver said. "I think that's where they're heading. They can put the herd in there, sort out the cows and calves, brand the calves, cut out the steers they need to castrate and the animals ready to make the drive north. We can circle around these dogies up there and get to the canyon in about four or five hours."

"Let's try it. We just might get lucky."

They got to what Oliver called Blackberry Canyon four hours later and worked up the side of it. There had been no sign of activity at the mouth of it and Spur had seen no fencing work. They left their horses halfway up in some trees and climbed the rest of the way up the slope until they could look down inside.

All they saw was a pleasant valley with a small stream running through it and half a dozen patches of green where springs watered and surrounding area to produce grass, but the moisture was quickly absorbed by the dry ground before it could reach the stream.

"Not a single damn steer," Oliver said. He shrugged. "Well, it was a gamble. They might be coming here with those they have. Not much chance a batch like that would include the Rogers cattle."

They went back to their horses and watched the sun sinking low as they angled back up a brushy valley well away from the potential cattle pen. An hour later they holed up in a thick copse of cottonwood and willow. The herd was ten miles behind them.

Oliver proved to be a good cook. He opened a tin of baked beans, added a tin of canned beef and put together a meal a hungry man couldn't turn down. They had a loaf of bread and some spread, coffee and an apple. They dined like a pair of swells.

Spur had set up camp early so their fire would be out well before dark. They lay down fully dressed on their blankets, with both rifle and pistol by their sides.

"How long we gonna be looking, Sheriff?"

"How long is it going to take us to find those Flying R cattle?"

"Just wondered."

They both fell asleep quickly.

Spur woke up about one A.M. and walked to the edge of the woods. He saw only the moon high in the sky, heard a coyote howling for a mate, and a few night birds calling. He went back to his blanket and went to sleep.

They rode half the next morning to get to what Oliver thought might be another possibility for holding the rustled cattle. This valley had over two hundred head in it, with plenty of room for another thousand. The narrow mouth of the valley was no more than a quarter of a mile wide. Posts had been planted at sixty foot intervals and four strands of smooth wire were strung across the entrance.

Oliver looked at the fence in surprise.

"Should hold them in unless they get riled," he said. "When we get that new barbed wire, it's going to hurt the critters to push against it, and they'll back off. Barbed wire is gonna make a whole damn big difference in how cattle are handled around Texas."

They went through a gate and rode inside. All the cattle were either unbranded or with the

Circle G prominently burned into their hips.

The rest of the morning they checked out two more small valleys leading off the Clear. Only one had been set up to hold stock, and both were empty.

"Where else?" Spur prodded as they ate a cold lunch of the rest of the loaf of bread and a jar of home-made crabapple jelly.

Oliver stared out over the Texas range, took off his low crowned black hat with its crushed wide brim and scratched his head.

"Hell, they could be almost anywhere. Maybe they moved them several places. Now if I was doing this, with all the shit flying around, I'd probably move them closer to the home ranch, where they could be watched better, where somebody like us couldn't find them easy if we tried."

"Where would that be?"

"The Blue Crick valley. Leads off the Clear about a mile from the main ranch. They should have three or four thousand head in there just before they move them out to start the drive. It's big enough to graze them for three or four days, maybe a week. Usually hold a big batch of steers there just before the trail drive."

"Let's go."

They rode on. Spur agreed that they would have to approach the valley from the far end. They rode north, across the unmarked boundary of the Galloway ranch, then turned west and rode until dark. They found a thicket with an open space for a camp, made a small, smokeless fire

120

and brewed coffee and fried up the last of the bacon before it spoiled, then doused the fire and ate the bacon on the last of the bread. Oliver dug out a tin of peaches for dessert.

"I got maybe one other spot we could check after this one," Oliver said. "But it's a long shot. We're also running out of food. We can live off the land if we can risk a rifle shot or two for some rabbits."

"We might just have to do that, unless we can find a nest of three or four big rattlesnakes. Ever eaten them?"

Oliver nodded. "I got to be damn hungry, but I can do it. Not one hell of a lot of meat, but it can keep a feller alive for a time."

They were so close to the Circle G that they took turns standing watch that night. Each one got about six hours of sleep and headed out the next morning after three cups of coffee for breakfast.

By ten o'clock, a light ran began falling. They pressed on. The light rain turned into a downpour and lightning crackled around them, but there was no shelter. They rode on. By noon they were soaked through to their boots and the storm had blown on east. The sun was out half an hour later and they dried from the outside in.

Ahead Spur saw a hill, a ridge of some kind, and Oliver pointed it out.

"That's our target—backside of the Blue Crick canyon. It don't lead nowhere, just from the Clear River to the slightly higher plateau beyond, but it makes a nice little valley."

By two that afternoon they had ridden to the top of the little rise and looked down into the area. Parts of it were still green, irrigated naturally from springs along the sides. Spur guessed the valley was about three miles long. At the far end he saw the brown milling mass of a herd of Texas Longhorns.

"Paydirt!" Oliver said.

"Not unless you're in California. Looks like cattle to me. Want to bet they have the Flying R under fresh Circle G brands?"

"Not a betting man, Sheriff. But my guess is we finally found the Rogers herd."

There were a few scrub pines along the rim of the valley, and the pair of riders worked forward carefully, staying out of sight as much as possible. At times they were forced to cross over the top of the ridgeline where there was no growth to cover their advance.

They left their horses a quarter of a mile from the herd and moved up cautiously. From a distance they could see no herders, no cowboys around at all. Now, a hundred yards away from the animals, they still could see no men.

Oliver and Spur crouched behind a stunted white pine and watched the herd.

"Looks like they penned them in here and left them," Spur said.

" 'Pears you're right."

Spur wished he had brought a good pair of binoculars. He was going to buy some next chance he got.

"We can get within fifty yards of them under cover. Then I'll walk out and take a look at the brands. You cover me with your rifle."

Oliver nodded and they moved again.

On the third animal Spur examined closely, he saw the new brand on its hip. It was raw, scabbed and unhealed. At the top, just outside the circle, Spur saw the edge of a flying bar. It could be the Rogers herd. He checked a dozen more. Most of the cattle had been recently branded and all were two-year-olds, so that meant they had been re-branded. On half of them he found evidence of the old brand, an R with the bar on top. He was satisfied.

Back at the edge of the ridge, they got back onto their horses and move cautiously around to the mouth of the valley.

It was the smoke that warned them first. The blue column lifted almost straight into the sky from a hidden campfire.

Ten minutes later, Spur had worked his way on foot to a position where he could see the camp. There were three men and a small tent, set up like a line camp, and it looked like they would be there for a while. Each man had a rifle and a pistol and there were extra horses in a rope corral.

Across the face of the valley was a fence, partly made of poles and partly of newly strung smooth wire on strong posts. The men were obviously guards against the cattle escaping or anyone trying to steal them.

"All we need is one as evidence," Spur said.

"Hell, Sheriff, you know you can't lead a steer.

123

Put a rope around their horns and they'll fight you all day."

They had been talking about the best way to get some of the steers to take back to Clearwater.

"No cowboy in his right skull would try to lead one of them steers. Even a young one would plant both feet and hold its head down until the rope came off. Not a chance."

"We could cut out about ten steers and drive them up over the rim, then head back for town," Spur suggested.

"Longhorns ain't afraid of nothing, but hills will spook them. This ridgeline is too steep. They could walk right up it if they ever decided to, but try to drive them up and they'll run the other way. We'd play old Billy Hell getting one of them up to the top, let alone a dozen."

"Then there's only one other way," Spur said. "We wait until it gets dark, and we stampede the herd straight at the wire. First few will go down in the wire and the rest of them will go right over them, break the wire, knock down the posts, wipe out the guard's camp and be off running like hell for about five miles."

Oliver was nodding. "Sounds good. I could use my rifle and take out one, maybe two of the guards on front if you want me to—just like in the war."

Spur considered it. But he wasn't here to kill Texans. These men were simply cowboys doing a job. It wasn't a war, not yet anyway.

"Don't think we need to go that far, Oliver.

Once we get the stampede started and breaking through the wire, we can ride on the far side and the guards will never see us. Now, say you want to stampede those cattle down there. How many do you think are there, and how do we get them moving?"

"I'd guess we have about five hundred, some cows, steers and a few calves," Oliver said. "Far as getting a stampede going, it's easy. We carry torches made of pine pitch and we shoot off our six-guns and rifles and scare the hell out of a bunch on one side. We get them moving downstream, then circle and scream and yell and shoot and wave the fire torches. They'll move, all right."

Spur sat on his horse and looked at the cattle below. They probably all belonged to Matt Rogers, and he probably would never get a cent for them, but one or two of them could be the last bit of evidence needed to cinch the case against Doak Galloway.

He looked at the sun. "We've got three hours of daylight left. That should be plenty of time to find some pine tar for our torches. Then we'll pick a spot to launch the stampede. Too bad we don't have some of that lightning from this morning now when we need it."

It was just before dusk. Spur and Oliver had found pine tree limbs, lathered them with pine tar and leaned them against a tree. They had dismounted and were waiting for darkness.

But when Spur turned to look at the cattle

again, he saw a six-gun muzzle three feet in front of him and a cowboy behind it with a rabbit in one hand and a surprised expression on his face.

"What the hell you men doing here?" the cowboy asked. "You sure as hell ain't Circle G men. Don't touch that iron, cowpuncher, or you're one dead hombre!"

# CHAPTER ELEVEN

Spur McCoy grinned easily, staring at the black hole of death.

"Hey, you must be Anderson. Boss told us to find somebody named Anderson out here and we're plumb lost. We both just signed on and he sent us out here. *Are* we lost, for Christ's sake?"

Oliver pointed to the torches. "Yeah, we been working our butts off making these torches. Why in hell would a guard shack in a valley full of critters need torches like these? Hell, we didn't know. We just follow orders. Got to go where there are some pines to get pine tar, right? So we stopped here. Now where the hell is Anderson? I want some chow before he closes up the damned chuck wagon."

The cowboy with the six-gun looked more confused at each moment.

"What the hell you talking about? Ain't no Anderson on this crew. Maybe out in the west end of the range. And what's this about torches?"

"Let me get one and I'll show you," Spur said. The gunman nodded.

Spur walked to the stack, picked up a branch and brought it back to where the cowboy stood. Spur saw a thin line of sweat showing on his chin.

"See this stuff here? This is the pine tar. We smear it on and the blamed thing burns like it had coal oil on it. Smell that stuff. Clear out your nose in a rush."

The man leaned forward to sniff the pine tar and Spur jolted the three-inch thick limb upward, smashing it into the gunman's gun hand and knocked his weapon to the ground.

Oliver tackled the stranger the moment he hit the ground, but the cowboy was already unconscious.

"Close," Spur said. They tied him up loosely enough that he could get undone in three or four hours, then waited once more for darkness to fall.

"Guy must have been out hunting," Oliver said. "Wish we'd had that rabbit this morning. I would have cooked it. Too late now—be dark in half an hour."

When they could no longer see the steers below in the valley, they each took three of the pine-tar torches and rode down. They worked together, riding right up to the edge of the herd, then lighting the torches from matches, waving them and shouting.

Two steers near Spur reared up and snorted. He shoved the torch at them, almost touching their sides, and they bellowed and ran forward. He had his six-gun out now and shouted and fired into the air. Nearby, Oliver did the same and they saw the whole herd wake up and rise and start to mill around frantically.

They lighted more torches and threw them into the bawling mass of steers, emptied their pistols and loaded and emptied them again; then they heard the sound of two thousand hooves beating against the ground. The pounding became louder and louder as the beasts began running hard, away from the noise, away from the fire, away from the explosions of the firearms.

Spur threw his last torch at the stampeding longhorns and yelled at Oliver, "That's it, let's follow and fire once in a while to keep them running."

They rode.

The steers and cows thundered forward. Spur rode past a calf or two that couldn't keep up. He heard the wire sprang away as it snapped as the first cattle crashed through it. There were some shots from the mouth of the valley, then the wave of terrified beasts swept past he guards, trampled down the fence, and thundered through the tent and cooking area. Spur and Oliver followed on the far side and were past the guards without being noticed in the blackness.

Spur saw only a few ropes left on the temporary corral and hoped that the cowboy's entire remuda had been swept away by the rampaging cattle. It would make pursuit much harder if they had no horses.

The mouth of the valley angled south, and Spur and Oliver chose a group of fifty head and ranged behind them, firing once in a while, charging at them, keeping them running. After what Spur guessed was five miles they let the fragment of the herd they chased slow to a walk, but kept them moving south toward the river. They would walk them all night, drive them toward the smell of water, and hopefully would have them almost off the Galloway range by sunup.

Just after dawn a bone-weary Oliver rode up to Spur and shook his head.

"We got four or five miles to go to the river. What should we do?"

Spur looked at the cattle. They were tired, getting hard to drive. They needed water and rest. He checked them in the dim light. Almost every critter had a fresh re-brand on its hip.

"Let's cut out ten with the new brands on them, and try to move them faster. When we hit the river, we'll find a place to ford and get them across, and then we'll look for some trees for cover so we can let the animals rest."

"Sounds reasonable."

It had been a long time since Spur had done any cutting, so he sat on his horse and watched as Oliver cut out ten beasts that looked strong and that had the double brand. Spur kept the group together, then they yahooed the critters south, leaving the rest of the herd to rest and graze.

It took them two hours to urge the ten animals to the river. It was low this time of year and Oliver drove the steers into the hock-deep water where they drank their fill then moved to the other side.

Once there, Spur got them moving again. Ahead he saw a stand of cottonwoods and heavy brush. He pointed at it and they had the ten critters concealed inside the brush a half hour later. Oliver herded the steers into a small area and as soon as they were left alone, they lay down.

"Get some rest yourself, Oliver. We could have company at any time."

Oliver sat down beside a tree and was sleeping at once, his rifle across his legs, his pistol by his right hand.

Spur stood and kept walking to stay awake. He heard distant shots and voices from across the river. Then he saw one cowboy rounding up some strays that had probably come from the stampede.

A half hour later, Spur caught himself nodding as he leaned against a tree. He shook his head and saw Oliver sleeping. The steers were quiet, some of them chewing their cuds.

The sound of hoofbeats came to him slowly, and he realized he had dropped off to sleep standing up. Spur shook his head and stared into the sunshine. Two riders were coming toward him, both carried rifles. Spur was alert at once. He sent a round over their heads from his Winchester, and they pulled up for a consultation. Then each fired twice into the woods, bent low over their horses and charged.

Spur waited until they were two hundred yards away. He put his first round into the first rider's bay and saw her go down and roll, taking her rider with her. The attacking cowboy jumped up, screaming. The other rider turned and looked at him, but didn't slacken his pace.

Spur put a round over the rider's head and then another. The cowboy swung around, fired twice more into the woods and returned for his unhorsed partner. The man caught a hand and vaulted onto the back of the horse. They rode away fast.

Spur roused Oliver, who had slept right through the shooting. He looked at the dead horse and nodded groggily.

"Not really a war—I got to remember that."

They moved the ten steers out, kicking them to get them up and walking. Oliver was good with the animals. He understood them, and Spur's limited trail drive work had not made him much of an expert in herding cattle. They pushed the critters hard and saw no one following them. Just before dusk, Spur found another copse of willow along the Clear River and they hid the steers in it.

"We're not more than five miles from town," Oliver said.

"I've got to get some sleep before I fall out of

the saddle," Spur said. "I doubt if anyone will follow us this far, but you better keep watch. Wake me in three hours and we'll drive them on into the livery and put them in that back corral."

Spur lay down on the grass and fell asleep before he could pull his six-gun and lay it by his hand.

Later Spur heard an owl, and wondered what it was doing, hooting inside a hotel. Deeper into the night he heard a cow bawling, and his fuzzy mind couldn't figure that out either.

When he woke it was dawn.

"Damn!" Spur said. Oliver sat beside a tree, snoring. Fine watchman he turned out to be, Spur thought. He roused Oliver and they drove the animals the last five miles to town, put them in the back pen and told the livery man not to let anyone come near them.

Spur staggered into the hotel, found his room and vaguely saw Holly as he walked through the door. He saw the bed and made a lunge for it. He was asleep almost before he hit the mattress.

Something tickled his nose. Spur blew it away. It happened again and he pawed at the offending fly with his hand. The offending fly caught his hand and giggled.

Spur pried one eye open. He saw only a fuzzy blur. The fuzzy blur kissed him, caught his hand and pressed it against her bare breasts.

"Hey you, big handsome guy. You still alive? You've been sleeping for almost eight hours. It's seven o'clock in the evening and I have a huge steak dinner and all the side dishes for you. Hungry?"

Spur blinked again. Slowly the mist cleared from his eyes and he saw Holly, bare to the waist, smiling at him. He pressed forward and kissed her lips, then kissed her breasts and her lips again.

"I died."

"Surely and truly you did, sir."

"Is this heaven? No, I don't think angels have big tits like these."

Holly laughed. "I can cover them up if they offend you."

"Don't you dare!" He sniffed. "Did you say steak?"

"Yes, sir. On the table."

He blinked again and saw the little room service table with a layout of food that made him crawl out of bed. Surprised to discover that he was buck naked.

"You undressed me?" he asked, astonished.

"Yes. I enjoyed it. I even made you get hard. Then I let you alone so you could rest."

"Thanks for the favors." He pulled on his pants and sat down to the steak. He had never eaten such a delicious meal in his life. It had been nearly thirty-six hours since he had eaten a bite.

When the steak was gone, he ordered another one, also more mashed potatoes and gravy, more carrots and more of the sliced and browned parsnips. They were delicious.

By eight o'clock he was full, rested and ready to take on his weight in wildcats. He went to see Paul Victor. Quietly they disbanded the local militia. Spur said he needed three more deputies, and Victor said to hire them at a dollar a day, thirty dollars a month. Spur also found out there was no brands inspector this side of Fort Worth and no telegraph.

Not much had happened in town during the three days Spur had been out of circulation. Galloway had not been to town. His rider had been in to the bank, but that was normal, and a Circle G supply rig had come to the Mercantile for its usual monthly stocking up on food and supplies.

"I want to charge Galloway with rustling the Rogers herd," Spur told Victor. "We can prove that easily. I also want to charge him with the murders of the Rogers clan and their two hands. We ought to be able to make that stick because of the drawings little Rogers boy made. Isn't cattle rustling a capital offence in Texas?"

"Yes, indeed. We'll get the papers drawn up tomorrow. When should we go out to bring him in?"

"Not quite yet, but get ready. I want all but one of the steers I brought in slaughtered and the meat given to the nine poorest families in town. No—give a quarter of beef to the thirty-six poorest families in town. You work it out. Tell them it's courtesy of Matt Rogers."

"Yes, Sheriff, we can arrange that."

"I just wish Matt was here to appreciate it. Oh, and I want to bring civil action against Galloway as well, in the name of Matt Rogers. Estimate the value of his ranch buildings, and add $24,000 for the value of his livestock. Then add on to that three hundred thousand dollars for the wrongful death of his family members. Get it all drawn up right and legal, and we'll have Matt sign it as soon as I can find him."

"That's more than Galloway's whole ranch is worth," said Victor.

"You're getting the idea. Any other county business we need to talk about?"

"I think that about covers it, Sheriff."

"Good. It's well past time I had a drink."

Spur had more than one and got back to the hotel late.

# CHAPTER TWELVE

Matt Rogers had forgotten how long he had been
on Zane Smith's trail. The days blended together.
The second horse he had came up lame before he
overtook the killer. His tracks meandered and
were hard to follow. Once Smith had stopped at a
ranch.

By the time Matt got there, a woman and two
hands had been killed and Zane took off with two
fresh horses and a sack full of supplies and food.
The rancher was preparing to go after the killer
and now both he and Matt were on his trail. The
rancher's name was Jennings and he had only
been in Texas for a year.

By four o'clock the second day after the new
killings, they thought they had him. Zane had
stolen two horses, including one flashy stallion
that was temperamental and had one bad leg.

Matt and Jennings had found the stallion shot to death near the end of the first day. Now they were closing in, since the big sack of supplies had slowed Smith down.

Jennings was a small man, with a soft, kindly voice, piercing brown eyes and a sharp wit. But now he was totally dedicated to avenging his wife's murder. He spoke little, made certain Matt knew he was going to kill Zane when they caught him, and was open and fair about everything. Matt liked the other man at once and they worked well as a team.

Jennings nodded at the small hill ahead.

"The trail flattens out up there and there's a five mile straight stretch along a section line. If he's anywhere around, we'll see him. I got a feeling we'll close with him today."

And they did. Jennings spotted Zane on the dun horse half way down the trail. The small man nodded and turned off the track into the prairie slanting at a forty-five degree angle to the wagon road.

"The route here goes almost straight north for six miles, then mades a right-angle turn to the left. We can cut across the hills here, save three miles, and beat him to the crossroad. Then we sit and wait for him."

It turned out that way. They spurred their horses on, knowing they would be able to rest just a ways farther. Jennings set up the ambush. He had a shotgun with him, and his rifle. He wanted to be closest. Matt would be farther back as insurance, with his own rifle.

Jennings lay behind the tree and waited. His hands were sweating. He hadn't killed anyone since the war ten years ago. Then he had to. Now he had to. He watched the road. For just a moment he asked himself, Why him? Why had *his* ranch been the one the killer had stumbled upon and shot everyone he saw? Tears seeped down his cheeks as he waited.

But his resolve was firm. He would take out the bastard with the first barrel of the twelve-gauge, then walk up and blow his head off his body with the second blast.

Down the road he saw a man coming on horseback. Jennings signaled Matt, who lay on the other side of the road farther along. They had a good crossfire pattern, but Jennings had asked Matt to hold his fire until he could get in the first shot.

Jennings offered a silent prayer for his wife and his family, and then his eyes turned cold; the sweat vanished from his forehead and he felt strangely chilled. He was going to kill a man, one who deserved to die.

The rider came on. He did not look behind him, but his head turned now and then as if checking the trail, the wagon road. He seemed confident that he would get away again. Only this time he was wrong. He was a hundred yards away—an easy shot for a rifle, but not for a shotgun with double-ought buck. Jennings had to wait until the man was as close as possible. When he was in the middle of the road directly opposite the tree, Zane Smith, the killer, would be only ten yards away.

Jennings took a deep breath and waited.

Fifty yards.

Forty yards.

The horse walked at an even pace but it seemed so slow to Jennings. He waved at Matt Rogers, who could see both of them now. Jennings lifted the shotgun and slid it through the green leaves that shielded him.

Twenty yards. Close enough. No, closer for a better killing target.

Fifteen yards.

*Now!*

Jennings had been tracking his target, and now he pulled the trigger slowly, squeezing it. A rattlesnake slithered over Jennings' arm where it lay on the ground, the snake's forked tongue stabbing at the air in surprise at the sudden heat of a human body.

Jennings saw the snake coiling to strike just as his finger stroked the trigger, and he spun backwards away from certain death. The shotgun went off, pointing straight in the air.

Matt had waited, realizing that in a few seconds Zane would be dead. He planned to take the murderer's head back to Galloway and make him hold it as he killed him. He had his rifle sights on Zane's chest, which he expected to splatter in all directions when Jennings' shotgun blasted.

The firing caught Matt by surprise, and when

he saw that Zane was not hit, he was too late to adjust his sights. He fired, but Zane had already jerked the horse around and rode directly at the shotgun blast. His .44 was into his hand and he saw the man by the tree. He fired three times as he raced the fifteen yards to him, then fired once again directly into the man's face as he looked up from the ground.

As he galloped past, Zane realized a rattlesnake had its fangs sunk deeply into the man's neck. The ambusher was already dead.

Then Zane bent down low on his horse's neck and pounded away into the countryside, away from the other man, the one with the rifle. He had been lucky, Zane realized. He had escaped death with the unexpected aid of a rattlesnake. At that moment Zane made a vow never to harm another snake of any size or kind. He rode low in the saddle for a mile, then turned and swung low again, hunting a swale or riverbed that would put him out of range of the rifle.

Ten times the slugs from the rifle flew past him. The man with the gun was not taking time to aim properly or he could at least have hit the horse. Then Zane was away and riding hard for the maze of hills with more woodlands now where he could hide.

Behind him, Matt Rogers had caught his horse and mounted. He stopped for the shotgun, then took Jennings' pistol and rifle. He wouldn't need them anymore. He saw the snake and killed it, then took the scattergun and the twenty rounds

141

from the dead man's saddlebags. He tied Jennings' horse to the back of his own saddle and rode hard for the point where he had last seen his quarry.

It was two days later before Matt picked up the trail as Zane continued his general northward route. They had passed through a small town where Matt sold the rifle and a pistol in order to buy food, and asked if anyone had seen another lone rider heading north. Two people had and they said he was now riding a sorrel, that he had on a white hat and dark clothes, and that he had plenty of money.

Zane had killed again, Matt knew. He had to find him soon, to stop this rampage of death. His chance came the next morning when Matt stopped at a small stream to drink and wash his coffee pot. A pistol shot sounded a hundred yards away and Matt took the shotgun and his rifle and worked through the brush slowly. He found his target skinning out a rabbit beside a small cooking fire on which he intended to roast the meat.

This time Matt was determined to have his revenge, once and for all. He did not bother to conceal his approach, and Zane put down his skinning knife and turned with two six-guns in his hands. He blasted twelve rounds into the brush in Matt's general direction. One round creased Matt's shoulder; the rest were high. He had no shot as Zane jumped behind a tree. With his rifle, Zane killed the sorrel with one head shot, then chipped wood off the tree.

"Give up, Smith. You've got nowhere to run!" As soon as he said the words, Matt rolled behind a downed log and heard four rounds clip through the brush where he had been. He remained silent.

The only sound he could hear was one stick breaking. Matt rose to his feet and saw that Zane had used the tree to shield his exit directly behind it to the stream bed. Now it was a race on foot as Matt ran along the top of the low bank, searching for the killer.

A pistol shot gave away his location, but bored through Matt's left arm, knocking him down. Matt sent one barrel of the double-ought buck into the woods where Zane had been. There was no shout of pain, which meant the killer had probably moved.

A startled grouse flew up from further down the stream and Matt rushed that way, pushing a fresh round into the shotgun. As far as Matt knew, Zane did not have a long gun with him. He had been forced to leave his rifle behind. That helped.

For a moment Matt wondered if he should run back and get his horse. He rejected the thought at once. He was in hot pursuit with the enemy. He had to maintain that contact, locate him and kill him. Simple. The day was young. He had ten hours before dark. There would be a proper time and proper place.

The small stream tumbled through a rapids as

the land slanted off on a downgrade. Matt paused behind a tree and scanned the entire area in front of him for movement. He sectioned the brushy area around the stream, skipped the open places and then concentrated again on the brush and trees along the winding stream.

A blur a hundred yards down.

Movement, then nothing.

He stared at the spot until he was seeing double; then another movement. Now he could spot the man. Zane was lying near a tree. There seemed to be something unnatural in his position. Matt decided Zane might be wounded. He brought the Winchester up and sighted in on the man. But before he could fire, Zane was up and running.

Matt fired three times as fast as he had ever worked the lever on the Winchester. He saw the first round catch flesh—a leg he thought—and Zane tumbled into the brush and out of sight.

Matt was running too now, the shotgun in his right hand, the rifle in his left. He moved through the open country for fifty yards, then darted into the cover of the trees and charged toward the spot where he had seen Zane fall.

The last twenty yards he came up slowly. He couldn't let Zane have a shot with his six-gun. The animal had killed enough people already. Slowly he worked forward. Ahead, he heard a groan that seemed to come through gritted teeth.

He moved up to the next good-sized cottonwood. Beyond it he could see Zane lying in a small patch of sunshine. Zane gripped his right leg, and he was trying to put a bandana around it to stop the flow of blood.

Matt didn't say a word. He lifted the shotgun. But before he could fire, Zane spun around, his left hand holding a pistol, and he thumbed off two shots, sending Matt diving behind the tree. A sudden agony burned in his body and Matt knew he was hit. As he fell, the shotgun discharged, but was aimed into the air. He tumbled into the grass and lay there unable to move. He had no idea where he was hit. The pain came in surges and billows and he wondered for a moment if he were dying, or dead. No, if he were dead he wouldn't be hurting this way.

Matt Rogers tried to sit up. He couldn't. His hands worked all right. He pulled out his six-gun and watched his horizons. At any moment he expected Zane Smith to hobble toward him with his pistol fully loaded and finish the job he had started at the Flying R ranch.

# CHAPTER THIRTEEN

Holly Kane sat in bed watching Spur as he woke up. She was topless—he knew she always slept naked. It was an interesting sight to wake up to.

"Good morning, Mr. McCoy."

"Good morning, Miss Kane."

"I was just trying to figure you out. I know now that Paul Victor and the county people brought you in to settle this thing with Galloway. Which presents me with a damn big problem."

"How is that a problem for you?" Spur asked, reaching across and kissing her lips. She pulled away.

"Don't—I'm thinking. My problem is that I figure you're some kind of a fiddlefoot who wanders around getting people out of trouble, and that you're a grown man and ain't never got married, so how in hell am I gonna lasso you and hog-tie you and get you to a church and a preacher?"

"You *do* have a problem." Spur tried to kiss her again and again she pulled away.

"Like my old granddaddy used to say, Why should a man buy the heifer when he's getting the milk for free?"

"Nicest little heifer I've seen in a long time."

She slipped out of bed with her back to him and pulled on her clothes quickly. "No more free milk. You like me, you buy me with a ring and a preacher and the whole marriage thing."

"What's got into you this morning?"

"*You,* Spur McCoy, too often, and too damn nice! I'm moving into my own room and try to find a job. Maybe Mr. Victor needs somebody to work here in the hotel."

"You're serious!"

"Damn right!"

"What can I say?" Spur got out of bed. He was naked. "I am a cad and a bounder. A complete heal. I've been taking advantage of you, and you'll be a hell of a lot better off without me. Don't have anything to do with men like me. How could I steal all that free loving that way?"

She turned and looked at him, her absolute decision wavering. Holly stared at his hard body and his genitals and she shivered.

"Well, I guess I did kind of ask myself in. I mean, I didn't say no anywhere down the line."

"No. It was my fault, I was the aggressor."

"I wasn't a trembling virgin, that I know." She

sighed. "Damnit, McCoy, I am right about one thing. You will be leaving Clearwater as soon as this trouble is over, right?"

He nodded.

"Oh, Christ! I knew it!" She ran to him and threw her arms around him, holding him tight. Tears trickled down her cheeks. "I have you for another week or two. That's better than playing the wronged woman." She nodded as if convincing herself. "Yes, I'm going to love you for as long as I can!" Her hand slipped down between them and found him and soon Spur was hard.

She squealed and pulled him on the bed.

"I'm not very good in the mornings," he said. "I should warn you."

"You are fantastic anytime, I can testify to that in a law court!"

"Little darling Holly, you don't have to testify just on my account."

She laughed, pulled off her clothes and sat naked on his chest. Then she moved off the bed and pulled him up. She leaned back against the wall and drew him to her.

"Show me how to do it standing up. I always thought it couldn't be done standing up, but I heard a girl once say it wasn't so hard. Show me!"

Spur laughed gently, kissed her sweet lips and showed her.

At about the same time Spur was instructing Holly in the art of vertical lovemaking, a rider from the Galloway ranch came into town and went to the bank. He made a deposit of funds from the ranch, spoke kindly to the teller and the cashier, then briefly with the bank president, Clint Bascomb. As they talked, the rider, Ian Dunning, passed the banker an envelope. He said goodbye and drifted outside, went to the saloon his boss' son used to own, and soon vanished out the rear door into the alley.

Dunning moved quickly then, down the alley and into the residential section, up another alley there and then quietly he tried the back door of a two-story house. Even from the back, anyone could tell it was the finest house on the block, well cared for and with a garden in the rear that was drying up from lack of rain.

Dunning did not bother to knock. The door was open and he slid inside without a sound. He went to the kitchen, saw it was empty and continued on to the living room. A pair of watchdogs came off the carpet in tandem, their hackles lifted, jaws open, showing gleaming white fangs.

Like good attack dogs, they made no sound. They sprang at him as a team, one going for his throat, the other after his right arm. Dunning had known the dogs would be there and was prepared. He brought up two Cavalry short swords, met both dogs with thrusts of the blades and drove the twin knives into their throats before they knew what hit them. One died at once; the other staggered off to one side and Dunning thrust a second time into the dog's chest, killing it.

The only sound had been one dog pushing a

living room chair a foot across the floor when the animal fell.

Dunning put down one of the swords and listened. The house was deathly still. He moved to the stairway and went up the steps silently, walking on the side of the treads to avoid any loose or squeaky boards. Upstairs, he moved to the second door which he knew was the master bedroom.

Dunning had found his niche in the Galloway ranch quickly. Galloway had learned of his background and had brought him in from Forth Worth. He had been in the war, riding with an independent group of freebooters for the South, raiding around the Kansas and Nebraska area, burning, looting, and raping, but never turning anything over to the Rebel cause.

Dunning had been in trouble in Forth Worth when Galloway made one of his infrequent trips to the big town. Galloway paid his fine, his damages at two bars and one bordello, and took him back to the Circle G as his enforcer. No one gave Dunning any trouble on the ranch. He was available for any dirty job that Galloway might have. He had missed the Rogers massacre because he had twisted his ankle on a roundup. Now he was healthy and ready.

The door squeaked as it opened, but when Dunning looked around the edge, he saw that it had not wakened Agnes Bascomb, wife of the banker. She wasn't pretty, but she was a woman—about forty, Dunning decided. It had been too long

since he had used a woman. He decided he would
have her no matter how ugly she was. She took a
nap every morning at this time, right after she
got her husband fed and off to work and the house
cleaned.

Dunning pulled his short knife with the thin
blade, the one he used for skinning, and pressed it
against Agnes's throat. Then he shook her
shoulder. She awoke with a start and a little cry.

"Quiet!" Dunning hissed. "Don't say a word or
I'll slit your throat and you'll be dead in two
minutes. You understand?"

She nodded.

He pulled back the comforter and saw that she
was dressed but her skirt had been pulled up and
her blouse was open, showing her breasts. In her
right hand she held an inch thick pink candle with
the end carved into a phallic point.

Dunning snickered.

"Upright citizen, pillar of the community, go to
church and everything and here you are, Agnes,
fucking yourself with a candle! Christ, you must
be needing it." He looked at her again. She was
short and fat with sagging breasts. So what?

"Sit up and take your dress off," he told her.
"Any sound at all and I'll cut off one of your tits,
understand?"

Agnes Bascomb shivered. She had often
dreamed of something like this happening, but it
never did. She had no children. The doctor didn't
know why. Her husband wasn't demanding at all
in bed—she wondered if he used the girls down-

town, but she never asked. Now she watched the dangerous-looking man. He was unshaven, and there was a bulge at his crotch. Strangely, it excited rather than alarmed her. She had no idea why he had come to her, but she pulled the dress off quickly, and the chemise.

"Them underthings too, you old cunt," he said.

She blushed. She had never heard the word used before. Quickly she kicked out of her drawers and sat there, feeling fat, old and naked.

Dunning took a watch from his pocket, checked the time, then opened his fly. She stared in fascination as he erect penis came out.

"Oh, my!" she said softly.

"You like that? Good—have a bit or two." He straddled her, pushed her down on the bed on her back and lifted her head, forcing his penis into her mouth. At first she sputtered and fought, but then she relaxed and he saw she was enjoying it.

"You old whore!" he said. "You do like to suck cock! I'll be goddamned!" He looked at his watch again, pulled out of her mouth and moved lower, pushing her legs apart.

"You like to fuck, don't you, old whore?"

"Yes," she said softly.

Dunnings laughed and drove hard into her dry nether lips, searing past them, hurting himself as well as her, bringing tears to her eyes and then a soft moaning as she worked her hips against his.

Dunning didn't wait for her. He slammed into her hard and fast and just as he felt that he was about to climax, he slid his knife into his right

153

hand and put the blade across her throat.

"Don't make a sound!" he warned her. Then the power of the human animal's instinct for the perpetuation of the species overpowered him and he pumped the final climaxing thrusts at her and at the same time slit her throat, jerking a pillow over her head to staunch the blood. Christ! He had climaxed just as he was killing the old bitch! He had never felt that kind of a surge of power and sex all mixed in together before. Fantastic!

He panted a moment, came out of her and buttoned his pants. Then he found her clothes and folded them neatly, put the big candle in her hand and wrapped her fingers around it before they stiffened, and folded the top blanket neatly at the foot of the bed. Then he sat by the window that let him watch down on the street.

He still had ten minutes before the banker and the sheriff were set to arrive. Bascomb wouldn't have a hint what this was all about. The note from Galloway which Dunning had delivered said it was time they talked in private, and he wanted him to come home and bring the sheriff with him. It was time for a clearing of the air with the sheriff so they all could go on living here and working in peace and harmony. The note would intrigue Bascomb; he would have no choice but to come.

Bringing the sheriff into it was a master stroke by Galloway. Dunning smiled and nodded as he thought about it. His own part was simple. Just the killing. As he waited, Dunning cleaned his knife on the curtain.

Five minutes before eleven, the appointed hour, he saw Bascomb walking quickly down the street. Nothing unusual about that, he always walked fast, and always came home for lunch. Today he was a little early.

But where was the sheriff?

Dunning frowned. They were supposed to come together. He had to have them together! Change of plans. He was planning on letting them both come up the steps hunting Bascomb's wife until they found her here. Then it would be too late.

Change of plans. Flexible. He had to do it differently. Dunning hurried down the steps, put the knife away and adjusted the .44 on his hip. He would have to play it as the cards were dealt to him. He would still win the pot, he was sure of that, but he would have a different hand.

Bascomb came in the front door, looking around nervously.

"Dunning. What are you doing here? That was a strange letter from Galloway. What the hell did he mean by all that?"

"Don't know, Mr. Dunning. I just brought the message. Mr. Galloway will be coming in the back way, and he's a little late. We better wait here."

"I'll see Agnes and then be right back."

Dunning shook his head. "No, Mr. Bascomb. I'm a cautious man. I want you to stay right here where I can see you until Mr. Galloway gets here. That's my job. Don't ask me to do something that would stop me from doing my job."

Bascomb frowned, then lifted his brows in resignation. He sat down and watched Dunning. "I still don't understand."

"I don't understand either, but that's not my job. Mr. Galloway will be coming soon. You were early."

"But why meet here and not at the bank?"

"That one you know. Do you want everyone in town to see you meeting with Galloway? It would cause lots of talk."

"Yes, I can see that." Bascomb looked at Dunning, then past him and his brows lifted in surprise. He glanced away quickly, but Dunning had noticed. He shifted his position slightly and his right hand came free of his belt. He moved like a lightning bolt, hand to his gun butt, and spinning on his left foot to face whoever was behind him.

He was three quarters of the way around when a .45 roared and the big lead slug pounded into Dunning's right shoulder, slamming him back three feet, knocking the six-gun from his hand and bringing a bellow of rage from his mouth. He stumbled and fell on the floor.

Bascomb screeched in surprise and fear, cowering against the wall. He looked down and saw Dunning bleeding all over his expensive carpet. Then he looked at Sheriff Spur McCoy, who still had his pistol pointed at Dunning.

"Don't move, Dunning, or you're a dead man," said Spur.

"Christ, help me! I'm bleeding to death!"

"Good."

"What the hell you mean, asshole?"

"I've been upstairs."

"What do you mean?" Bascomb asked at once.

Spur sighed. He had to know sometime. "This seems to be some kind of a trap, Bascomb, aimed at you, or at me, or at both of us. Can you tell me why?"

"No. Upstairs? That's where Agnes is!"

Spur caught Bascomb as he tried to run past. "Don't go up there, Bascomb!" But the banker wrenched away from Spur and ran up the steps. Spur took two steps to Dunning and picked up the fallen six-gun, took a derringer from his boot and a knife from his belt.

"Who was the trap for, Dunning? A sex scandal with both me and Mrs. Bascomb dead in her bed, naked of course."

"Stop my bleeding and I'll tell you."

Spur took a pillow off the couch and pushed it hard into the shattered shoulder. Dunning screamed. Then he held the cloth over the wound.

The animal-like tortured wail from upstairs came in a billowing roar, an agony that could not be comforted. Spur got to the bottom of the stairs in time to grab Bascomb and push up the doubled barreled shotgun he carried just as it went off. It had been aimed at Dunning, but shattered a lamp and the ceiling instead. Bascomb dropped the shotgun and charged Dunning, kicking him in the side and the wounded shoulder, then once in the head before Spur pulled him away.

Spur slapped Bascomb hard across the face,

and shook him.

"Bascomb! Come to your senses! Dunning will pay. He'll hang, and since Galloway ordered him to come, Galloway will hang, too."

Dunning laughed through his pain. "Sure, Bascomb! Tell him how you and Galloway have looted the county treasury. Tell him how you and Galloway split up the county, with each of you taking half and bleeding everyone dry. Tell him, Bascomb!"

Bascomb sat down heavily on the couch. He looked at his hands, then glanced up the stairs and began sobbing.

By the expression on Bascomb's face, Spur knew Dunning's accusations must be true.

"Mr. Bascomb. I'm sorry about your wife. Dunning will hang for it, I guarantee you. Do you want to send the undertaker around?"

Bascomb nodded.

Spur McCoy picked Dunning off the floor and marched him down to the doctor's office. Then he would be locked in the jail. Spur had to find out when the judge would be in town again. He had an airtight case against Dunning.

But Bascomb? Working with Galloway? He was going to have to have a long talk with the town's only banker.

# CHAPTER FOURTEEN

Spur McCoy sat at his desk sharpening a pencil that didn't need sharpening. He shaved the lead down to a fine point, then to a blunt point and began sharpening the wood part again.

Toby had been gone for two hours. There couldn't be that many places in town to check. When Toby came in a few minutes later he was smiling and a little unsteady on his feet. The glint was gone from his eyes.

"Toby, have you been drinking on duty?"

"Just a smidgin, Sheriff."

"And you found out what I wanted to know?"

"Oh boy, sure did!" His grin was now a mile wide as he sat down on the chair beside Spur's desk in the sheriff's office.

"Got the information." He laughed and his voice went high.

"Toby, you're drunk."

"Yeah, guess you're right. Not the right person to send out to a whorehouse."

"You didn't have to patronize each one of them!"

"Best way to find out things. Jeeze, have you seen this little colored girl they got over at Bertha's? She's got tits. . . ." He stopped and looked at the ceiling. "Lordy, my Georgia pappy probably turned right over in his grave!"

"What about the man you were asking about?"

"Oh, yeah. He was a steady customer. At least twice a week around town somewhere. He never caused no trouble, always paid and the girls liked him. Said he treated them like ladies."

"Good. Now go sleep it off in the first cell. I'll lock the door and you just ignore anybody who knocks. Got me a call to make."

Spur had given Clint Bascomb four hours to control his grief; now he went to the bank for a chat. The president of the bank was at his desk, looking suller, and a little defensive. One thing he was *not* was grief-stricken.

"Bascomb, is there an office where we can talk?"

Bascomb nodded toward a small room at the back where they counted money and used for storage.

"Seems like we have something to talk about," Spur said. "First, I want you to know *I* know there wasn't much love between you and your wife, and that you used the fancy women in town at least twice a week. So don't give me the bereaved husband story. Also I want you to know that when I found your wife she was naked on top of the bed with a candle in her hand. I figure I was to be the other person found dead in her bed. But that part didn't work. Do you have anything to tell me?"

"I really don't understand what you're getting at, Sheriff."

"So that's your approach. Fine. I want you to know that this noon I sent a message to Fort Worth, asking an accounting firm I know there to send out a man to audit the county books. There should be someone here within a week. Until then, I've locked up the county treasurer's books."

Bascomb paled but he said nothing.

"Now, if you don't want to talk about that either, what is your connection with Galloway?"

"He's a depositor. Has a good bit of money in the bank. He has one of the new safe boxes where he can put valuables inside our vault." Bascomb shifted on his feet. "Two years ago Galloway lost a lot of cattle in a flash flood on his way to the railhead. Cost him over $40,000. I made good on some of his debts, loaned him some cash. He didn't want anyone to know."

"Anything else?"

Bascomb shook his head.

"What about you and him splitting up the county and looting the county treasury?"

"The man who said that is a killer. Who'll believe him?"

"I do, because it's the kind of thing Galloway would do, only he would need a secretive inside man. Somebody who was on the County Board."

"I don't know what you're talking about."

"All right. The auditor won't be here for a week. The judge will be here the week after that. We have plenty of time to work up our case against you. And Bascomb, don't try to run. There will be a man watching your house and your bank twenty-four hours a day, a member of that militia you helped set up last week. Handy. I'm not familiar with the Texas prisons, but somebody told me they are the toughest in the Union, with maybe an exception made for the Arizona Territorial Prison at Yuma. Have you heard that?"

"Sheriff, I have no intention of running."

"Good, because I would find you. Have you heard about the new law service that is getting into use? It's called the Criminal Information Service. There's a central point in Chicago where every wanted criminal is listed, along with a picture or description, his habits, his type of crime, what he is wanted for and a lot of biographical information. Just send in a letter and find out about anyone on the wanted list. A damn fine service."

Bascomb nodded, but Spur saw a trace of perspiration on his forehead.

"That's about it, Bascomb. I hope you won't be leaving town, and if you have anything to tell me, my office is always open." At the door Spur turned. "We could try something. I see that they do it quite a bit back East. Say you did step out of line here and there with the county, but could make full restitution. The County probably could be talked out of prosecuting on most of the crimes. There could be a chance that you could get off with a suspended sentence and put on immediate parole. Think about it."

Spur closed the door and walked out of the bank. He went past the Mercantile, then retraced his steps and stopped in. Katie was waiting on two customers and when they were served and had left, she crooked her finger at him and walked behind a screen that separated the front of the store from her quarters and some storage areas.

She wore a brown and white print dress with bows on the sleeves and at her throat. The bodice swelled enticingly, and Spur remembered the lovelies that lay just underneath. Her hair was that deep red he loved and she smiled with honest pleasure.

"How would you like a home-cooked supper tonight?" she asked.

"A big party?"

"Plenty big—it's for two. I can find some good wine and do up my specialty, steak and scalloped potatoes."

Spur nodded. "You know the right words to say. That's my favorite menu." He leaned in to kiss her.

Their lips met and she slid away.

"Oh, no. Don't put your arms around me or I

might melt right on the floor and flip my skirt over my head and spread my legs."

"That sounds like dessert," Spur said. He caught her by one arm and pulled her slowly to him. She pressed hard against him and he felt his pants start to bulge as he held and kissed her. His hand found her breasts and he fondled them, then opened a button and pushed his hand inside.

"No, don't," she said softly. "Then, if anyone comes in, you button me up real quick."

He nodded. He kissed her again and their tongues battled. Someone looked in the front window, but didn't come inside. She stood against him with her legs spread slightly. Spur bent and picked her up by her thighs and pushed his crotch against hers.

"Do you know how quickly I could make love to you right here, holding you this way?"

"Only if you bit a hole in my drawers!"

"I've been known to do that, too." He put her down and lifted her skirt. She was smiling and her breath quickened.

Just then the little bell on the front door jangled and she pulled down her skirt and fastened the button of her bodice, blotted her forehead against his shirt and giggled.

"Saved by the front door bell," she said. "You be here at six tonight. That's when I close up." Then she was gone into the store to wait on the customer. Spur left the back part of the store when the woman buyer couldn't see him and eased out the front door.

Back at the office, he roused Toby and fed him two cups of black coffee, then left him there and walked the street. It was a nice little town. With more ranches and some dirt farming, it could blossom into a real town. Or it could if he got rid of Galloway.

The one piece of hard evidence he was still missing was Zane Smith, the man who had been on the killing spree at the Rogers ranch, the one they had missed in the raid on the Galloway Circle G. He would put the final nail in the gallows that would hang Galloway. Spur shrugged. There was a good chance for conviction anyway. He had obtained the two pictures that little Will had drawn of his killers. They would help sway a jury. And he had the rustled cattle. That was strong evidence.

Spur walked past the bank. He saw Bascomb sitting behind his desk, but the banker never looked up. He went into the nearest bar and ordered a beer. It was cold.

"Ice house?" Spur asked.

The barkeep nodded. "All the bars went together and built it. We cut ice every winter and bury it in the hole, cover it with straw between the layers of ice blocks. It keeps things nice and cold. Roof over it, 'course, and tight around the edges. Last year we used the ice right through to the end of August."

Spur nodded, gave thanks to the bar owners who planned ahead, and sipped at the beer until it was gone. He was getting more cases than he could handle—Galloway for multiple murders, Dunning for one kill and now Bascomb for grand theft and embezzlement. At least they all tied in together. Then he wanted to push the civil suit against either Galloway or his estate, whichever one was left by that time.

It was a quarter after five. Soon he could go for an old-fashioned home cooked supper. That sounded good, and so did the charms of Katie. It should be a pleasant evening. No, more than pleasant—an exhausting but great night.

Somebody rammed open the front door and a head poked in. Spur made a reach toward his pistol.

"Trouble down at the bank, you better come!" the man's voice screeched, then the head vanished.

Spur was on his feet running. He got to the bank fast but already there were thirty people outside the door. A man Spur remembered as an employee at the bank had locked and bolted the front door. He saw Spur and called through the glass, "Tell everyone to stand back and I'll open. The bank is not failing or going broke. Their money is safe. We've had an accident inside. Please come in quickly."

Inside, Spur saw the man lock the door behind him, then point to the back room where Spur had talked with Bascomb. He started to draw his gun, but the teller shook his head.

"You won't need your gun, it's too late for that."

Inside the room, Spur saw why. Clinton Bascomb's body lay on the floor. The side and back of his head were missing. Powder burns ringed a black hole on the right side of his head. The left side had been carried away by the heavy pistol round. Blood, brains and bone tissue had sprayed the wall. Evidently he had been standing when he shot himself. *If* he shot himself.

"Tell everyone in the bank when the gun went off that I'll need to talk to them. Is there any other way out of this room?"

"No, sir. No way out except the way we came in."

"Did you see Bascomb come in here?"

"Yes, sir. He came in alone. He had been unhappy and brooding all afternoon. We all thought it was because of his wife."

"Did anyone talk to him this afternoon after I left? Any strangers, anyone other than regular customers or the bank staff?"

"No. Just you. I think he was mighty depressed."

"What's your position here?"

"I'm vice president and cashier. That's the number two man in the bank. I've been here for fifteen years."

"Then you know the records pretty well."

"Better than anyone else."

"I want you to tell me how much cash, securities, property, everything of value that Mr. Bascomb owned. Second, did the county have its account here? How much of a balance does it have? When are taxes collected, and are there any irregularities with the county's account.''

"That's going to take some time.''

"You have all night. I expect you to be open for business as usual tomorrow. When is your opening time?''

"Ten A.M.''

"Hire an extra person if you need to, but have that information ready for me. If we make a public announcement we should be able to stall a run on the bank. I'd guess you don't have enough cash on hand, both paper and coin, to cover your total deposits.''

"No, of course not. A bank can't operate with that much cash on hand.''

"True.''

"Sheriff, why did he do it?''

"Fear.''

"What could he be afraid of?''

"Public ridicule, failure, prison.''

"I don't understand.''

"Evidently Bascomb had been looting the county treasury for years. He also did the annual audit. In fact, I would guess he did the audit without charge to save the county money.''

"Yes, I helped him sometimes. It's a big job.''

"It's bigger when you have to cover up corruption and a massive shortage of funds. Get the undertaker over here to clean up. I'd say Clearwater is going to have a double funeral tomorrow.''

Spur went out the front door and nodded at the

crowd which now numbered over a hundred.

"Ladies and gentlemen, the bank is closed now, but it will be open for business as usual in the morning. This bank is solid and safe. There is nothing to fear. Clint Bascomb is dead by his own hand. As most of you know, he lost his wife today, and evidently it was more than he could stand. His death has no bearing on the solvency of this bank. Now please go home since there is nothing you can do or gain by being here. Remember, the bank is solvent, your money is safe. This is one of those tragedies that happen now and then."

Spur put on his hat and walked down the block to the sheriff's office. Ten minutes later the crowd in front of the bank had dispersed. He told Toby he was going for supper and might not be back until late. Then he walked down the street to the alley in back of the Mercantile, found the right door and slipped inside.

Katie was waiting for him.

"I thought you'd probably be late so I waited to fry the steaks. Medium rare or rare?"

# CHAPTER FIFTEEN

Spur leaned back from the table and smiled at Katie. "I'm not sure that I believe this. All that luscious, sexy, glorious body, that beautiful face and sparkling personality, and in addition to all that you can still cook like a goddamned French chef."

"That must have been a compliment," Katie said, brushing a curl of long dark red hair off her shoulder. "Want to cut cards to see who does the dishes?" She laughed. "Just joshing you. Spur McCoy, I can do dishes anytime. It isn't often that I have a big, handsome stud like you captured in my house and all to myself."

"Sounds like it's time to take off my boots and move to your couch."

"If you don't take off a lot more than your boots, I'll be a most disappointed woman."

"We'll see what we can do about that."

They went to the couch and she sat beside him, leaning against his shoulder. His arm went around her.

"How did you wind up owning a store?"

"I thought I told you. My father began it, and built it up, then he died one day. Heart, the doctor said. So I inherited it, and I'm determined to make it pay."

"Looks like you're doing fine so far."

"I am. How did you happen to come to Clearwater and get yourself named sheriff?"

"Just ran out of luck, I guess." He kissed her and they forget about talking. She kissed him back and pushed her hand inside his shirt.

"Sweet Spur! I want this one to just last and last. Let's go real slow, all right?"

He nodded and kissed her again, his hands finding her lovely breasts and slipping underneath the cloth of her bodice to her warm flesh. They kissed again and she sighed.

"Love it when you pet me!" she said. "I just get so soft-feeling, and my willpower evaporates, and I want more and more petting." She kissed him hard on the mouth. "Yes, yes!"

He took off the dress she was wearing, and the chemise, and bent to kiss her full breasts.

"Spur, I get the feeling that you won't be around here much longer. As soon as you have this situation straightened out, I suspect you'll be moving on. You seem to be some kind of expert problem solver."

He kissed her right breast, then nibbled at the nipple until she shivered.

"The big problem I have now, is which of these two beautiful orbs I should chew on."

"No problem," she said giggling. "Have both of them."

Spur thought how easy it would be to stop his travels and settle down in a little town like this, move in with Katie and stay with her. Hell, maybe even a wedding band and a family sometime . . . He shivered. What was he thinking about?

She had worked one hand inside his pants and was playing with his scrotum.

"Just marvelous, a man. This little sack is where the seeds of the future generations come from. Amazing! A man always fascinates me. And to see your cock get big and hard is like magic. A woman can't do that."

"Your nipples enlarge, get hard and hot. Feel them."

"Just a little. They don't triple in size."

"I'm glad you like it."

He was in a rush then. He pulled her drawers off and stared at her naked body there on the couch. He put one of her legs up on the back of the couch and began undressing.

"No! Leave all your clothes on. I want to pretend. Just go ahead and take me, fast and hard, like . . . like you were making me fuck you even if I didn't want to."

"I could spank you too."

She nodded, her eyes lighted up and she turned over on her stomach, pushing her little ass in the air. He whacked her with the flat of his hand, building it up from slow to faster and then harder until she wailed.

"Right now, sweetheart! Fuck me now, right now!" She turned over on the couch and he jolted into her in one quick stroke bringing a wailing shout of rapture from her. Then she was humping, jolting and gyrating and bouncing until he had a hard time staying inside.

The fire built and built and Spur thought sure they both would burn to cinders. The longer they worked at it the higher their temperatures rose until at last Katie let out a scream and dissolved into a writhing mass of flesh and bones as her climax riveted her to the couch and sent a thousand spasms rushing through every nerve in her body until she was weak and spent and could barely lift an eyebrow.

Somewhere in the process of her giant climax, Spur had also come. As he thought back, he could hardly remember when it had been. A strange one, but he relaxed and could feel the throb of post-climax reaction as his body began cooling down.

He started to say something but she shushed him and shook her head and closed her eyes. Her arms went around him then and she pulled his shirt against her breasts and hugged him tightly. She held him that way for twenty minutes, then sighed and looked at him.

"I just wanted to remember that, to plant it firmly in my mind how I had the best fuck of my life with Spur McCoy, even though I know he's going to be running away in a week or so. A woman needs memories like these."

She relaxed her hold around his back and he lifted away from her and helped her sit up.

"I don't suppose we could get any hot water. I would really like to have a bath."

"Great! I'll wash your back. I'll wash your front, then I'll wash your crotch!" She giggled and stood. "Not only do I have hot water, I have a bathtub. A genuine steel clad, nickel-plated bath tub that is practically long enough to lie down in. Come on, let me show you."

She stood, entirely at ease in her naked, just-loved state and caught his hand and took him to the kitchen. She had a stove that had been modi-fied so copper coils ran through the top of the fire-box, just under the lids. Water circulated through them and went to a lower copper boiler holding tank on the back of the stove where the already hot water could be kept warm indefinitely. A drain at the bottom of the tank permitted anyone to draw water from the holding tank into a bucket to transfer to the bathtub.

Spur smiled when he saw the tub. It was better than any he had seen in the fanciest hotel.

"Remember, I'm in the market. I buy and sell bathtubs to anyone who wants them. Naturally I have to set the tone with one of my own. Al-though I don't invite just anyone into my quarters to see it, or to have a bath with me. Do you think we could both get in there if it were half-filled with water?"

"Easy," Spur said, found a bucket and carried seven bucketsful of hot water to the tub, then put in three more buckets of cold water to temper it.

Spur pulled off his clothes quickly and stepped into the water beside her.

"How do we sit down?" she asked.

"Together," Spur said, then held her hand as she sank into the water. She crossed her legs and sat at one end, and he went down in front of her.

"See, plenty of room," Spur said. "You can put that on your advertisement for your new bathtubs. Plenty of room for two to bathe at the same time."

Katie snorted. "I can just see our church women reading that sign! They'd never shop here again."

"We won't tell them. But I bet you could sell one to every bawdy house in town."

Katie grinned. "I'm going to remember that. Think I'll order two more tomorrow when the stage goes through."

"What does one of these cost?"

"The six foot model, like this one, is nine dollars and twenty five cents, plus freight from Chicago of about a dollar."

"You mean some clerk is going to spend half a month's pay on a bathtub like this?"

"No, but some madame probably will, offering the cowboys a bath before and a bath after. It could be a good sales idea for the ladies of the night.''

"Shut up and wash my back." He gave her the soap and turned around. Later he washed her back, and then her front. Soon they had washed everything that was above water and tried to wash under water, but it didn't work.

"Now you're getting silly," she said.

He pulled her hand down to his crotch. "Does that long hard thing down there seem silly to you?"

She looked at him. "Can we fuck under water?"

"Been known to happen. Last time I heard, a couple tried in Forth Worth. Only one of them drowned.''

She hit him in the shoulder.

"Me on the bottom," he said, turning over and boasting her above him.

"It won't work," Katie said.

"Try it. We may like it."

She laughed and slid down toward his upright shaft. It took her three tries before she yelped and his shaft slipped into her and she lowered gently into the water impaled to the roots of his member.

"Now what do we do?" she asked.

They both began laughing so hard they couldn't stop. After a half dozen abortive tries to get some action going, Katie pulled away from him and stepped out of the tub.

"Now I see why half the partners drown. Also, we splashed water over the whole room."

"The maid will clean it up tomorrow."

"I don't have a maid."

"Then hire one. Anybody with the fanciest bathtub in town should have a maid, a butler and a driver."

She threw a towel at him. He caught it and used it. An hour later, they were back in the living room. They had dressed and were sipping some port wine.

"You are a complete crazy character, do you know that, Spur McCoy? Will you marry me?"

Spur chuckled. "*Now* who's crazy? I'm the one who is supposed to ask that question, not you. No, I won't marry you, but thank you for asking. I was getting worried. That's only my second proposal and I'm almost thirty."

They both laughed and concentrated on the wine.

"I have this new friend who says she likes to make love with men and women too. Isn't that weird?" said Katie.

"Have you ever played with her?"

"No, of course not!"

"You should try it. The lady absolutely will not get you pregnant."

Katie giggled and hit his shoulder. "I don't know. I think that it would be strange at best, and absolutely disgusting at the worst."

"You mean you would feel different if a woman was petting your breasts rather than a man?"

"Of course."

"What if you didn't know if it were a man or a

178

woman? Wouldn't just the physical touch have an effect on you?"

"Yes, I guess so. But if I did know, my reaction would be different, I'm sure. Somebody told me once that sex was basically . . . what was the big word he used . . . ? Yes, psychological. He said enjoying sex, getting sexy and excited, was ninety percent in your head, and the other ten percent was the physical responses of your body."

"Sounds reasonable. I've seen some beautiful women I just couldn't get excited about. It turned out that I knew too many unhappy facts about those women. I didn't like them. So you're right, my lack of response was mental, not physical at all."

"That's why you get me sexy so fast. I'm mentally ready!"

"Glad you bring this fascinating, sexy body along with your mental preparedness."

They both laughed and went into the bedroom.

"You think we're both mentally ready for another try at it?" asked Katie.

He sighed. "It's a struggle, but I'll try once more."

She punched him in the shoulder again and he fell on the bed, laughing.

They made love again, gently this time, with lots of whispers and confidences, and much quiet talk. Then Katie cooked a midnight snack of fried chicken. Spur ate half the bird, both drumsticks, the gizzard and the heart and liver.

"It's a wonder you don't get fat, the way you eat," she told him as she watched.

"It's all the exercise I get between the sheets that keeps me trim," he said smugly.

"I'll be sure you get a good workout again before morning," Katie promised.

They made love twice more, silly and wild the first time, then soft and loving and gentle the next.

"I wonder if this will be my last time with you," Katie said as they rolled over to go to sleep at about three in the morning.

"It won't be, I promise you," Spur said. That was a promise he was going to keep.

# CHAPTER SIXTEEN

The next morning in his office, Spur found a pile of paper work he needed to do, routine matters that needed to be taken care of. Toby slept through to noon as he was supposed to, then came to duty.

Spur met the incoming stage along with what seemed like half the other residents of the town. It was the highlight of the day. Spur wasn't sure how often the stage came through now, but he was interested in this one coming from Fort Worth.

On it was a package of papers from the state capitol for the sheriff, with word that Judge Harley P. Johnson would be arriving a week from that day for the trial of any and all accumulated cases, both civil and criminal.

That was the way they did things in outlying

areas. When the judge got there, things moved quickly. Spur went on to the Hotel Galloway where he talked to Paul Victor in his small office.

"How is your militia doing?" Spur asked.

"Not much need lately for one."

"I'd like to take a ride out to the Circle G ranch, and I need a forty man posse again. Think you can round up a crew for this afternoon? I want to get out there before Galloway knows that we're coming this time."

Victor smiled. "This must mean the judge is coming. When?"

"A week from today."

"Good, we can handle all our problems at once. I'll have the posse assembled by 12:30, ready to ride. You want sixty rounds per man for both rifle and pistol?"

"That should do. Have the men bring one meal and enough water for the round trip. We might run into some armed opposition out at the ranch."

The lookouts outside town had been pulled back; now Spur sent Oliver out to keep watch until the posse picked him up.

"Just don't let anybody ride out of town heading for the Galloway ranch," Spur told him. "We want to be damn sure we surprise them this time."

Oliver took his rifle and rode.

There was no trouble rounding up the forty members of the posse, and everything went smoothly as they came upon the Galloway ranch.

Oliver remembered where the Galloway lookout had been when they raided the ranch before, and he rode up alone while the rest of the posse kept out of sight. Five minutes after Oliver rode into the woods, he came out waving his rifle over his head. All clear; there was no lookout.

Spur watched the ranch from the cover of the copse of willow and cottonwood. (He had bought a pair of used binoculars from Katie at the Mercantile.) As he swept the ranch from about a mile away, he could see no sudden activity. He saw only a half dozen men, who were doing normal daily chores.

Spur broke his force into two halves. Half under Paul Victor he sent down a draw for a mile to the west so they could come in from that angle. Spur and the remainder would ride straight up the trail to the ranch buildings.

"When you get to that far lightning-struck cottonwood, I'll be able to see you. Put two riders by the cottonwood with rifles held over their heads, then we'll move on the ranch together."

Victor nodded, took his men and rode through the draw out of sight of the ranch. It would take them about half an hour to get there. Spur saw by his watch that it was nearly five-thirty. They had two hours of daylight left.

"Let's go get them," Spur said. He had warned all his men that he wanted to pick up Galloway without a shot being fired, but it wasn't likely. No man was to fire until Spur did. They rode.

They came in at a steady trot, and when they

were a quarter of a mile from the buildings, Spur sank the rowells into his black and charged forward at a gallop.

Two cowboys looked up, and ran for the bunkhouse. Another headed into the main ranchhouse. When the posse was a hundred yards away, rifle fire came from the main house. Spur sent his men in at a jagged line so there wouldn't be any one group to shoot at. He saw one horse go down, and saw a man catch a bullet in the shoulder. Then they were past the bunkhouse and surrounding the main house. Spur put a pistol round through the downstairs window where he remembered Galloway had his office.

"Galloway, this is the sheriff. You are under arrest. It will be best for everyone concerned if you tell your men to put down their arms and surrender quietly. No one will be charged with resisting arrest if you come now. Otherwise every man who fires a shot in your defense will be considered an outlaw and dealt with accordingly."

Two men with hands over their heads and empty holsters came from the bunkhouse. Two of Spur's men quickly patted them down for hidden weapons and told them to sit on the ground with their hands on their heads.

Another man came from the barn. Then another lifted up from behind the well, a rifle in his hands. Spur saw him, spun around, and sent two rifle rounds into the man before he could fire. He was dead on the spot.

Victor had arrived with his twenty men,

discouraging those in the house.

There had been no shots from the house, but neither had anyone else come out.

"Galloway, you only make it worse for yourself and your men by remaining inside. We can stay out here and slam three or four hundred rounds into your house, then burn it down. Is that what you want?"

A figure showed quickly at the window that had been broken by Spur's round. Then a voice boomed out that could only be Galloway's.

"What you got there, a lynch mob, Sheriff? How do I know I'll ever see town? You could lynch me half a dozen times on the way to town."

"The county doesn't operate that way, Galloway. That's the way *you* think, what *you* would do. We abide by the law. These forty men are all citizens of Clearwater; they all want to see justice done. Hanging you out here would be worse for them than letting you go free.

"You come out or we'll come in and get you. You have two minutes to decide."

Spur talked with two of his men. They circled around the house, came up on the blind side and crawled to a spot on each side of the front door. They had pistols ready and flattened themselves against the wall.

The voice came from the window again.

"No chance, Sheriff. I will shoot it out with you, though. Just you and me in the yard out there. Move all your men back a hundred yards. Then I'll come out for a showdown. I'm not as fast as I used to be, but I think I can take you. If I do, you ride back to town, and I'll ride the other way, moving west, California probably. Better than hanging."

Spur saw his men near the front door. He stalled.

"Why should I make a deal with you? I've got all the evidence I need to go to trial."

"Because you think you can beat me, and save the county the cost of a trial. And because if you're a man, you can't ignore it when I call you out. It's a matter of pride and being a man. That is, if you *are* a man."

Spur smiled. He had him on the line. Now all he had to do was set the hook and reel him in.

Spur talked with Victor, told him to get ready to move the men back.

"I don't want to do it, Galloway, but looks like it has to be your way. You'll die quickly. You don't have a chance to order me backshot here. My men will be watching every roofline and building in the area. If anybody tries a backshot, they will be blasted into dust."

"Big talk, big man. I'll see you at the front door just soon as I get my gunbelt on."

"Hurry up. I have a long ride ahead of me."

Spur looked at his men near the door. They both knew what to do. When Galloway came out the door they were to knock the gun from his hands and capture him as efficiently as possible.

Spur ordered his men to pull back. He gave the orders loudly so they could be heard inside. Then

Spur walked to a point fifty feet from the front door. Much too long a shot for a pistol. Spur moved to one side, then back, then to the other side. He was thinking about a rifle inside the front door aimed at him from the dark interior. He moved farther to the side so there was only wall showing behind the section of the door he could see. Better.

He waited. After five minutes the white door with the Galloway Circle G crest on it swung open slowly.

Galloway stood there. He wore a Rebel military jacket and cap, had a sword at his side, and carried a long-barreled pistol in one hand. He stood just inside the threshhold and stared at Spur, then at the men who had drawn back. Slowly he nodded.

"You seem to be a man of your word, McCoy. I hoped I wouldn't have to do this. Once I kill you I'll have to run, but that is the agreement."

He stepped forward two paces and at once was slammed to the side as one of Spur's men outside the door blocked him with his shoulder, driving him to the ground beyond the open door. Spur saw movement in the door and dove into the dust, rolled and came up and put four shots through the dark hole of the doorway.

"All right, men." Spur bellowed. "Every man take aim at the house, safeties off. Be prepared to fire on my order."

He faced the house.

"I want every person in the house to come out,

now! You have ten seconds to get out here, then we open up and kill everyone inside. Now, move it!"

Three men raced out the door, hands over their heads. A cook came out the back door along with a Mexican girl.

Spur ran to the three men and glared at them. "Anyone else inside?"

"No, everyone is out," the closest man said. A rifle shot came from the upper window at the same time the man spoke. The slug could have been aimed at Spur, but it caught the speaker in the throat and drove him sideways, his life's blood spurting from the ruptured veins in his neck. He was dead in two minutes.

Spur raced for the doorway, charged inside and found he had two men behind him. The two at the door had Galloway down and his hands tied behind him.

Spur stopped just in back of the big stairway.

"You upstairs! You've still got a clean bill with the law. You can lay down your gun and walk away free. If we have to come up and get you, you'll either be shot down or hung."

"Don't shoot! I'm coming down. I just did what the old man told me. I didn't hurt nobody."

The man was in his twenties, wild-eyed, with a look tht indicated he had always been slow-witted.

"Hold your fire!" Spur barked to his men. He went up the stairs and brought the man down, checked to see that he had no weapons, then they all went outside.

Spur checked his troops. One man had caught a rifle slug in the shoulder. A second man had a broken leg he had suffered when his horse was shot out from under him and rolled over on him. The ranch hands had two dead and three wounded.

It was almost dark. He found the cook in the cookshack near the bunkhouse. She was a big Mexican woman with two helpers.

"Everybody eat," she said matter of factly. "Plenty of food for all."

Spur had not relished the idea of the ride back to town. He made a decision quickly.

The foreman came forward and said he had twelve men in line camps getting ready for a roundup. There were nine men at the head-quarters camp. Spur told him to get them fed first and bedded down. Spur put the foreman, a man named Billy Utley, in charge of the ranch and told him to run it in a normal manner, sending a daily rider to report all factors to the sheriff's office. The messengers would ride in one day and ride back the next, so he would need two men on permanent duty.

The foreman nodded and said he would hold things together until the trial was held.

The forty members of the posse ate until they could hold no more: steak, potatoes, vegetables, fried chicken, bread and jam, and all the coffee they could drink.

They bedded down in the bunkhouse or under the stars as they preferred, and soon all except the posted guards were sleeping. Spur let Galloway sleep in his own bed, after checking the room carefully for weapons, but kept the rancher's hands tied and a guard on duty all night.

Spur relaxed in a spare bedroom and lay with his arms folded beneath his head in total relaxation. The worst part was over, the dangerous part. Now all they had to do was get a conviction. The boy's drawing would help. In the morning he would talk to all the men who worked for Galloway and see if any of them would testify against him. If he could find even one man who had heard Galloway's orders to attack the Rogers spread, it would be a big boost.

Spur cursed himself for not going with Matt Rogers after Zane Smith. Smith was a key witness and could have put the noose around Galloway's neck. But he would have to make do with what evidence he had. He would be a witness himself. It should be enough, depending on the judge. Spur drifted off to sleep, hoping that the judge had not received any favors from Galloway in the past.

The morning brought a big breakfast, and the Circle G riders got to work. Spur talked to each of them individually, and found two who said they had heard Galloway talking to the five men, then had seen them ride off in the direction of the Rogers place. It wasn't much, but it might help. Spur told them to get ready to come to town with the posse.

Galloway said he couldn't ride, and his men affirmed it. Spur had a buggy hitched up, assigned a driver, and bundled Galloway on board. The posse mounted up and at ten that morning rode for town. It would be a slightly slower trip with the buggy along.

Spur maintained the posse formation until they were a mile from town, then let the men break ranks and ride home any way they wanted to. Half of them raced, shouting and calling to each other. It had been a picnic, an outing for them, one that might very well change the future of Galloway county for all time.

# CHAPTER SEVENTEEN

Once back in town, Spur cleaned up, changed clothes and went to the county offices where he found the legal papers all ready for his signature as complainant against Dunning for the murder of Mrs. Bascomb, and against Galloway. The rancher had been complaining of shortness of breath when Spur stuffed him into the second cell at the jail, but Spur ignored it and put the legal machinery into motion.

The judge would arrive in six days.

Back in his room, Spur kissed Holly, and found out she had been buying clothes and making herself beautiful while he had been gone. Spur took her to a late lunch at the hotel and told her about arresting her former boss.

"Now, what are you going to do with the rest of your life, Holly Kane?" he asked over their meal.

"Why, find a husband, raise a family."

"Maybe not in this town. People have long memories."

"And probably no man here would have me?"

"Possible, but I'll keep my eyes open for you."

"What about you, Spur. Will you marry me?"

"Not with my job. I move around too much."

"And besides, you aren't ready to get married. I know. I've heard that line before." She pouted then sighed. "Well, I guess I'm used to it. Maybe I *should* move to another town."

"How would you live? I don't want you in some dance hall."

Her eyes twinkled. "You know I would be good at that kind of work."

"Almost any woman is good at lying on her back and being used. I want something better for you."

She sobered, blinked back tears, then smiled. "Thank you. That was a terribly nice thing you said."

"You are a terribly fine person." He shook his head. "Now shut up and eat your lunch before we both start crying."

Before they had finished eating, Toby came with news that the auditor had arrived from Fort Worth. He was early but wanted to get right to work.

Spur excused himself and went to the county offices where he put the man on the job. The auditor looked at the simple set of books and said he should have it all worked out in a day, two at the most.

"Good," Spur said. "When you finish here I want you to go over the local back records. The president just shot himself and I think this mess is mixed up with the bank and a big local rancher who's now in jail. Sound like fun?"

The auditor was a small town man in a black suit with a black string tie. He wore spectacles and had a thin line of moustache. He had no sense of humor and merely nodded.

"I shall endeavor to do a satisfactory job. If there are any legal problems I'm sure your local officials will initiate the necessary legal action."

"Right, I imagine so. Thank you."

Spur turned and left, knowing the situation would be well taken care of. He went to the bank, found it open and running smoothly. Taggart, the man Spur had talked with after Bascomb's suicide, came up to him.

"I have that material you wanted on Mr. Bascomb's holdings. They are extensive, as you figured. I really don't see where Mr. Bascomb got all that money."

"He stole it from the county," Spur said, accepting the large sealed envelope from Taggart. "Any problems here?"

"No. We assured people we were solvent, paid out a few hundred dollars to account holders and then it settled down. No problems now."

"The county has hired an auditor from Fort Worth. When he's done there, I am ordering an audit of the bank. Do it quietly. We don't want to stir folks up again. I want you to make an estimation for me. If the court said the bank had to pay

the county say ten or twenty thousand dollars,
could it do it without going broke?"

Taggart nodded at once. "Oh, yes. Mr. Bascomb has letters of credit and accounts in two
Fort Worth banks that could cover such an
amount from his personal accounts. That's one of
the things I don't understand."

"Being a first class thief and embezzler can be
highly profitable—but you have to live long
enough to enjoy it. Bascomb didn't. I'll talk to
you about this later. Not a word to anyone else,
not even your wife." Spur turned and walked out
of the bank.

The county prosecutor was preparing some
civil cases and the lawyers in town were bustling
around with other civil suits, getting them ready
for trial. The judge would probably be in town for
about a week, maybe more.

Spur went back to the sheriff's office, and sent
a report to his boss in Washington, D.C., to
Capitol Investigations, the cover name for the
Secret Service. He gave a brief report on his
progress and the upcoming trial and added that
he should have everything wrapped up in a week
or so and would wire them from Fort Worth. He
took the letter to the stage office and had their
assurances that it would be on the next stage
east.

Back at the jail, Spur heard Toby yelling at
someone. When Spur walked in, Toby jerked his
thumb at the cells.

"Old man Galloway is screaming back there

196

that he has to see you. He gave me this twenty dollar gold piece to make sure you went back.''

Spur took the coin and marched back to the jail cells.

''Well, well, the important sheriff can take time out of his busy day to come see me,'' Galloway said. He was sitting on the hard bunk, his expression furious.

Spur tossed the gold coin between the steel bars. It fell to the floor in front of Galloway.

''Next time you try to bribe one of my men I'll ram the gold down your throat! Now, what do you want?''

''Easy, Sheriff. We're both reasonable men used to getting our own way. I'm sure you realize I don't plan on sitting here and letting some bunch of assholes on a jury send me to the gallows.''

''With the evidence we have against you, that is an appealing possibility, Galloway. You've ridden roughshod over this county for too long. You've had too many people killed.''

''Sheriff, you're a man of the world. You've been around and know how things work. I think you're the kind of man who is broad-minded enough to talk sense here.''

Spur looked up quickly. Galloway stood up, his one shoulder higher than the other as he walked to the bars.

''I think we can make some kind of arrangement so I could have an overnight head start on a breakout, and then you and your posse would ride the wrong way after me."

"Why would I do something as stupid as that, Galloway?" Spur asked grimly.

"So you wouldn't have to work another day in your life."

"It would take a lot of convincing, Galloway."

"But we're still talking, aren't we?" He smiled and Spur could see the evil oozing out of him. "Why don't we say we start talking about twenty thousand dollars. Think what a time a man could have with twenty thousand dollars in Chicago!"

Spur shook his head. "Not nearly enough. It would hurt my reputation as a lawman. I'd be hunted. I'd have to have at least $40,000 all in cash, federal greenbacks."

Galloway frowned. "I'm not sure I can get that much cash. Not in a week. When is the judge coming?"

Spur snorted. "You would try it, wouldn't you? Galloway, I wouldn't take forty cents from you, let alone forty thousand dollars. I want to see you hang. Besides, you don't have twenty dollars left. An auditor is here going over the county books. You know Bascomb blew his brains out. Your partnership is finished. When we get done auditing the county and the bank's books, I don't think you're going to have twenty-five cents left in your pocket."

Galloway went back to the cot and sat down.

"Audit? The county books? God damn!"

"Right. Bascomb can't do it this time, and we'll find out exactly how much you and Bascomb have stripped out of the county in the last fifteen years."

"No! It can't be. Nobody knew!"

"Bascomb knew. And when you killed his wife he knew how loyal a friend you really were."

Galloway glowered through the cell bars.

"You're a dead man, Sheriff. One of my men will get you. I've still got men all over. One of them will get you—it's an open hunting season on you. Dead or alive, double for dead. You're a dead man!"

Spur came out and slammed the connecting door between the cells and the office.

"No visitors for Galloway," Spur said. Rage tightened his throat so that he could hardly speak. The man was an open sore festering on the clean flesh of the county. The sooner he was cut out and buried, the better.

Fifty miles to the north, Matt Rogers sat beside a small fire. He had just finished eating half a roasted rabbit, and licked off his fingers and threw the bones into the woods.

"Damn good," a voice said from across the fire.

"Shut up, Smith. I'm still thinking about you. I should have killed you when I had the chance. You are garbage. You're a hired killer. You murdered my family. I should squash you like a rattlesnake under my heel."

"But so far you haven't. And you gave me half the damn rabbit."

"I should be locked up for stupidity," Matt

said. He should have gunned down Zane Smith with the shotgun and had it over with. He slammed his hand against his thigh. Now he had his enemy tied hand and foot, and still he was dangerous. It was like living in a barrel with the rattlesnake he'd just mentioned.

"Told you, hombre. Had nothing to do with the rape or killing of your people. I was holding the horses. That Weed was the crazy one. He liked to kill."

"Shut up!" Matt screeched. "I don't want to hear it!" He pulled out his six-gun and waved it at Smith. "I could put a slug right through your gut and watch you die slow. It hurts like hell to die that way, with your insides all torn up."

He breathed deeply to get control of himself. Then he moved where Smith could see him more clearly.

"Let's play a game, killer. They call it six to one. Chances are six to one you live. Good odds." He took four rounds from the cylinder of his revolver and showed Smith the one bullet.

"You ever play this game, Smith?"

Smith frowned, then shook his head. "That's no game, that's crazy!"

"Then why are you playing it, Smith. Why?" Matt closed the cylinder and spun it, pointed the .44 at Smith's head and pulled the trigger. The hammer fell, charged toward the center fire cartridge in the cylinder. Only this time it fell on an empty one.

"Jesus! You're loco!"

"You helped kill my family, you bastard! You expect me to pat you on the head and turn you loose? I'm trying to figure out the most painful way to kill you."

Matt spun the cylinder again, aimed at Smith's heart and pulled the trigger.

Smith's eyes widened, his face blanched and his chin quivered as he watched the finger on the trigger. As the hammer began to fall he screamed and leaped to one side just as the hammer hit on an empty chamber.

Matt shook his head. "You spoiled that one. You move and it don't count. You won on two, but now we're gonna do it five more times. See if you can be lucky six out of six times. Yeah, your odds are gonna get lower and lower each time you win, but don't worry—it only takes one time to lose it all. Might say you'll lose your head over this game if you ain't careful. And every second I want you to suffer, Smith. You suffer the way my wife and my son and my daughter did those terrible minutes when you and Weed and the rest were torturing them. You goddamn bastard!"

"Hey, Rogers, I got some money. You want some money? I got me a whole trunk full buried. We hit a train and got away with a lot, but then we got chased and had to bury it so they couldn't prove it was us who robbed the train. My two buddies got killed and hell, I'd be glad to let you have the whole thing. Just forget this fucking game with the pistol."

"Forget it? This is the most fun I've had in

years. Watch the cylinder spin, killer. Is this the time you go down and die right here by the fire? Is this the time you cash in your last poker pot? Think about it!"

Matt put the gun at the man's head, so close that the mental touched his temple, then smiled and pulled the trigger. Smith started to lunge away, then shivered and stayed where he was. Matt laughed as he saw Smith's face.

"Scared, Smith? You might get lucky. Just four more after this one. 'Course, you might be *un*lucky and die within sixty seconds. Which one is it going to be this time?"

Smith screamed as the hammer fell.

It clicked on an empty chamber.

"Damn, Smith, you're lucky again! Wonder if your good luck can hold out for four more? Odds are against it, you know that. Just consider that rabbit your last meal. Do you want to spin the cylinder this time, killer?"

# CHAPTER EIGHTEEN

Three days later, Judge Johnson arrived on the stage, had a bath and dinner at the hotel, then opened court in the big meeting room at the county offices. It wasn't a regular courtroom, but there were plans to build two in the new court house, if they ever got enough money ahead.

Judge Johnson was a large man, as tall as Spur and twice as wide. He had heavy, bushy brows, thick black hair, and a big nose that had been broken and left with a bend to the right. His mouth was firm and hard, his chin jutting, and his eyes told you at once that he put up with no disruptions or nonsense in his court.

He called the court clerk to open the proceedings and when the spectators in the room quieted, he stared at them for a minute.

"Some of you don't know me. For those, let me

give you a few quick suggestions. I am the judge here. I interpret the law, make the decisions and rule on everything. I'll stay in town as long as I need to to handle all the cases that are ready for trial. I don't want a lot of fancy fol-de-rol. Let's just have the facts and move on. First case, clerk.''

Ian Dunning was on trial first for the murder of Agnes Bascomb. The district attorney, Ted Oxley, had his case well documented. He quickly showed the letter supposedly written by Doak Galloway, which Dunning had given to Clint Bascomb. Spur testified that he had gone with Bascomb to his home.

"I went in the back way, Your Honor, up over the woodshed and in the second floor window. I found Mrs. Basdomb dead in the master bedroom, and came downstairs where Dunning was talking to Bascomb. Dunning saw me and attempted to fire his revolver at me, but I wounded and captured him.''

"Did the accused say anything?'' The attorney asked.

"Yes, he kept saying that Mr. Galloway would be there for the meeting. Then after Bascomb found his wife dead upstairs, he returned with a shotgun and tried to kill the accused. When that failed, Mr. Dunning screamed at Bascomb, told him he would tell everyone how Bascomb and Galloway had looted the county treasury. How they had split up the county, each taking half of the graft, and that Galloway was closing out the partnership."

"Thank you, Sheriff. Now, did the suspect have a knife in his possession when you captured him?"

"Yes, and it had fresh blood on it that had not dried yet."

"How was Mrs. Bascomb killed, Sheriff?"

"Her throat was cut. She bled to death."

"Could the knife Dunning had in his possession have made the wound in Mrs. Bascomb's throat?"

"Yes."

"And were there any other disruptions in the Bascomb house that day?"

"Yes. We found two large guard dogs that had been killed with a knife of some kind, a large knife."

"Could it have been a cavalry short sword?"

"Yes. That would give the killer enough distance from the dogs to avoid their jaws."

"Did you find such a weapon in the Bascomb house?"

"Yes, sir. We found two cavalry short swords, both with blood on them."

As was often the case in early court trials in outlying areas, Dunning had no defense attorney. He couldn't afford one, and most new states could not afford to furnish one to every defendant. Galloway had not provided counsel for Dunning, nor would Galloway let his Fort Worth attorney help the man.

Dunning refused to take the stand in his own

defense, but acted as his own attorney and showed he had either been in court before or knew something of the law. He cross-examined Spur extensively.

"Then you did not actually *see* anyone kill the dogs or Mrs. Bascomb, Sheriff."

"No."

"The blood on the knife you said you took away from me—was it from Mrs. Bascomb?"

"Blood is blood. We have no way of knowing."

"Could it have been my own blood I got when I cut myself cleaning my fingernails, Sheriff?"

"It could have been."

"Did anything in the letter from Mr. Galloway say anything about a death taking place?"

"No."

"Would it be illegal for a depositor, such as Mr. Galloway was, to write a letter to his banker, Mr. Bascomb?"

"No."

"Would it be illegal for Mr. Bascomb to meet with Mr. Galloway in a bar, a theatre, a church or Mr. Bascomb's house?"

"No."

"Have you presented any evidence here whatsoever that positively shows that the defendant harmed anyone that day, let alone killed Mrs. Bascomb?"

"No, sir, I have not."

"Thank you, Sheriff."

Dunning had earlier waived his right to a jury trial, and now he made his summation to the judge. He was soft-spoken and more eloquent that Spur had expected. He hit hard on the fact that the prosecution had no evidence that he had been the one to kill Mrs. Bascomb, that he had done no such thing. He had merely delivered the letter and stopped by to tell Mrs. Bascomb that her husband would be home shortly. He had been admitted by Mrs. Bascomb and she had told him to wait. He didn't even know she was upstairs. He said he had seen the Sheriff kill the guard dogs with the sabers.

Spur sat in the row of chairs with a scowl on his face. A good lawyer could have done little better defending Dunning. The man sat behind his table relaxed, smiling, sure that he would be acquitted.

The judge listened to the summary of the prosecution and Spur realized they had little hard evidence against Dunning. He was certain that Dunning was guilty. He had opportunity, motive, and means. He was working for Galloway who evidently wanted Bascomb out of the way.

The judge now studied his notes, and looked at the evidence that had been brought in. Often a judge would accept the evidence and testimony and come back one to six days later with a verdict.

Judge Johnson did not seem that type. He rapped his gavel. The spectators in the improvised courtroom hushed. He looked up, stared at the district attorney for a moment and shook his head.

"This is an unusual case. There is almost no

evidence. The prosecution has failed to produce anything but a circumstantial mass of facts. There is little hard proof of any kind against the defendant.

"However, the defendant has chosen not to take the stand in his own defense, to tell his side of the story. The law states absolutely that a defendant is not obligated to take the stand, and that no conclusions can be drawn from that act. However, it has been my experience that whenever such a defendant takes this action, he hurts his own case.

"I am now ready to rule on this case. Will the defendant rise?"

Ian Dunning stood up, grinning.

"As presiding judge in this matter, in and for the county of Galloway, state of Texas, I, Judge John F. Johnson, do find the defendant Ian Dunning guilty of murder. I hereby sentence him to . . ."

"Noooooooooooo!" Dunning screamed. He leaped off his chair, charged the table ten feet in front of him where the judge sat and dived over it, grabbing the judge's throat with both hands and squeezing hard. The judge roared and surged backward from the table, dragging Dunning with him. He slammed both fists into Dunning just below his rib cage and slightly in back, jolting both kidneys. The blows brought a shriek of pain from Dunning, who loosened his hands and rolled to the floor, his legs drawn up to lessen the pain as he turned his head and vomited on the floor.

By that time Spur had charged from his own seat to the front of the courtroom and pinned Dunning to the floor on his stomach, one knee jammed into his back.

Deputy Toby rushed up with a set of manacles and secured Dunning's hands behind his back. Then he was dragged to his feet and pushed back to his place. Spur stood beside him this time, one big hand tight around Dunning's arm.

The judge had righted himself, sat down in the chair again and hit his gavel twice on the oak board in front of him to enforce silence.

"Ian Dunning is hereby found guilty of murder, and shall receive the mandatory sentence of death by hanging. Due to the violent nature of the defendant, the execution will take place tomorrow morning at ten o'clock. Baliff, does Clearwater have a gallows?"

"No, Your Honor."

"I suggest you start building one at once." The judge looked at Dunning and shook his head. "Mr. Dunning, there are still a few of you around, men who think they can take, and maim, and kill when they wish with impunity. That kind of life is all over in Texas. We have laws, and by God, we will live by them or some of you will die by them. You shall be hanged by the neck at ten A.M. tomorrow, until you are dead, as testified to by the local physician. Is there a doctor in town?"

Head nodded.

"Remove the prisoner. Next case."

The clerk read the charges, a criminal case of

the county of Galloway versus the estate of Clinton Bascomb and Doak Galloway for fraud in the amount of $78,485, perpetrated over the past twelve years.

The district attorney informd the bench that Mr. Galloway could not come to court, but he had an attorney to represent him.

The trial lasted fifteen minutes. The auditor had been ordered to stay for the trial. He quickly showed records that proved that Bascomb and Galloway had worked in tandem to defraud the county of the amount in question. Bascomb had covered it up each year by doing the auditing of the county books as prescribed by law for the sum of one dollar, and thereby concealed the corruption and the theft.

The judge quickly have a verdict of guilty and ordered Galloway and the Bascomb estate to reimburse the amount in full, half from each party.

The day was over. The judge went to have dinner in his room at the hotel, and Spur worried about his upcoming case which was set for tomorrow morning. He still wished he had the testimony of Zane Smith. But what he had would have to do.

He wondered where Matt Rogers was. He would be a good witness himself, coming and finding the bodies as he had. Idly Spur wondered if Matt had ever found Zane Smith. If he had found him, he wondered if he had killed him. Suddenly Spur hoped that the death had been slow and painful, tremendously painful. Smith deserved it. He went over in his mind the case the district attorney had put together against Galloway. Even with the pictures little Will had drawn it seemed weak. Johnson seemed like a hanging judge, but his kind went on emotion as much as fact.

Spur knew the judge had been here often before. It was possible that Galloway had reached him with some of his envelopes filled with stacks of hundred-dollar greenbacks.

Spur could only shake his head, and hope the judge would see it his way tomorrow.

# CHAPTER NINETEEN

Spur slept little that night. Holly knew he was worried and insisted that her ministrations would settle him down and help him sleep, but the stimulation seemed to make him even more wide awake.

He had talked with the district attorney again about their case against Doak Galloway which was set for the next day. They went over everything they had. Spur knew that it might not be enough, depending on the judge. Everyone knew Galloway was guilty as hell, but proving it might be a different matter. On this one they didn't know if Galloway would want a jury or not. The D.A. thought he might prefer to take his chances with Judge Johnson.

Spur was bleary-eyed and his nerves were raw when morning came. He felt like diving in the river for a swim to get himself pulled together, but there was no time.

The trial was set for nine A.M., and the courtroom was already crowded when Spur arrived with his prisoner. Galloway had been talking only to his lawyer from Fort Worth. He glared at Spur now and tried to pull away from Spur's grip. Spur had put manacles on him and he disliked them.

To Spur's surprise, Galloway's lawyer chose a jury trial and a panel was quickly selected from those in the courtroom. The basic charge was the murder of five persons at the Rogers ranch. The district attorney tried hard to show the connection. Early he called on Spur McCoy to testify, and Spur told everything he knew about the case; how they had found the drawings by little Will and how one of those drawings depicted one of the attackers at the ranch, and the other two men pictured were found in the bunkhouse at the Circle G ranch.

"Would young Will have had a chance to see these men at any other time than when they attacked his father's ranch?" the district attorney asked Spur.

"No, sir."

"And they were good likenesses?"

"The drawings were in pencil on a tablet, but they were immediately recognizable. Anyone could have matched the drawings with the men and as far as I'm concerned, they show positively that those two men were at the ranch and participated in the killings."

"You then went to the Circle G ranch, and so as not to start a range war, you went in at night and arrested the two men and took them back to town."

"We *started* back to town. One of them tried to kill Matt Rogers, tripped and fell into our bonfire and was dead before we could get him out. Believe me, we wanted him alive to testify here today."

"That was Raoul, the man of Mexican extraction?"

"Yes. He was one of the ones pictured by Will. The other man was named Weed. We were taking him to town when we were bushwacked and Weed was killed by a person or persons unknown. We could not find the attackers."

"Who would want Mr. Weed dead?" the district attorney asked.

"The defendant, Doak Galloway. Then Weed could not testify against him."

"And the fifth man on this raid on the Rogers ranch. Did you find out who that was?"

"Yes, his name was Zane Smith. He also worked at the Galloway ranch. But we didn't know that when we arrested the first two. He evidently heard us take Weed and Raoul, knew he was in danger from us as well as Galloway, and took off for the high trails."

"He ran away?"

"Yes." Spur said.

"Where is Zane Smith now?"

"I wish I knew. Matt Rogers left as soon as Weed died, searching for Smith. I haven't heard from him since. I have no idea if Smith is still alive or not."

The trial dragged on. Spur listened to towns-people tell of Galloway's mistreatment of the citizens, how he rode roughshod over them, how his son ran the saloon and whorehouse, and how four of the previous sheriffs had been gunned down, all in the back in setup shootouts.

Galloway's defense attorney rose time and time again to object, saying none of this was relative to the case and that none of it implicated the plantiff in the Rogers ranch murders. Often the judge agreed.

The district attorney continued to show that Galloway was the kind of man who was capable of such behavior. He showed how Galloway had tried to get his boundaries extended to include the Rogers' Flying R ranch three times, but the county had firmly maintained that the Flying R was a proper homestead and not on the Circle G's rangeland. The Rogers cattle with the Circle G overbrand were also introduced into the case.

Twice the defense council asked that the case be dismissed for lack of evidence, but the judge indicated that there had been enough information presented to let the jury decide, but instructed the district attorney to confine his presentations to hard evidence that had a direct bearing on the case.

Toward the middle of the afternoon, the prosecution rested its case and the defense began. The defense lawyer again moved for dismissal, but was denied. He then brought on two witnesses to affirm the defendent's law-abiding nature, and indicated that he had only one more witness, and that the defendant would not take the stand against such trumped up charges as these.

The district attorney frowned. He touched Spur's arm.

"It doesn't look good. We have a completely circumstantial case. Everyone knows that Galloway ordered his men to wipe out the Rogers' ranch. But we don't have a single, solid, living witness!"

There were shouts in the street. Somebody came bursting in the door to the courtroom. The defense attorney frowned and watched in surprise.

More shouts came from outside, then a tall figure walked into the courtroom. Over his shoulder, he carried a man with blood on both legs and on his shoulder.

The tall man was Matt Rogers. He looked around, saw Spur and lowered his burden to the defense table.

After Spur had informed the district attorney of Rogers' identity, the D.A. said, "Your Honor, an important witness for the prosecution has just arrived. We request a fifteen minute recess while we talk to him and then we wish to call him to the stand. This man who has just arrived is Matt Rogers, owner of the Flying R ranch, father and husband of the victims. I'm informed that the man he has brought in to the court is Zane Smith, the missing participant in the slaughter."

An hour later the trial was over. Zane had sworn under oath that Doak Galloway had ordered his men to go to the Rogers ranch and burn them out and not leave any witnesses—kill everyone there. Zane swore that he had not killed any of the victims. He had been setting the buildings on fire. He was immediately charged with murder, arson, flight to avoid prosecution, and the attempted murder of Rogers, and put in jail.

Galloway was sentenced to death by hanging the next day. Due to the continuing trials, the judge had moved Dunning's hanging to a later date to coincide with the Galloway hanging.

Galloway's lawyer tried to present a motion to appeal the verdict, but the judge shouted him down.

"This isn't one of your big city courts. We don't hold with a lot of legal clap-trap. The man is guilty as sin, and by God, he's gonna die tomorrow! Any more comment by you, sir, and I'll throw *you* in jail for thirty days for contempt!"

A loud cheer went up from the onlookers in the court. Afterwards, all four bars in town gave a free drink to every man who asked for one. It was the beginning of a new day in Clearwater!

Spur took Matt Rogers to the hotel, rented a room for him and had bath water sent up. Spur then bought a new set of clothes for him from the Merchantile, and when Rogers was shaved, bathed and dressed, Spur treated him to a steak dinner. Holly came along, and when Spur introduced her to Matt, he saw her eyes light up.

"Matt Rogers, this is Holly Kane. Holly, you saw Matt in the courtroom, but he looks a lot better now."

Holly blushed. She bobbed her head. "Nice to meet you, Mr. Rogers."

Matt looked at her for a minute and nodded, then smiled.

"Holly. That's a nice name. Are you from here in town?"

Holly looked quickly at Spur, then smiled back at Matt. "Yes. I'm looking for some kind of a job."

"I'm sure you'll find something. A girl as pretty as you are should be on the stage, one of those touring theatre companies I used to hear about."

Holly thanked him quietly and looked down at her hands.

Their steaks came in, and Spur and Matt ate while Holly watched Matt and picked at her food. Spur had never seen her so affected by a person. It could prove interesting.

After the meal, Spur hurried Matt over to the county building and got his signature on the civil suit which would be filed the next day and tried the following day.

"I don't see what good that's going to do," Matt said.

"It could mean a lot of money for you so you can buy another ranch," Spur said. "Galloway owes you that. You have to pick up your life and get going again. I know you had a tremendous shock, a blow I'll never be able to appreciate. But you've come through it. The fact that you didn't blow Smith's head off proves that."

"Damnit, McCoy, I tried! Played the old one-bullet-in-the-cylinder game with Zane. He won seven times. Spun the cylinder and the cylinder came up on an empty chamber seven times in a row, so I brought him on back. Figured somebody was trying to tell me something."

From the clerk's office, they went outside and found the carpenters putting the final bracing on the gallows. The judge had ordered two gallows to be ready by ten the next morning.

"A double hanging! That will make some folks around here sit up and take notice," Matt said. They watched the men testing the first trap with a bag of sand on it. When the lever was pulled, the trap door fell away and the sandbag fell through to the ground. The platform was four feet off the ground to give plenty of room for the death fall.

Matt looked at the twin gallows and shook his head.

"Never seen me a hanging," Matt said. "Guess I will tomorrow. And another one when Smith gets his necktie party. Christ, Spur, you'll never know how much I wanted to kill that little bastard!"

Spur nodded. "I have some idea. I've been in a killing rage a time or two myself, and I never had as much reason as you. It's hell to try to control."

He pointed at the closest bar. "I think it's about time we settled that steak down with some firewater. I feel a good drunk coming on."

Matt laughed softly. "Glad you said that. I was getting ready to grab a bottle and head up to my room. But I don't like to drink alone."

It was after midnight that evening when Matt and Spur got back to the hotel. For the first time since he rented the room for her, Holly was not in Spur's room. There was a hasty note saying she wanted to be by herself that night and was sleeping next door. Spur lifted his eyebrows and fell on the bed. He could get undressed anytme—like in the morning. He went to sleep at once, thinking about the hanging the next day.

# CHAPTER TWENTY

Spur was at the jail at 5 A.M. He had not wanted any breakfast. Jody and Phillips had been up all night protecting the two prisoners. Both were given anything they wanted to eat at eight that morning. Galloway had a big breakfast and two shots of whiskey. Dunning said he wasn't hungry.

A crowd began gathering outside the jail at nine o'clock. Dozens of rigs Spur had never seen before rolled into town. The word was out about the hangings. The gallows were moved to the side of the courthouse by a pair of heavy draft horses. Spur went out with the district attorney for one last check of the gallows.

The ropes had been stretched all night with 200 pound bags of sand. The knots had been carefully crafted so they would break the victim's neck, killing him instantly, rather than leave him strangling to death.

One lever would drop both traps. Spur was satisfied. It still had not been decided who would spring the trap. The district attorney said it was the sheriff's job. Spur insisted there should be another hangman.

Back in the jail, Galloway still could not believe it.

"You'll never hang me, you bastards!" he shouted from his cell. "Some of my men will come swooping down on the gallows and pull me off and we'll ride out of town, laughing like hell!"

Spur had thought of just such a possibility. He had recruited twenty of the posse he had used, and all were armed with repeating rifles and set up on roofs around the gallows. There would be no last minute rescue today.

Spur took out his watch a dozen times, and at last nodded to Toby, who went for the prisoners. Spur had brought eight men to escort the condemned men to the gallows. Four men marched close to each victim, surrounding him, and rushed them quickly to the gallows.

The crowd had swelled. Spur guessed that every man, woman and child in town and for fifty miles around had come to the double hanging. There were over 300 people crowded into the square. A silent path opened through the throng as Spur led the sober group of men forward and soon Galloway and Dunning stood on the platform.

The court clerk read the execution orders in a clear and ringing voice. He finished and stepped back. Spur moved each man over the two foot square trap and helped Deputy Toby slip the hangman's noose over their heads. He pulled the slip knot up tight and placed it exactly against the left side of the jaw. The slack was adjusted on the rope and it was secured on the strong beam overhead.

Spur stepped back and informed the clerk that all was ready.

There still was no hangman. The clerk nodded to Spur.

"It's up to you, Sheriff. Pull the level and spring the traps."

Spur wanted to refuse, but he stepped to a position between and in back of the two condemned men and put his hand on the lever. The crowd began chanting something. Men shouted, and a clamor arose in front of the raw lumber of the gallows.

Spur McCoy took a deep breath and pulled the lever forward.

There was the spang of a spring; then the traps opened and both men dropped two feet, coming to a sudden stop. Spur heard the snap as both necks broke at almost the same time. He stared at the backs of the men, saw their heads at an unnatural angle.

The crowd gasped and was quiet. Spur could hear a faint squeak as Galloway's body swung slightly. The deadly silence stretched out until a woman near the front row screamed and then fainted into her husband's arms.

That broke the spell and the noise surged up as the people pressed close to the front of the gallows to look at the men. Spur waited for two minutes, then motioned for the doctor to come up. He checked both men, feeling for a pulse, testing for breathing with a little tubed device he had in his ears.

He stepped back and shook his head.

"Both these sinners are now in heaven or hell," he said, and walked down the steps.

Spur walked down, left a deputy at the top of the steps and one on the far side, and turned and looked at the faces of the dead men.

Galloway's eyes bulged, eyelids open, his tongue extended from his mouth, ruining any remaining dignity he might have possessed.

Dunning's body turned gently, as if surveying the whole crowd, which had come closer now. His eyes seemed still alive, still filled with hate.

Spur frowned. Something bothered him. Not the bodies—he had seen plenty of them. Another point. Then he knew. He had not given the men a chance to speak any last words. He shrugged. Just as well; neither deserved any. Let the next hangman do the job better. He would be out of town by then.

He moved slowly back to his office, signed the execution papers and filed them, then looked up as the court clerk came in.

"Mr. McCoy, the judge has decided he will hold

court right after lunch. One o'clock. The first case will be the civil suit brought by Mr. Rogers against the estate of the late Mr. Galloway."

Spur thanked him and went to find Matt Rogers. He and Holly were having a talk in the hotel lobby. Spur grinned when he saw them. It just might work out. He told Matt about the upcoming court schedule.

"What do I have to do?" Matt asked.

"Nothing, Just answer any questions the judge may ask you. As you can see, justice is rather informal here. You can get a lawyer if you want one, but he wouldn't know much more about it than you do."

"Will you be there?"

"Can be."

"Please." He motioned to Holly. "I like this lady. I don't know where you found her, but I'm glad you did."

Spur smiled. "I'm glad *you* found her. See you at the trial."

Spur went to find Paul Victor. The hotel owner was in his office.

"Victor, I'm almost finished with our little project here."

Victor stood and shook Spur's hand. "And a fine job it has been. The Senator will get a letter commending you. This county had been just about milked dry by Galloway, and now we find out about Bascomb too."

"One thing you'll need is a new interim sheriff until you can get your election going. You might consider one of the deputies I have now. Or someone else. If you could make the announcement today I would appreciate it."

"So fast?"

"I have other work to do. See if you can take care of it—I would be grateful."

Victor asked Spur to stay to lunch. Spur begged off, saying he never ate after a double hanging. The hotel owner nodded.

"That was a surprise for you, but we never have had a hanging in the county before, that I can remember. Thanks again. Be sure to see me before you leave."

Spur went to the bar across the street, drank two shots of whiskey and sat down and stared at the wall for an hour. Then he got up and went to the courtroom. It had not been one of his better mornings.

Judge Johnson had been given the papers and he called Matt Rogers to the stand.

"This is an informal court, Mr. Rogers. I know of your tragic loss and your present situation. It appears that you are asking for damages for your buildings and cattle, in the amount of eight thousand for the buildings and a fair market value of forty dollars a head for 500 cattle for $20,000. These amounts are granted, in cash if such is available."

"Thank you, Your Honor," Matt said, surprise on his face.

"In the matter of the wrongful death claims, we at first reasoned that these requests were exces-

228

sive. However, due to the viciousness of the attacks, we are inclined to agree. The court has no evidence of the cash position of the estate of the late Doak Galloway. However we understand he has no living relatives, that the land is free and clear, and that he has several accounts the bankers will trace to Fort Worth.

"Therefore, I hereby grant the award of $100,000 each for the three deceased members of your family, such monies to be paid in cash if available. If not, the value of the Circle G ranch, the cattle and buildings and land are to be applied against the total sum hereby granted.

"Any surplus over and above the $328,000 shall revert to the Doak Galloway trust to be utilized by the county of Galloway unless any living relatives are found who then may make claim for such funds. If no relatives appear within five years, the Galloway trust reverts to the county to be used as it deems worthy. Case closed."

Spur watched Matt's troubled face. "Rogers, don't say anything real dumb for a minute. Look at it this way. If you had been killed, wouldn't you have wanted your survivors to have been taken care of by the courts if possible?"

Matt looked up, his eyes still a little glazed. He nodded.

"And don't you think that your wife would want you to be able to pick up your life and move forward?"

He frowned, then at last nodded. "Yes, I think

Gloria would have wanted that. I guess you're right. But a spread like the Circle G—can I handle it?"

"Damn right," Spur said.

Holly touched his arm. "Of course you can, Matt. You said you took a homestead and built it into a ranch from nothing. Now you'll have something to use the same way, build it into something bigger. And I just bet you can do it without pushing the little ranchers around and raiding the county treasury and killing people!"

Matt was touched by the confidence his two new friends showed in him. "Well, if both of you think I can do it, maybe I just better give it one hell of a good try. Only one trouble as I see it right now."

"What's that, Matt?" Holly asked.

"Well, I've seen that big house out there, and I don't know anything about a house or running one or anything like that. And you did say you were looking for a job. I mean it might not be the most important job in the world . . . "

"I'd love to!"

"I haven't even said what the job is going to be yet," Matt protested, grinning.

"I know." She smiled and reached out and took his hand. "But I really don't care what it is, if I can be there with you. I could be the housekeeper, and I could be the upstairs maid, I could be the second cook or wash the pots and pans. I'm not very good on a horse, but I could learn."

Matt shook his head, his face a little grim. "No,

I'm sorry, on a big spread like that, we can't use people without experience."

Her smiled dissolved, and she sighed.

"However," Matt went on, grinning, "I do have an opening for mistress of the ranchhouse. Of course, you would have to marry me to keep idle tongues from wagging."

Holly spun around, surprise, then wonder, and at last joy flooding her face. She leaped into his arms and kissed him.

"Whatever took you so long?" she asked.

"Could we maybe go into the hotel where it's more private to talk about this?" he asked, embarrassed. People on the sidewalks were watching them, smiling.

"I don't think you people need me around right now," Spur said. "Matt, don't leave town until you check with the court and the county clerk. No problem, but it might take a few days. Then when you ride out to the Circle G, it will be all legal and proper."

Matt nodded, but didn't take his eyes off Holly. She linked her arm through his and they hurried toward the hotel.

Spur checked another item off his list, and knew that it was the last big problem he had. He didn't even have to stay for Zane Smith's trial. Matt was the witness there, he could handle that.

Spur turned in at the Mercantile and walked to the back where Katie was wrapping up two pounds of eight-penny nails for a customer.

"And thank you, Mr. Streib." The man walked

toward the front door and Katie caught Spur's hand.

"Think you could find time for dinner tonight? A friend shot a pair of pheasants this morning and said he can use only one. Little buckshot in the dark meat, but who cares?"

Spur nodded. He remembered that he hadn't had any lunch—he would be doubly hungry. His depression after the hanging had been swept away by Matt's good fortune, and the way he and Holly had been drawn to each other. They would probably establish some kind of Texas dynasty.

"Pheasant, with some current jelly, fresh baby peas and buttered carrots, and the bird jammed full of sage stuffing? Yes, I think I can work it into my busy schedule," he said.

She looked around the big store, saw no customers and kissed Spur on the cheek. "I close at six. You can help me cook after that. Be here at six."

He kissed her lips hard and firm and backed away. "I'm almost never late for that kind of menu, as long as I get you for dessert."

"We'll see how well you clean your plate."

He laughed and went out the door toward the county offices. Paul Victor was there in his small room, as Spur figured he might be.

"Found my replacement yet?" Spur asked.

"Matter of fact, we have. One of the deputies had done some law work in Kansas. We hired him on as a temporary. He said he wants to run for election in three months. Sounded fair. Officially

232

you are no longer our sheriff."

"Good." Spur took the star off his shirt and gave it to Victor. "That is a load off my mind."

"Who are you really, Mr. McCoy?" asked Victor shrewdly.

"Let's just say that I work with some of the federal people, but I am not a U.S. Marshal. They work strictly with a U.S. District Court. I earn my pay, and I get to see a lot of the country. Do you need to know any more?"

"Not really. How did Matt Rogers come out in his lawsuit against the Galloway estate?"

"Won. He gets the cash right after the county gets its share from the estate. Then the balance of everything Galloway owned is going into Matt's name."

"Seems fair. But I wouldn't trade places with him. You going to be in town much longer?"

"Couple of days. The stage will be through Thursday heading for Fort Worth."

"Have a good trip."

Spur walked the street, stopped by and wished the new sheriff good luck and picked up the few personal items he had left at the office. Then he went to the hotel, had a long, hot bath and dressed in a crisp white shirt, string tie and his black suit and headed for the Mercantile. It was five minutes past six when he got there, and Katie was tapping her foot at the door as she waited.

As soon as Katie locked the door and pulled the blind down, Spur kissed her, a hard, demanding,

233

kind of a kiss that elicited a moan of desire from her.

"You do that once more and I won't be able to walk to the back of the store," she whispered.

He kissed her again the same way, capturing one breast with his hand and stroked her deliciously as he kissed her. She sagged against him, and he picked her up and carried her to the back, opened the door and stood her up on the floor inside her apartment.

"You have no scruples at all," she said.

"I had some last week, but I lost them in a poker game."

"Are we going to cook supper, or what?"

"We could try 'or what' first, and then cook the pheasant."

"We could."

He reached out and opened the buttons on her dress top and spread it apart, then found both her big breasts under the chemise and caressed them tenderly.

"Or maybe we should just feel around a little, and undress a little, as we cook the supper."

"I don't know if I could cook naked or not," she said.

"Hell, let's try!"

"I have a better idea," she said.

"Sounds interesting." Spur opened the rest of her buttons on her dress and helped her get it off over her head. When that was accomplished, he took off his coat, tie and shirt.

She pulled off her chemise.

"Damn but I love good tits!" he said. He kissed them.

"Sweetness, they love you too!"

Spur kissed each one.

"I hear you got fired as our sheriff."

"True."

"Then if you try to rape me, I can scream and call in the new sheriff?"

"True. Or I can claim you were raping me."

"That's never been done."

"I could try."

"Let's cook later," Katie said grabbing his hand.

"You going back on that supper invitation?"

Katie grinned. "Well, it all depends just what you want to eat. Come on in the bedroom and let me show you the menu."

Four days later, Spur wired his home office from Fort Worth, and two hours after that he had received a message to stay right there. General Halleck was putting together the final details of his new assignment and would contact him with complete details the following day.

Spur read the wire and nodded. Another day, another dollar in the Secret Service of the United States. . . .

SPUR

THE MINER'S MOLL

# CHAPTER ONE

Carl Mond knelt behind the rain barrel. He heard Jedidiah's scuffling feet next to him but didn't take the time to glance at his partner. The streets were deserted. All good folk had been in bed for hours. Even Ma's saloon—The Motherlode—was silent.

Oreville, Nevada, slept under a silvery, crescent moon.

"Carl."

Mond waved him off.

"Carl!" The voice was louder. Too loud.

"Quiet. What the hell is it?" Mond whispered as the cool desert air swept around them, driving stinging particles of sand into his eyes. He rubbed them out and continued surveying the street.

"Mebbe we—"

Carl sighed at the tremor in Jed's voice. "You ain't turnin' yellow on me, is you Steele?"

"But hell! Don't you want yer hundred bucks? It'd

take you months to prop'rly earn that much! Quit yer bellyachin'. We got a job to do."

Mond turned, catching Steele staring at the ground. He grabbed the man's shoulder. "Right?"

"Okey. Okey, Carl! It just feels bad."

The two men crept along the street and halted at the corner of Woody's Dry Goods.

The street was still clear. Their destination was just across the street. Mond snapped his head in both directions. No one moved down Main.

Energy surged through him. Carl tapped Jed's shoulder. As they hurried across the broad, dusty avenue, Mond retrieved the three skeleton keys from his coat pocket. They softly jangled. He muffled the cold steel with his fingers and pushed on.

Rattle. Hooves clomping into the dirt. Leather twitching.

A carriage.

Mond grabbed Jed's plaid shirt and yanked him from their target into the gloom surrounding the assayer's office. They melted into the shadows and waited.

Jed Steele's breath was so loud Mond thought the men could hear it at the silver mine across the desert. He clapped a hand over his partner's mouth and froze as the one-horse carriage clunked by them. The sound of its passing died out.

"Dang near choked me!" Jed said as Carl removed his hand.

"Better than being seen." He wiped his palm on his knee. "That carriage must've turned onto Main from Parker. Come on. We got work to do!"

After a quick look, they ran to the small, wooden

structure. The front porch squeaked as Mond slipped the first skeleton into the lock. It wouldn't budge.

Wouldn't you know it, he thought, trying the second one. Another breeze sent the smell of Jed's fear into the air. Carl Mond cursed and yanked out the useless second key.

"Come on!" Jed whispered into his ear.

"Shut up!"

Carl's hands were chilled. The small ring slipped from his fingers and crashed onto the porch. His face flushed as he picked it up and studied the keys in the thin moonlight.

Which ones had he tried? Which ones wouldn't work? No time for thinking. Mond slid a likely key into the lock and tried to turn it.

To the left, no go.

To the right, a slight hesitation. Then success.

Mond smiled and pressed against the knob. The two men hustled inside and quietly closed the door.

The dim light that shone through the windows made everything inside the building a dull grey.

"Whew!" Jed said. "When you dropped the keys I—"

"Shut up. This thing ain't over yet!" He stuck out his chin. "Draw yer weapon, Jed. Eyeball outside the winders. We were on that damned porch for too long. Someone might'a seen us."

"Okay."

Carl Mond leaped over the long, waist-high counter, amazed at how easy this had been so far. Just like they'd been told. He stared back at the barely visible wooden boxes, stacks of U.S. stamps, receipts, pens and bottles of inks that littered the counter.

He never figured it'd be this easy to break into the post office.

Carl frowned and stood before the left door behind the counter. That was the one he wanted. That was the one he'd been told to go into.

The first skeleton key easily turned the lock. He pulled on the knob and went inside.

It was a small, black room. Unable to see but unwilling to strike a light, Carl Mond kicked through the darkness, searching for his prize. His boot banged into two soft objects and sent them sliding away.

The heavy one, he remembered. Take the heavy one.

He plunged a hand into the void. Carl's fingers raced along the dusty floorboards. He felt a smooth, polished object and gripped it. Too narrow, he thought.

Then it moved.

"Sheeit!" Mond stormed from the storage room and threw the creature. It sailed across the counter and landed at Jedidiah Steele's feet. The snake slithered away.

"Hurry up!" Jed said, stepping back from the window. "You was the one in the rush and you're playing with snakes. Find it yet?"

"Shut up!"

Carl grimaced and returned to the closet. He found the two sacks, weighed them in his hands and chose the undeniably heavier one. He hauled it from the small room.

Jed went to the counter. "You shore that's the

right bag? I don't wanna come back here again."

"Yeah." He climbed over the counter. "Let's go."

The canvas bag was so heavy that Carl Mond had to sling it over his shoulder. He gripped Steele's arm as the man stretched his hand to the doorknob.

"Check outside first, damnit!"

"Oh, right."

Carl leaned over Jed's shoulder as Steele cracked open the door.

"Don't see nothing."

"Then let's git!" he whispered back.

Steele pushed the door fully open.

The elderly Chinese man stared up at them in surprise from where he crouched on the porch. Jed Steele cursed. Mond dropped the sack, drew and fired a slug into the man's heart. He'd already retrieved the mail sack as the Chinese groaned and flopped onto the boardwalk. His pigtail flipped across his face.

"Run!" Mond yelled as the explosion echoed around the buildings.

They stormed down the alley beside the assayer's office. Doors banged open behind them. Mond put everything he had into his run and urged on Steele who was somewhere behind him.

The heavy canvas bag slammed into his shoulder, carving a dent into the muscled skin.

"Damn!" he said under his breath.

Mond's boots kicked up clouds of dust. He cleared the last ten feet and meshed himself in the thicket of cottonwoods that choked the Merrone River.

"Mond!"

"Right here."

Steele crashed over to him.

"Stop!" he said.

They listened. The whole town was rising. Light bloomed in scattered windows. Men ran past the alleyways through the distant buildings in their nightclothes. A woman screamed.

"Okeh, Steele, we've gotta make the delivery."

"What?" Jed shook his head. "I ain't never moving from here. Never!"

"What you gonna do, swim?" He snorted. "Come on!"

The two men tramped through the saplings and underbrush as Oreville discovered the Chinese man's body and the Merrone River covered the sounds of their movement.


"I don't like it." Julie Golden shook her head and stared at her reflection in the cracked mirror. "Hear me? I don't like it!"

The middleaged, lean man smirked as he pushed the Stetson onto his head. "Too late for your womanly concern, Julie. I'll be back in the morning, and you'd better have it."

She turned to him, crinolines rustling. "Just a minute, Lionel Kemp!" The raven-haired young woman stormed up at him. "You think I'll do anything you say?"

He nodded. "If you wanna keep your pretty little head out of jail."

Julie stepped back at his words, fixing her green eyes on his. "You don't own me."

"I do now. Don't you forget it, woman!"

"But—"

"Shut up, Julie. Open the door for me!"

She took a breath, ran a hand through her hair and sighed. "Open it yourself. I got better things to do."

Lionel Kemp laughed. "You sure are pretty when you're mad. If you didn't have company arriving, I just might—"

"Get out. Get out!" Julie grabbed the silver hairbrush from her table and flung it at the man.

"Careful. You know what'll happen if I get bored with you?"

She sank into the chair in front of the mirror and sighed. "I know what you say you'll do. You don't have any proof. Besides, I didn't do it and no one would believe you."

"So you say. I know better. Keep your skirts clean, Julie. See you in the morning." He looked at the ceiling. "Bacon and eggs sound fine."

"You bastard!"

Lionel Kemp laughed as he walked out of her bedroom.

When he was gone, Julie wiped her eyes. How had she gotten herself into this situation? It was so absurd. But it had happened.

She sat and fiddled with her perfume bottles until the knocking on her door brought her back to reality.

Julie quickly checked her appearance—old habit, she thought with a wry smile—and went downstairs.

The knocking from the kitchen hadn't let up and was so incessant, so loud, that she was infuriated when she opened the door.

"Come in!" she snarled.

Carl Mond and Jedidiah Steele pushed past her.

Their clothing was torn and leaves poked out of their pockets, but Julie ignored that and stared at the canvas bag in Carl's hands.

"Is that it?"

Carl shrugged. "Don't know. Didn't have time to check it."

"We had some trouble," Jed added.

Julie shook her head. "Never mind about that now." She ushered them into the kitchen and checked the heavy, floral draperies that completely covered the windows. They wouldn't be seen.

"What kinda trouble?" Julie asked as Carl laid the bag onto the oak table. "Hell! How we gonna get this thing open?" She flipped the small padlock that secured the top of the canvas bag.

Carl produced the skeleton keys and soon tore the padlock from the grommeted holes.

Despite her anger at Lionel, Julie couldn't resist the urge to see her booty. Maybe he was right. Maybe all women are born criminals.

She reached for the bag and tried to lift it, but a life spent on her back hadn't toughened her arms. "Dump it out on the table!" she said to Carl.

The man upended the mail bag.

Cards and letters spilled from it. A series of small, well-packaged parcels slammed onto the wood. Carl shook it twice to make sure it was empty and threw the canvas sack onto the ground.

Julie ripped open the closest parcel. She tore away the paper and unwrapped the cloth. Ten dazzlingly bright ingots of pure silver poured out from it.

She caught her breath. "You did it." Her excitement died as the men revealed the rest of the silver.

"What was this about trouble?"

"Had to kill a man," Steele said. "Actually, Mond here killed him."

Julie stared at the two. Her face reddened. "Well? Who was it? Who'd you plug?"

"Chin Wah," Mond said, fiddling with the precious metal. "Ran into him right outside the post office. Nothing else to do. He saw our faces."

Julie ignored the surge of emotion. She nodded. "Okay. Don't talk about it."

Mond glanced at Steele. "You aren't, ah, too happy about that?"

She shook her head. "No." Lionel's words bounced around in her head. Julie straightened her back. "No! Of course not! What should have been a clean little robbery's gotten so complicated. Honestly!"

"Didn't you hear the commotion outside? The whole town's up in arms, lookin' for us."

Julie sighed. "I was, ah, busy."

"You got yer silver," Mond said, banging his hand onto the table. "When're we gonna get our money?"

"Right now. Just like I promised you."

Jedidiah Steele rubbed his hands together and licked his lips. Julie sighed and walked to the salt-ware crock where she kept her egg and butter money. She reached into the jar but hesitated.

Did she really trust these men?

A faint scraping sound behind her convinced Julie not to take foolish chances. She slipped the folding money into her hand.

"We'll just take this here silver and be on our way, miss," Carl said.

Julie also grabbed the small, cold object she'd

hidden in the crock and spun to face them. "Sorry, boys. We agreed on a hundred each. Take it or leave it!"

Carl and Jed stared at the deadly little pistol, their mouths open. Each had one hand at his holster, the other on the silver.

"Surprised? You shouldn't be. Just because I'm a woman doesn't mean I'm stupid! Stand back, boys."

They did as they were told.

"Very good!" Smiling, Julie threw the bills onto the table.

Mond and Steele exchanged glances.

"Well? You taking or you leaving? I don't have all night, boys!"

Carl laughed. "Heck, didn't mean nothing by that. Just, ah—ah—" He looked at Steele for help.

"Ah—"

"Testing me?" Julie brightly suggested. "A feeble attempt to see if I have what it takes?"

Mond brightened. "That's it. Just testing you."

"Then I passed. Take the money and get out there. Mix with the crowd that's assuredly gathering, eager to be in on the excitement. I'll be in touch, but stop in the Motherlode Saloon every day to see if I've got more work for you. Gentlemen, I have the feeling this is the start of a beautiful relationship. Just behave yourselves."

"It's beautiful, alright," Carl said as he grabbed his share of the money. "So're you."

"Yeah!" Jed picked up his cash.

Julie smirked. "I'm surprised at you, Carl Mond! This is strictly business. Besides, you can have all you want from my girls at the Motherlode—on the house, like I told you. What would you want with an old woman of thirty? Now git your behinds outa my kitchen!"

"Yes, ma'am." Carl stared down at the money in his hand, folded it and carefully stuffed it into his coat pocket. "We're going."

Julie watched the men walk toward the door. "You sure that Chinese man's really dead?"

"I guess so. We didn't wait to find out," Carl said with a grimace.

The door banged shut behind them.

Alone again, Julie looked at the silver that was scattered across the table top. She laid the derringer in the middle of it, rubbed her eyes and yawned.

It had started. She'd done what the man had told her to do. They had that mine owner's silver. She was safe from Lionel Kemp for another night.

But they'd killed that man . . . .

Julie fought off the revulsion and the tears that threatened her eyes. She locked the kitchen door, gathered up the silver and hid it in the bottom of her pie safe. No one would think to look there, she told herself.

Her work finished, she turned down the kerosene lamps plunging the kitchen into darkness. Julie Golden walked through her silent house, her bootheels clicking on the wooden planks beneath her.

She stifled a yawn, stretched and went to her bedroom.

She never realized she'd lose so much sleep being a criminal.

# CHAPTER TWO

He'd seen more Godforsaken towns, but the tiny speck on the map that turned out to be Oreville, Nevada, seemed to be barely alive. Spur McCoy dislodged himself from the stage, collected his carpetbag and stood on the well-packed dirt.

Heat shimmered from the ground and pounded onto him from above, but the air wasn't still. It twisted and banked all around him, sluicing off the nearby mountains like hell-driven demons.

Didn't it ever rain here?

It was a desert town, alright. The buildings hadn't been painted so every wooden plank was the color of dust. The windows at the post office—where the stagecoach's driver was handing over the mailbags—were caked with dirt. Men walking past were similarly coated.

A wind picked up and deposited a pound of dirt on Spur McCoy's face. The howl of millions of

particles of sand scraping against each other in the
dust devil only increased his dislike of the place.
As he brushed off his coat and face, Spur wasn't
happy to be in a dying mining town.

But it was his latest assignment as an agent of
the Secret Service. Wiping the grit from his eyes,
he looked at the two armed men who carefully
watched the transfer of mail from the stagecoach.
Just as his superior's telegram had informed him,
Oreville was in trouble.

Spur got a room at the Eastern Heights Hotel,
dropped off his bag and emptied the ewer into the
basin. The sound alone refreshed him. He vigorously scrubbed his face. The cool water felt so good
after his long stagecoach ride that McCoy finally
started to feel good about this case.

He ambled down the street looking for a barber.
He had to get some of his hair chopped off in this
heat. Spur tried hard to ignore the strength-sapping
temperature.

From the looks of things, Oreville must have had
a wild past. Money had poured into the place. He
saw three assayer's offices, five old dry goods
stores, the remains of half a dozen livery stables.

Of the twelve saloons lining Main Street, all but
two were abandoned. Their once proud walls
sagged. Windows and doors had been ripped from
them to furnish new buildings. Three had been
burned into huge piles of blackened rubble.

Spur McCoy glanced at the distant mountains. He
knew there were mines out there. Gold and silver
had brought men to Oreville. A year ago the rich
veins had been worked out. Most of the town's men
had left, taking their wives and children to more

promising hunting grounds. The only thing keeping Oreville alive was the last operational silver mine run by one Cleve P. Magnus.

Spur finally found the familiar red and white pole and walked into the barbershop.

"Blair's my name; hair's my game," the balding man said by rote. "Cut or shave?" His round face carried tired eyes. The barber stropped a razor.

"Uh, just a cut. My hair, I mean."

The barber smiled. "No miner surgery today?" He whisked the blade back and forth. "I'm Oreville's doctor, too."

"No. No thanks."

Blair frowned. "Sure. Think you can come in here and order me around!"

"Look." Spur fit his tall form into the chair. "I just got into town. Chop off some of my hair, or isn't my money good enough for you?"

The barber sighed and threw the razor onto the floor, where it sent a skinny dog yelping and scurrying out the door. "Sorry, fella. It's been tough. No work." He fondly smiled. "Used to be men lined up to get looking good for their ladies."

"Mine closings?"

"Yep." He grabbed a pair of scissors. "All my customers left town, and I'm gonna follow them. I'm gonna be on that stage one day. Never come back here again."

"Sorry to hear that." Spur removed his hat and placed it protectively on his chest.

"Yeah, sure." The barber laughed and fastened a towel around Spur's neck. "But hell, that's my problem. What's yours?"

"Nothing I can think of." He closed his eyes and

relaxed in the chair.

"If you're here, brother, you got a problem." Blair the barber chuckled and started clipping. "You in town long?"

"Maybe. Don't know."

"Hmm." Clip. Snip. "What you here for?"

"This and that."

"Hm. I'll bet you're one of those men who heard there's still gold hiding like a rattler out there in the mountains, waiting for the man with the right kind of luck to stumble onto it."

"Nope."

"Mmm."

The scissors clacked together. Reddish-brown hair rained around Spur's face.

"You always talk this much?" the barber asked.

McCoy grinned. "Yep."

"Let me give you a piece of advice—no charge," the barber said. "You'll probably want to be seeing the ladies here. Just stay away from Ma's place."

"Ma's?"

"Yeah."

Bored, Spur took the bait. "What's wrong with Ma's place?"

"She has the ugliest girls, the lumpiest beds and the highest prices."

Spur grunted. "Yeah? Then why in hell would anyone go there?"

The barber guffawed. "Shit, man, they got live shows. You know?"

Spur opened his eyes. "Huh?"

Blair's face lit up with steamy memories. "Live shows. You know, girls doing things to each other."

He made a face in the mirror. "Oh."

"Dirty things. Hoo-whee! I just go there for the shows myself—'travagances,' they're called." The bartender grabbed a fat hunk of hair. "You want all this off?"

"No. Don't scalp me! Just take off a little all the way around."

"Why didn't you say so? Jeez! I ain't no mentalist!"

"Just a barber and surgeon."

"Yep. And the town's doctor. You need to get a bullet dug outa your shoulder, you just come to me. Also the undertaker and the notary public."

The barber clipped in silence for a few more minutes.

"Done!" he said, and removed the towel.

Spur glanced in the mirror. He'd had worse haircuts. McCoy flipped a quarter to the man.

"You sure you don't want a shave? I could spruce up those mutton-chop sideburns of yours." Blair retrieved the dirty razor from the corner and held it toward Spur's face. His hand shook from side to side.

"I don't think so. Thanks."

"Right. And if you know what's good for you, stay outa Ma's!" He winked.

Spur tucked on his hat and stepped into the blinding sunlight. According to the telegram he'd received three days ago, Oreville had been a sleepy little town after the gold fury had passed. But in the last three weeks the post office had been robbed twice, both times on the night before the mail was to go out with the stage. Two men had also been killed.

The local mine owner—one Cleve Magnus—had

lost thousands of dollars when the silver ingots he'd been sending to New York had been stolen. The wealthy man had hired four guards to protect the post office. It hadn't been broken into but last week the stagecoach carrying the mail—and Magnus' silver—had been attacked, the driver and gunmen killed, and every last piece of mail stolen. The strongbox was also taken.

The passengers—two women—had been spared. Seems the thieves couldn't bring themselves to shoot them. They're still in town at the Eastern Heights Hotel, which is why Spur had hired a room there.

That was all he'd learned from his boss back in Washington. No possible suspects, nothing else. The Secret Service had a new job for Spur McCoy: find the men responsible for the murders and the thefts and haul them in.

He had little to go on. No one who had seen the men's faces had lived. From what General Halleck had written there were two men doing the robberies.

A young man strolled down the street. "Excuse me!" Spur yelled.

"Huh?" The boy stared at him, glassy-eyed, his nose red with burst capillaries.

"Where could I find the mayor?"

"Old Kincaid?" The youth snorted and threw his hat onto the ground. "Ma's place? Naw. Eatin'? Naw. Screwing a horse? Naw." He scratched his wild-haired hair. "Drinkin'? Naw. Skinny dippin'? Naw. Screwin' a—"

"Do you know where he is?"

The drunken boy shrugged and reeled on

unsteady feet. "You could try his shack. It's right there." He pointed.

McCoy smiled. "That's the livery stable."

"Huh?" The kid moved his gaze from his shoulder, along his arm and out from his fingertip. "Oh yeah. Um, hell! Where'd he put it?" He turned to Spur, curling his upper lip. "Why the hell'd you ask me all these questions?"

"Never mind. I'll find it."

"Then I think I'll take a nap." The young man crumpled onto the street onto a pile of horse droppings and snoozed.

Spur shook his head, asked a well dressed man, and quickly found Mayor Kincaid's home.

He knocked at the handsome two-storey house. No answer. Another knock finally brought a vision to the door—a young woman swathed with peach silk.

"Yes?" she said, primping her hair. "Sorry, I just took off my bonnet. I feel naked."

"Looks fine to me." He smiled at her expression. "I mean, I'm inquiring after Mayor Kincaid, Miss—"

"I'm Kelly Kincaid, the mayor's daughter. *Miss* Kincaid. My father's out somewhere, think he rode to Mr. Magnus' mine about something or t'other." The blonde woman broke into a smile. "My, you must be new in town."

He grinned at the beautiful young woman. "That's a fact. How'd you know?"

Kelly curled a lock of blonde hair around her little finger. "I'd remember you." She giggled and lowered her eyes, but not to Spur's feet.

He could feel her staring at him down there.

Three seconds of that made his pants uncomfortably tight. "Ah, well, Miss Kincaid—"

"Kelly." She looked up into his eyes. "Call me Kelly. Heck, call me anything you want!"

She was so delicious, so willing, but she was the mayor's daughter. "Uh, right, Kelly." Spur stepped back from the threshold. "Know when he'll be back?"

"Not for hours. It's a long ride out to the mine." Kelly moved toward him. "I'm all alone here in this big, old house, lonely and needing male company." She narrowed her shoulders and licked her lips.

Spur's throat tightened. "I guess I'll try again later."

Kelly pouted. "You're not going to leave me, are you? You just got here!"

"I really should be going."

She sighed. "Alright. Who should I say called for the mayor?"

"McCoy. Spur McCoy."

"Spur? What an unusual first name!" Kelly laughed and grabbed his hand. "Won't you come in for a cup of tea? It's the least I can do for you—and I do mean the least."

The contact of her skin on his was so erotic. Spur felt his control slipping. "Ah—ah—"

The determined young woman pulled him into the house and slammed the door behind him.

"Come on, Spur!" Kelly said.

"Come on, ah, what?" He removed his hat—a bit too late for being in the presence of a lady. A *lady*?

She rolled her blue eyes. "You know perfectly well what I'm talking about. I don't think we should waste any more time. Do you?"

"Time? Waste?" His crotch was unbearably tight.

"Yes!" Her eyes were alive. Kelly released his hand and stood in front of him, panting, her breasts rising and falling, straining against the thin material of her silken dress. "I've never beheld a man who did this to me, who could make me feel this way."

"Well, ah, Kelly, ah—"

"Can't you see I'm on fire?" she asked him, and tilted back her head.

He could see it alright. And he liked what he saw. The uninhibited young woman had set a blaze in his body as well. Spur took a stumbling step toward the woman, right there in the parlor.

The door banged open. "Kelly! Did that—oh, hello!"

Spur recovered his balance before he fell onto his face. Flushed, he turned and took in the short, dusty man who stood in the doorway. "Hello yourself," he said in slightly husky voice. "Mayor Kincaid?"

"Yep."

"Spur McCoy."

They shook hands. Spur fanned his face with his Stetson. "You order all this hot weather just for me?"

Kincaid laughed jovially and kissed a suddenly poised Kelly's cheek. "Nope. Heck, McCoy, we're having a cool wave. Normally, it'd be 112 by now." He hung his hat and coat on a rack beside the door. "I was just going out to the mine—Magnus' silver mine—when old Isabella threw a shoe. Had to come right back. Course, there wasn't much I could tell him anyway." Kincaid planted his hands on his hips. "I see you met my daughter."

Kelly beamed. "I was just going to make tea. Would you like a cup, dear father?"

Kincaid rubbed his sweaty face. "Might as well. I have some business to discuss with McCoy here."

"Fine. I'll be right back!" Kelly winked at Spur from behind her father's back and swirled away.

Kincaid led the Secret Service agent into his office. "Glad to see you made it to my little town in one piece, McCoy."

"No problem."

"Ain't it a regular Eden around here? An oasis?"

Spur grinned and lowered his voice. "It's a blooming garden."

Kincaid laughed out loud.

"Had any more robberies lately, Mayor Kincaid? Silver robberies? My information's three days old."

"Nope." The man lit a cheroot and puffed. "But the post office is too well guarded now, and the eastern stage isn't due to leave for a week yet. I don't figure anything'll happen until then."

"I suppose Magnus will put guards on the stage from now on. Right?"

"You can bet the farm on that. He's stocking the coach with gunmen. Cleve is determined not to lose another shipment of his silver."

"Where's he sending it?"

"A big bank back East. He doesn't trust our puny local bank. Sure, he keeps a small account. But the rest of it he ships out soon as he can."

Spur nodded. Justin Kincaid seemed a reasonable, intelligent man, McCoy thought, as he watched him puff away. He liked him. In one sense he was glad the mayor had walked in when he did. If he'd arrived back home a few minutes later he would have found McCoy and his daughter in a comprising situation, and position.

"You talked with the two female witnesses yet?"

Spur shook his head. "I only just got into town and wanted to see you first."

Kincaid nodded. "You know there's no law around here. The last sheriff quit a year ago when the biggest gold mine petered out and we haven't elected another one. No interest. And, until a few weeks ago, no real reason. Things were quiet here. Then this started happening." The mayor chewed on the end of the cheroot. "I don't understand it."

"Neither do I. But I'll find the men responsible. Trust me, Kincaid."

"I do. Your boss said you're the best."

Spur grunted.

Justin hesitated and set his smoke in an ashtray. "Did my daughter—well, did Kelly—"

The young woman burst into the room. "Tea, anyone?" she asked, bearing two cups.

Spur smiled as he burned his hands on the cup. Justin Kincaid shrugged at him.

"I'll be in the kitchen if you need me," Kelly said, waltzing out.

"She's quite a woman, that daughter of yours," Spur said.

The mayor spit out his tea.

Five minutes later, Spur walked with Kincaid to the front door.

"Sure hope you can clean up this little problem of ours," Justin said, removing his coat and hat from the rack. "Cleve Magnus is ready to shoot me if he doesn't stop losing his silver, and he's not a violent man." Kincaid opened the front door.

"Mayor! Mayor Kincaid!"

It was the drunken youth Spur had met in the street. Suddenly, he'd had no problem finding Kincaid's home. He reeked of alcohol and pulsed with excitement.

"What is it, Ephraim?"

"Ole Jake Connelly's holed up in a room at Ma's with two girls." The boy gasped. "Says he won't let 'em out until you get over there and forgive him for his carnal sins!"

"What?" Kincaid guffawed.

"It's true! Ma's hunkering around mad as a wet hen. She sent me out here herself." Gasp. Breathe. "You gotta get over there. The guy's gotta knife!"

"The damn fool!" Justin Kincaid turned to Spur. "He thinks I'm a damned priest!"

"Drunker than a skunk he is," said the inebriated youth. "Hurry up! Wait any more and those two girls—Kitty and Felicia—won't be giving you or me any more discounts, mayor!"

Kincaid gave him a stern look and shrugged on his coat. "Okay. Okay! Sorry, McCoy. Duty calls. I'll be back as soon as I can untangle things."

He ran out the door ahead of the sweating youth.

Kelly walked up beside Spur. "What was all that about?" she asked, peering through the doorframe.

He smiled. "Your father's, ah, needed elsewhere."

"Good. Because I need you here." Kelly Kincaid slid her hand between his legs.

# CHAPTER THREE

"Look, young lady. You are the mayor's daughter." Spur McCoy flushed as he gently peeled Kelly Kincaid's fingers from his crotch.

"Uh-huh." She wrestled from his grip and zeroed in on her target once again.

Spur flinched at the erotic contact. "He could come back here any time."

"Yes."

He backed away from her, inadvertently closing the door. "He'd be mad as heck if he saw what you're doing right—uh, oh—now."

"Positively livid." The blonde-haired woman fingered him below his brass belt buckle.

He caught her gaze, smiled, and let her work him over. "We really shouldn't be doing this. You're so young."

"Eighteen," Kelly said, furiously stroking the growing bulge between his legs.

"Really?" He groaned.

"Yes."

"Well then—" Spur shook his head. "Kelly, stop that!"

She used both hands, sliding them up and down his thighs and gripping the most sensitive part of his body. She was at him like a Pagan at an idol.

"You hear me, girl? You better stop that or I'll let you have it!"

Kelly squeezed him so hard that Spur's body convulsed. His head smacked into the kerosene lamp that hung adjacent to the front door.

"That does it. Come with me, young lady!" McCoy grabbed her hand, but she laughed, twisted away from him and ran up the stairs.

Spur followed her flying skirt and petticoats, taking two steps at a time, but she was fast. He didn't catch up with her until the girl had cleared a hallway and had disappeared inside a room.

"Kelly?" he said as he walked in.

Mayor Kincaid's daughter pounced on him from behind the door. The delicious attack threw him off balance. McCoy crashed onto the canopied feather bed as the girl giggled and laughed and rolled over his body.

Spur relaxed and gasped. Kelly was all over him, kissing, groping. She lay fully on top of him and rubbed her groin against him. The pressure at his crotch increased tenfold. Spur grabbed her head and pulled it closer.

He forced his tongue between her lips and sank it into the young woman's mouth. She ground her breasts against his chest and moaned as she took McCoy's thrusts, stabbing her own tongue between her parted teeth.

Kelly threw back her head and gasped.

"Let me guess. I'm your first man," Spur said, fumbling with the tiny white buttons that extended down the back of her silk dress.

"No time for small talk, Spur!" Kelly slid off him, bent and ripped open his belt.

He was halfway down her back when the mayor's daughter succeeded in hauling his pants and underdrawers down to his thighs. Kelly went crazy at the sight of his genitals, peppering them with kisses, licking and tasting everything in sight until Spur had to pull her mouth from him.

"Hold on, girl!" he said as the impending explosion subsided within him. "Jeez! You're worse than a—a—than anything I've ever seen!"

She looked up at him with glassy eyes. Locks of blonde hair veiled her face. "Spur, I've never wanted a man as much as I want you!"

He opened the last button. They looked at each other for a second and clambered off the bed.

Spur pulled off his boots, pants and underdrawers as Kelly removed her dress. Seconds later they were stark naked, rolling over and over on the carpeted floor, locked in a wet, plunging kiss.

He pumped his hips against her mound. Their bodies nudged the dresser so they reversed direction. Spur held her to the carpet and took her aroused nipples in his mouth, one at a time, left then right, slurping the succulent morsels with just enough of a bite to drive the woman wild.

The heat slickened their bodies. Kelly pushed him away and slammed him onto his back. She took him in her hand. Spur closed his eyes as the incredible sensation washed over him.

"You're good," he said as her blonde mane bobbed between his legs. "Oh, god—make that *real* good!"

The tight, wet, constricting feeling energized him. Oblivious to the intense heat, the open bedroom door and the dangerous situation he was in, Spur surrendered to the woman with the magic throat.

Up she went. All the way down. Again and again. He groaned and bucked his hips up to meet her liquid lips. Kelly pulled at his scrotum and sucked him with obvious relish for two minutes, slowing when he was on the verge, speeding when he'd regained control, repeating the cycle until he was out of his mind.

Spur helplessly groaned.

Kelly pulled off him with a loud pop and looked into his eyes. "Had enough, big boy? And I do mean big!"

Spur took her head in his hands. "I don't care if you are Mayor Kincaid's daughter," he said, his voice husky. "I'm gonna ram you, but good!"

She stretched out on her back, spread her legs and lifted her hips. "I don't care if I'm Mayor Kincaid's daughter either. Just do it. Do it to me!"

Their bodies fit together. Spur thrust into her, gently at first, then harder. Staring into her eyes, holding onto her hips, he pushed himself full-length into her.

Kelly's mouth hung open in the erotic expression of a woman who hasn't been with a man for awhile. She clutched his back and moaned, shivering, rubbing her hardened nipples across his hairy chest.

"I'm glad I didn't save myself for marriage."

He pulled out and slammed back into Kelly.

She winced. "Or become a nun."

Another pump.

The woman blinked. Her face flushed. "Or—or—ah hell, Spur! That's so good!"

He grinned at her. Their hip bones crashed together. The oak bed creaked. Spur pounded into the young woman whose astonished stares were periodically broken by moans. They sank deeper into the thick feather mattress.

Kelly held onto his hairy thighs, writhing and twisting, meeting his stroking hips. She squeezed around him to increase their mutual pleasure, breathing faster and faster.

She was so beautiful, so willing, that Spur felt himself losing control. He slowed down.

"Damnit, McCoy!" Kelly said. "I was almost there!" She dug her fingernails into his ass. "Do it as hard as you can! Jesus, let me have it all the way!"

He did, driving into her with quick, deep thrusts. Kelly wailed and urged him on with her hands. Spur mindlessly plowed between her legs, lost in an erotic world of warm, sweet flesh.

The mattress exploded. White feathers squirted out around them on both sides. Spur got onto his hands and toes and continued to plunge into her. The increased stimulation freed Kelly from that trembling moment of hesitation. She screamed and thrashed beneath him.

That did it. Spur had no choice. The room went blank. He exploded, spastically jabbing into her, grunting, kissing her forehead, revelling in the primal male feeling of seed spurting from his body.

His tight-muscled form vibrated and shook. Kelly moaned as he pumped into her again and again, stroking his back, clamping her legs around him, catching her breath in her throat. Spur finally sank onto her, spent, useless. They kissed as feathers floated down onto them from the air.

He snoozed for a minute or two, only to wake up to Kelly's laughter.

Spur opened his eyes and kissed her. "What— what's so funny?"

"You. You look like a chicken!" Kelly convulsed with giggles.

"Huh?" He twisted around and saw the feathers that had adhered to his sweaty back. Spur smiled back at her. "I'm the rooster. You're the chicken."

"Right. I never can remember which is which."

"Sure, Kelly. Sure."

She wiped off the feathers as he dressed. After their moment together, once his mind had cleared, Spur was anxious to get on with his mission. As much as he'd enjoyed it, he had work to do. He put on his professional attitude.

"Here!" Kelly said. "Don't forget your hat!"

McCoy took it from her with a kiss. "Ah, sorry about the room," he said, gesturing to the ruined mattress and the thousands of white clumps covering the floor.

"Not to worry," Kelly said. "It was worth it. You'll be back to see me before you leave town, right?"

"Right. I promise."

One last kiss and Spur was out the bedroom door. Fortunately, he didn't meet Justin Kincaid on his exit from the man's house. Spur smiled. Nothing like a midday romp in the hay to get him eager for work. Or, more correctly, a romp in the feathers.

He went to the Eastern Heights Hotel. The two women passengers who'd witnessed the stagecoach robbery were registered in room 23. They hadn't been cooperative with the Mayor's investigation but Spur knew they had something that would help.

Finding the room, he knocked.

"Go away!"

The female's voice didn't sound friendly. Undaunted, he banged again. "I'm here to help you!" McCoy said, trying to remember the women's names.

"Here to kill us, more likely!"

"No!"

Silence.

"Come on, ma'am! Just want to talk with you. Mayor Kincaid sent me here." He tried the knob. Locked.

"Well . . . ."

He heard feet shuffling in the room, the sound of women's boots against bare wood.

"How do I know you're not one of them men who attacked the stagecoach?"

"Ma'am, Mrs. Grieve, just open the door."

A key turned. The knob twisted. An elderly woman peered at him, her face pinched beneath the lace bonnet, eyes steely and active.

"Well?" she asked.

He removed his hat. "I'm Spur McCoy. Mayor Kincaid called me into town to investigate these robberies, including the one you were unfortunately involved with. May I come in?"

Emma Grieve shook her head. "Not yet. What do you want to know?"

"Everything, Mrs. Grieve, it would be so much easier for all of us if you'd just let me—" '

"Okay. Alright!"

Spur walked in as she stepped aside. The hotel room was identical to his own, save for the laces and petticoats strewn over every piece of furniture. A young girl with sad eyes huddled in a chair, meticulously working on a piece of embroidery. The girl was pretty, with a pert nose, huge blue eyes and ringlets of brown hair. Her face showed the last traces of the sunburn that she'd obviously received during her recent ordeal.

The old woman slammed the door behind him and locked it. "Hurry up. We don't got all day, mister!"

He turned to her—the girl's grandmother, if he remembered correctly. "Fine. Did you—"

"Save your breath, mister." Emma Grieve shook her head. "Can't remember a thing except that one man screaming at us the whole time, telling us he was going to kill us and leave us there for the blizzards to eat us up."

"Buzzards?" Spur guessed.

She frowned. "Blizzards, buzzards. See, I told you I can't remember!" The old woman walked to the girl. "Melissa here hasn't been the same since that day." Her face softened. "Neither have I for that matter. Had to walk five miles back to this hell-hole of a town after those animals left us alone in the desert. My arthritis flared up something fierce. Sorry, mister, we can't help you. Go away and leave us alone!"

"Were the men wearing kerchiefs over their faces?"

"I don't know. Yes, I guess so." Emma Grieve put a hand on Melissa's shoulder.

"And there were two of them?"

She nodded. Mrs. Grieve smiled tightly. "Now I'll have to ask you to leave again. And don't come back!"

"Thanks for your time, ladies." Spur sighed as Emma Grieve unlocked and opened the door.

"Find them."

The small, high voice behind him made McCoy turn back just as he stepped from the room. Melissa Grieve didn't look up at him.

"Now you shush, Melissa. Time to put some more cream onto those burns." Emma pointed into the hall. "Good day, mister!"

A rifle exploded in the hall, sending a messenger of death flying into the women's room.

# CHAPTER FOUR

Spur McCoy ducked as hot lead slammed into the hotel room's wall.

"Lock the door and stay there!" he yelled to Emma and Melissa. As he dashed out of the room, drawing his revolver, Spur caught a glimpse of two men flying down the stairs.

His boots pounded the floorboards. McCoy powered along the hall. He skidded, grabbed the railing on each side and half-ran, half-slid down the stairway. The gunmen disappeared outside, leaving the hotel's front door wide open.

Pumping his arms, he sped across the deserted lobby and rushed onto the porch, ready to fire, searching for a target.

The street was empty of people. A few horses drank at the trough in front of the Eastern Heights Hotel. A man wearing a minister's collar wiped sweat from his forehead as he trudged along with an armful of bibles. No one else was in sight. No sign of the two gunmen.

"Reverend!" Spur said, dashing up to the man of the cloth. "Two gunmen just ran out of the hotel. Must have gone right past you. Did you see them?"

The bespectacled man stared up at him above his unwieldly cargo. "No, my son. Nothing but the glory of this day that the Lord has made."

Spur was running before the man finished his sentence. He checked the wide alleys between the stores. He rushed straight through the livery stable. He searched through the piles of costly, imported timber stacked behind the "Fine Construction Supplies" building.

Nothing!

Spur stopped in the middle of the street, panting, his shirt soaked to the skin, fidgeting with his weapon. Where the hell had the men gone?

The barber who'd chopped off his hair earlier that day called to him from his shop.

"Who's dead?" Blair asked, hesitantly venturing from his place of business. "Or, who needs a bullet dug out?"

"No one. Damn! Two men just took a potshot at me and two ladies in the Eastern Heights Hotel! Seen them?"

The barber rubbed his face and sighed. "Nope. You and two ladies?" Blair chuckled. "At least you're staying away from Ma's place."

"Where the hell is everyone?" Spur asked, waving at the deserted street.

"Aint' much gunfighting in Oreville no more," the barber said, wiping his hands on his blue pants. "When a man decides to start shooting, citizens make themselves scarce."

"Great. So no one saw them." He dug his toe into the inch-thick dust that covered Main Street.

Blair shrugged. "If I'm not needed, guess I'll feed the dog." He walked back into his shop.

The two men who'd fired into Emma and Melissa's room had to be the same pair who'd robbed the eastbound stagecoach. They hadn't been after him. They'd been trying to silence them, Spur figured. He holstered his revolver.

But why do it in the middle of the day? It didn't make any sense. Unless—unless they weren't professionals. Unless they were experimenting around.

Or unless they weren't too smart.

As he stood there, thinking it through, Oreville returned to as much life as it could muster. Men appeared from the saloons, mounted up and rode off. Women walked with pails to the nearby river for water. Two boys in clean short pants—city clothes—threw rocks at each other.

Spur asked every passerby if they'd seen the gunmen, but no one had. They didn't seem to be lying, he decided. They simply hadn't.

He walked back to the hotel. The lobby was still empty, the manager nowhere in sight. On the second floor he knocked on room 23.

"It's me, Mrs. Grieve. Spur McCoy!"

"You git your butt outta here!" the elderly woman shrieked. "You sent those men to kill us!"

"No, I didn't!" Spur yelled back. "Use some sense, Mrs. Grieve."

"Sense? I'f I'd used sense I wouldn't have a hole in my wall and a shaking granddaughter! Now git before I blow you to hell with this rifle of mine!"

Spur started to knock again but heard the unmistakable sound of a rifle being loaded.

"Okay. But I'll be back."

He turned and walked to his room. Spur needed to sit down and do some thinking.


"You idiots!" Julie Golden said. She planted her hands on her hips. "How could you be so stupid? How? Answer me!"

Carl Mond and Jedidiah Steele stood with their hats in their hands and stared at the woman's kitchen floor.

"I told you to shoot them at two!" she continued, grilling them with her green-tinted gaze.

"But it was two, ma'am," Carl said in a low voice.

Julie slapped her bosom. "Two in the morning, not two in the afternoon!" She circled them. "What were you thinking, going into that hotel with your guns drawn, ready to do your dirty work while the sun's still up, in front of the whole wide world?"

"Well, I, uh—" Carl looked at Jed, who shook his head.

She sighed. "Did anyone see you running back here? I don't want to be connected with this."

"Certainly not, Miss Golden!" Mond pulled in his chin. "We're smart enough not to do that."

"I see. You just can't tell time." Julie shook her head. "Never mind. I'll take care of it my way." Julie had done her best to sound as fierce and angry as she should have felt. Inside, though, she could barely hide her relief that the man hadn't carried out the orders she'd passed onto them from Lionel Kemp.

"Okay. Stop standing there like a coupla boys who've messed your pants! You better lie low for a while. Stay here. Keep the doors and windows locked. Don't show yourselves in town, you hear? Heavens, you didn't even cover your faces!"

Carl burped.

Julie Golden tied the bonnet onto her head and adjusted it by feel. "It might be better this way," she said.

The two men glanced up at her.

"What—what you got in mind, Miss Golden?" Carl asked.

"Yeah, what?"

Julie reached for the kitchen door. "You'll find out soon enough. Just don't leave until I get back. Those girls will drop out of sight."

She strode down Camp Street, her boots kicking up the dirt that she hated so much. But Julie smiled as she walked to the Eastern Heights Hotel.

She'd figured Carl and Jed would be too dumb to do the right thing. She'd given them a stunning performance, telling them that the two women had told Mayor Kincaid that they'd identify the men tomorrow morning who'd robbed the stagecoach. Then Julie had told them that Emma and Melissa Grieve had to die as soon as possible. "At two," she'd told them. "And make sure you're not seen!"

Just as she'd planned, they'd gone ahead and hustled out to the women's room an hour later.

Lionel Kemp might have her livelihood wrapped around his finger but she wasn't his slave. There were things she could do, things he'd never dream of.

She hoped everything would go smoothly.

Julie Golden stopped in front of the hotel, stamped the dust from her black boots, smoothed her skirt and walked inside. It was just about summer time, after all, and she couldn't bear the thought of cooking.

A strange sight greeted her in the hotel's dining room. Five men stood with revolvers and rifles across their chests, backs to the wall, guarding the diners. They stared at Julie as she walked in.

The long table was empty save for an elderly woman and her young charge. She'd spot them anywhere, though she'd never seen them. Those had to be the two.

Julie seated herself across from the women.

"Good afternoon," she said, smiling.

The girl's hand shook as she lifted a fork to her mouth. The elderly woman nodded to her.

"Guess I'm not late for supper," Julie said, staring at the huge bowls of vegetables and the platter of still-steaming roast beef.

Once again the two women didn't speak.

They must have had a real fright, Julie thought, and she didn't blame them for acting like they were.

She leaned across the table. "Listen, ladies, I know all about your situation, and I think I can help."

Emma shook her head and murmured something into her glass of red wine.

"I know you can't leave Oreville until you can make up the money that was stolen from you on the stagecoach last week."

Melissa dropped her fork.

"Miss," Emma Grieve said, finally looking up at Julie. "You're upsetting the child."

"I'm sorry, but I heard about what happened, and I've figured out a way for you to get out of here as soon as possible. Interested?"

Emma nodded.

"I know it costs a small fortune to take the stage. Then you have to buy a ticket for the railroad. But I can get you the money. You can be back home in a week. Two weeks at most!"

Melissa picked up her fork and glanced hopefully at her grandmother. Mrs. Grieve set her glass on the table and studied the woman who was beaming at them.

She almost spoke, parted her lips and turned toward the guards behind her. "Okay, men. Thanks for protecting us. Those three killers won't be back. But stay outside the door just in case, will you?"

"Of course, Mrs. Grieve!" a burly man said.

The five shuffled out and closed the dining room door.

"I don't know why, you should care about us," Emma said. "We're strangers to you."

Julie smiled. "Why shouldn't I care? I'm a woman just like you. I was in a bad situation a few months back and someone helped me. It's simple."

Emma Grieve's lower lip trembled. "No one can help us. We're all alone. No relations, no friends. No one. All we have is each other."

Julie reached across the roast beef and clasped the woman's wrinkled hand. "You've got me! And I can get you out of Oreville. Guaranteed!"

She brightened but bit her unpainted lower lip. "Our kind don't cotton to charity," Emma slowly said.

Julie had caught the glimmer. The light of hope

in her eyes. "Who said anything about charity? I'm talking about work. You'll earn the money fair and square."

"I've done washing and scrubbing," Melissa said, turning her reddened face toward Julie.

"Well, it'll be something like that. Then it's settled. You two done with your dinner?"

Emma pushed away her place and wiped her lips. "Yes, we are. When can we get started?"

"Right now. Shall we go?"

Julie led them from the room, past the guards and out of the hotel. Dusk settled in on the town as they walked two blocks south on Main and turned down Fletcher.

"This street was named after the man who first discovered gold in the hills. Did you know that?" Julie asked conversationally.

"No. Come on, Melissa! Don't hang back! We've got work to do!"

"Don't worry about those men who were after you. I heard they rode out of town."

"That's a load off my chest, pardon the expression," Emma said.

Julie laughed. She turned left past the livery stable and led Emma and Melissa along the tree-choked waterfront, passing the rear of the largest buildings in town.

"Where are you taking us?" Emma asked as her boots sunk into the soft earth.

"My place. Or, one of them at least. You'll see soon enough."

"Oh my god!"

"What is it, Mrs. Grieve?" Julie was suddenly very wary.

"Land sakes, my dear! You're being so kind to us and I don't even know your name!"

She relaxed. "It's Julie. Julie Golden." They halted at the foot of a long, rickety flight of stairs that cut across the back wall of a two storey building. "And here we are. Up you go!" she said gently.

Emma shook her head in the fading light. "My arthritis might argue with you." She clutched the railing.

"Don't worry, Mrs. Grieve. You won't have to use these stairs very often. I just figured it'd be better to bring you in this way. The inside ones are much easier to manage."

They climbed. Melissa patiently followed her slow grandmother. As they rose from the ground, the elderly woman quickened her pace. The sun set below the horizon. An evening breeze ruffled the three women's skirts.

On the landing, Julie produced a key from her sleeve and unlocked the door. She ushered the women inside.

The smell of tobacco smoke, whiskey and cheap perfume hung in the air. The corridor was dark, lit by two lonely kerosene lamps. Fourteen doors led from the hall.

Melissa stared at her grandmother. "What—what kind of place is this?"

Emma turned to Julie as the woman locked the door behind them. "Why, child, this is the kind of place I used to work in. Remember? I told you all about it?" Mrs. Grieve heartily laughed and smiled at Julie. "Of course, that was a long time ago. Years and years back. Mrs. Golden, you are a sly one, you is."

"But I didn't lie to you. After all, where else can a woman make good money? Especially in a town like this?"

Melissa watched with wide eyes as a man walked past them, turned to stare at her and disappeared into room 12.

"Come on you two," Julie said. "Let's go to my office. We have some business to deal with."

"You don't expect me to—" Melissa tugged on her grandmother's sleeve. "Be one of *those* women?"

"Hush, child!" Emma Grieve said as they walked down the hall.

Most of the rooms weren't quiet. Erotic grunts and the sound of flesh slapping together emanated from them. Melissa tightened her grip on the elderly woman's sleeve.

"After all, Melissa. It's nothing you haven't done before. I mean, you're no virgin."

"Grandmother! How could you say that?"

"Because it's true. Stop acting like a little girl. You're all grown up. Act like it. Really, Miss Golden's doing us a favor."

Melissa squeakily cried.

Julie smiled as she unlocked her office. Everything was working out perfectly.

# CHAPTER FIVE

"Isn's that him?" Jed Steele asked as he peered out the window at Julie Golden's house.

Carl pushed him away and stared out the slit between the curtains. "Sure as shit is. That's the bugger that was there at the women's hotel room!"

Jed swallowed hard. "Think he saw our faces?"

"I don't know."

"Neither do I."

They watched him wander down the road.

"Maybe we shouldn't take no chances," Carl coughed. "Maybe we should—"

"I don't know. Miss Golden told us to stay put. I don't like the way she looks at us when we mess up. She's liable to shoot us with that derringer of hers!"

"Hell, boy," Mond said, snorting. "You afraid of her?"

"No." His voice was unconvincing.

"Right. C'mon. Use your pea-sized brain! She'd want us to plug that bastard! He's what got us in trouble in the first place! If we take him out she won't be near as sore at us like she just was."

"I guess."

The two men buckled on their gunbelts.

"Your piece fully loaded?" Jed asked.

"Yeah, yeah. Let's get him!"

They walked onto the front porch as dusk spread gloom over Oreville.

The chill in the air refreshed Spur. Even though it had been hours ago he was still searching for the two men who'd come after the female witnesses to the coach robbery. He'd been through most of the town, knocking on doors, talking to every business owner and clerk he could find. Absolutely no one had been able to help him.

This three-block square area of decaying yet opulent houses, obviously built during the gold rush days, was the only section of Oreville he hadn't been through. Spur sighed, walked up to a squat house and knocked on the door.

The door fell inside with an echoing crash, rusted off its hinges. Spur stopped and looked around. How many of these houses were occupied?

Kerosene light glowed in the windows of the house next to it, and in the one down the street. He moved to the monstrous, three story structure.

An explosion rocketed through the night.

Spur slammed face-first to the ground. Hot lead dug into the dust a foot from his head.

Shit!

He slithered over to the nearest cover—an

overturned, weather-worn buggy that had long since outlived its usefulness. The gunman fired two more rounds as McCoy drew.

Make that gun*men*, Spur thought wryly, as the sounds of the new shots were obviously made by a different weapon.

He peered through a hole in the floor of the old buggy. Dusk was melting into night. The shots seemed to have come from directly across the street.

Where was his target?

Another round splintered one of the buggy's axles. Spur clearly saw the flash of gunpowder and pounded two bullets into the area.

No response. He fired a third time, aiming slightly farther to the right.

A volley of ammunition pounded into the buggy. Spur cursed as the top half split off and crashed onto him. His cover was rapidly disappearing.

He threw the wood behind him and peered through a new hole. Still unable to see anything across the street, and knowing that no man could hope for accurate aim at that distance, Spur chanced it. He hunkered down and sped from the buggy to a woodpile beside the three story house.

More shots, more misses.

The woodstack was thick, well packed and perfect for use. With fast, practiced hands, Spur flipped open his revolver's chamber and reloaded with the spares he always kept in his coat pocket. He blasted another round into the area.

It was fully dark. The explosive flashes of the men's return fire showed that they had moved twenty or so feet. The sounds of their weapons richocheted around the abandoned homes.

This wasn't getting either of them anywhere. Who'd be crazy enough to shoot from so far away?

The men who'd messed up at the hotel? Definitely!

Three more rounds dislodged the top few logs from the wood pile, scattering them around him. Spur got a fresh bullet, laid it on top of the pile, set a log just behind it and reloaded.

He slipped back of the house, circled around it, ran up to the front and sped across the inky street, making as little sound as possible.

The unseen gunmen blasted the barely discernible stack of wood. One of their rounds hit the live bullet he'd placed on the stack. The resulting explosion gave the illusion that Spur hadn't moved. He smiled and moved cautiously behind the house where the men had taken up position.

It was a massive thing. Spur took slow, careful steps, careful not to betray his approach. The men stopped firing. He reached the far wall and started toward them.

McCoy flattened himself against the wall and listened. No sound issued from the front of the house. Breathing deeply, his revolver drawn and ready to fire, Spur McCoy lunged out of safety and riddled the area with lead.

He discharged all six rounds and slipped back around the corner, quickly filling the heated chambers with fresh ammunition.

No response.

A sinking feeling rumbled around in his gut. Spur boldly walked into the area.

The men had gone.

He twisted his head in both directions. The darkened street didn't reveal their location.

He'd lost them.


Julie Golden grinned as she unlocked the door to her house, sniffing the odor of gunpowder in the air. Must have been some shooting around here, she thought.

|Everything had gone well with Melissa and Emma. She'd assigned them rooms right next to each other. Emma would just stay in her room and Melissa would work.

Of course, she hadn't told them that her guards had been instructed not to let the women leave the saloon. They were trapped and didn't even know it. Not only did she have a new girl but she'd also successfully gotten the women out of the way, for the moment at least.

Lionel Kemp would think they were dead. If necessary, she'd tell him she'd killed the women herself. Her place was off-limits to him anyway; the man would never know.

She'd decide what to do with them later. Now she had Carl and Jed to deal with.

They weren't in the kitchen. "Carl?" she yelled as she closed and locked the door.

Julie's face flushed. If they hadn't stayed there in the house she'd—she'd—

"Up here, ma'am!" a weak voice called from the second floor.

Curious, Julie raced up the curving staircase.

Carl and Jed were sitting back to back, bound together with rope. They turned expressionless faces to her.

"What on earth happened here?" she demanded.

" 'Bout time you got back!"

Lionel Kemp rose from the chair behind the door.

Julie gasped, unable to mask her surprise at seeing the man she hated so much.

Kemp spat. "I never should have trusted a woman to do this job."

"Why not? I haven't done anything wrong!" Julie unbuttoned her ankle length coat. "I've handed over every piece of silver. Every last bit!"

He stared at her with pointy, intense eyes. "That's not what I'm talking about."

"I see. Ah, why'd you tie them up?"

"They're no good, Julie. Just like I warned you. They're piss-poor excuses for men."

She shrugged off her coat and untied her bonnet. "What makes you say that?"

Kemp rolled up his sleeves. "Don't try to outsmart me, woman! You don't have the brains to do it. They tried to kill the women in broad daylight. They just got done shooting up the whole area trying to plug the man who stopped them at the hotel." Lionel spat on the floor. "They're worthless, Julie. Besides. We don't need them anymore."

"We don't?" she asked, glancing at the two men. She didn't like the tone of his voice.

"No." Lionel Kemp stood three feet from her. "I've got new plans."

"Oh." She forced a smile. "So, so pay them off and send them out of town."

"I'll pay them off alright. In the meantime, come on, Julie. Take 'em off. Strip!"

Julie paled. "Now? In front of the men?"

"Come on. Bashful or something all of a sudden?"
He leered at her. "Hell; more men have seen you
naked than have ever seen you wearing a dress! You
were a whore for fifteen years, bitch! Now do it!"

She hesitated.

"Remember, I own you. Lock, stock and barrel."
Lionel stomped to her and held his face an inch
from hers. "Get naked. Now!" he thundered.

Julie shivered as she undressed. Carl and Jed
didn't glance at her, not even when she'd completed
the simple action.

"What now, sir?"

"On the bed. Do it!" he said, rubbing his crotch.
Drool dripped from his lower lip.

Shivering in the breeze blowing through the
windows, Julie went to the bed and sat on the edge
of the mattress.

"On yer back!"

"Lionel, I don't really feel like it right now," she
said, stretching out beside the bound men. Carl's
dirty pants scraped against her thigh as she tried
to get comfortable. Impulsively, she spread her legs.

"You still don't unnerstand, do you, girlie?"
Lionel Kemp shook his head. "It doesn't matter
what you want. You'll do as I say or else!"

He loomed over her, staring down with a tense
face.

"Now, Julie, watch. Watch what happens to
people who don't follow orders."

Lionel produced a Bowie knife from his back
pocket. Julie flinched as the gleaming steel blade
flashed through the air.

"You men aren't worth *shit*!" Lionel said.

Carl tensed. "Please!" he said. "Don't!"

"Shut up!" Lionel looked at the woman. "Watch this. Watch this and remember!"

Carl and Jed kicked on the bed, struggling against the rough rope that bound their hands and torsos. Lionel laughed with relish. He pushed off his hat with his left hand and toyed with the knife as the two men thrashed and pleaded for mercy.

"You're enjoying this, Lionel! You're actually enjoying this!"

He ignored the naked woman. "Check out time, boys. This hotel's closed."

Carl Mond jabbed his boot between Lionel's legs. The big man doubled over and howled in agony as pain shot through his testicles. Julie fought the urge to smile.

"Goddamnit!"

He gasped and shook his head, massaging the damaged tissues. Lionel Kemp plunged the knife into Carl's chest.

"Take that!" he said, as steel pierced bone and flesh and vital organs.

Carl screamed.

Julie cried and turned her head.

The mattress bounced violently as Lionel stabbed Carl Mond, sheathing the knife in his body so hard and so many times that it finally slumped lifelessly against the rope.

"Now for you," he said.

More screams. More bounces. Then nothing.

Julie held back the revulsion that rose within her. She breathed through her mouth to avoid the horrid smell of death. Tears squeezed from her eyelids.

Grunting, panting, Lionel grabbed her head with bloody hands.

"Look at me, goddamnit!"

She opened her eyes.

"If you don't want to be next, do exactly what I say. Is that clear, girlie?"

It was.

# CHAPTER SIX

Just after the shooting, Spur stood in the light in front of the Motherlode Saloon, shaking his head. He really could use a whiskey, he told himself, even though he wasn't much of a drinker.

McCoy saw a familiar face walking toward him.

"Kincaid!" he yelled. "Mayor Kincaid!"

"And stay out!" a male voice roared from the Motherlode.

"Goddamn shit-faced sumbitch!" an airborne man said as he was pitched from the saloon and plowed into Spur. McCoy slammed his left leg to the ground to support his body. The drunk slid onto the dirt.

"McCoy!" the mayor asked as he stepped over the drunk, "you know anything about all that shooting?"

"Yeah. As it happened, I did some of it."

Justin Kincaid shook his head. "Ever since you

came into town ammunition sales are up by fifty percent. What was it this time?"

The ousted drunk got to his knees, wiped the dirt from his face, groaned and crawled onto the corner of the boardwalk fronting the hotel. He promptly snoozed.

"I was out knocking on doors, searching for someone who'd admit that they'd seen the two men running from the Eastern Heights Hotel after the shooting earlier today. Just after it got dark, two men started firing at me. Never saw them. I returned fire for a while then tried to surprise them. By that time they were gone. Vanished into the darkness."

"I see." Kincaid moved into the light that spilled from the saloon's batwing doors.

"I figure it's the same men I was looking for. They just found me before I found them."

"You mean the ones that almost killed Emma and Melissa Grieve? I heard about it. They must be powerfully bad shots to have missed you. After all, they had the valuable advantage of surprise."

"Distance," Spur said. "Too far for any real accuracy. That's why I couldn't hit either of them, even when I pinpointed their location from the gunpowder flashes."

Kincaid nodded and looked inside the saloon. "You, ah, riding out to Cleve Magnus' mine tomorrow?"

Spur nodded thoughtfully. "Think it's time I paid the man a visit."

"Good. Stop by and see me. I'll give you directions." He glanced inside the building. "Well, I should be going in. Have to see Ma. Strictly business, of course."

Spur laughed and put up his hands. "Of course. You're the mayor, after all."

"Yeah. Right."

A buxom young woman walked from the saloon, holding up the left shoulder of her dress.

"Justin!" she said smiling. "Justin, this big-handed oaf ripped up the new dress I bought this morning! See?" She released the cloth. It dropped away, revealing her bare shoulder and half of her left breast. "All my other dresses are out to be cleaned. Ma's not here so she can't help me. I can't go around like this all night, can I?" She turned to Spur. "Well? What do you think?"

He grinned. "Depends on if you're gonna wear the rest of it or not."

The woman smiled. "Justin, dear heart, is Gertie still at her shop?"

"Ah, I doubt it, Michelle." The mayor fidgeted as the woman grabbed his arm.

She dropped her sweet girl ploy. "Dangit! That seamstress'll charge me double if I call at her house, especially after sundown!"

Two cowboys whistled at the woman as they walked into the saloon. One of them slapped her rump. The whore squealed in delight.

"Look, Michelle, maybe I can help you out. But cover yourself, my dear. Don't want the men of this town thinking you're a loose woman."

"But I am, Justin! You know that better than anyone within a hundred miles." She smirked but pulled up the front of her dress, concealing that portion of her offendingly delicious anatomy.

Spur smiled at the mayor's obvious discomfort.

"Sorry, McCoy. Duty, ah, calls."

"Of course. I could use some sleep. I'll see you in the morning, mayor."

"Sure."

"Oh, honey, your friend ain't comin' in with you?" Gertie asked. "The show starts in just a few minutes."

"Sorry, ma'am. I'll be leaving now."

"Ma'am. Ma'am?" Michelle shook her head. "Such manners! Then come on, Justin. I've got something to show you. Ma just bought me a nice new set of ropes and chaps!"

Spur laughed as the mayor hustled the whore into the saloon. He returned to his hotel for a much-needed dose of sleep.


Julie Golden hadn't been surprised when Lionel had changed his mind about bedding her. Not only had Carl managed to temporarily put *that* out of commission with his boot, but the bed was a mess. She glanced at the two lifeless forms that lay there and at the brick-red stains that covered the quilt her mother had sewn for her in her youth.

Lionel Kemp snorted and swung on a bottle of whiskey. "I'm leaving. Leaving town."

She looked at him in shock. Though he'd stayed in Oreville, Lionel had lain low, rarely moving around when anyone could see him. He'd told everyone he was leaving and no one had suspected. "Where are you going? When? For how long?"

"West, in the morning and I don't know." He spat on the floor.

Julie's mind filled with ideas. If he was gone long enough she could cash in her business, clear out her bank account and be gone before he returned to Oreville. She'd take the next stage coach, east or west, and find her fortune elsewhere. Anywhere but Oreville!

"I see."

Lionel Kemp took another swig. "Things are getting too hot around here for my tastes. Besides, I got some investing to do. All that silver sitting there doing nothing. And don't think about runnin' out on me. If you do I'll track you down and kill you myself!"

Julie stared quietly at him. "I see."

"Cheer up, darling. You know you'll miss me, but I'll be back soon. I hope you can handle things here alone. I'll be sending you telegrams every day, telling you what to do. And you better have carried out my orders when I return. If not—" He nodded toward the dead men.

She hugged herself, suddenly cold.

"Besides, I wouldn't have to actually do anything to you. All I have to do is have lunch with Mayor Kincaid. Or hand Cleve Magnus a rifle and point him in your direction."

"Alright. Alright! Leave town!" she said, exploding. "I'll be a good little girl. Don't you worry about me." Julie hardened her voice. It was easy; she'd had so much practice. "What's next on your Christmas list? Robbing little old ladies? Maybe the fund for the church building?"

He raised his eyebrows. "Interesting. I knew you had potential—even if you are a woman."

"Come on, Lionel! I've done things for you that most men wouldn't do."

He snorted and guffawed.

Her cheeks reddened. "I don't mean—"

"Just keep yer skirts clean, girlie." Lionel planted his hat on his head and walked toward the bedroom door.

"What am I supposed to do with those bodies?" Julie demanded.

"You'll think of something." Lionel kept on walking.

"Okay. Okay! Jesus!" Spur yelled as he stumbled from the bed and answered the insistent knock.

"Open up, McCoy! You awake?"

"I don't know if I'm alive." He barked his shins on the chair. "That you, Kincaid?" He turned the key in the lock and swung open the door.

"Yes!" The mayor was breathing hard.

Spur yawned. "What the hell time is it?"

"After eight, but that's not important." He pushed past Spur. "McCoy, a prospector found two bodies in the desert this morning just after sunrise."

He rubbed his eyes. "Bodies?"

"That's what he says."

"So?"

"Tarnation, man! Wake up! The two men who shot at you last night. Remember them? They might have wound up dead in the desert."

"Could be them, or a couple million others."

Kincaid shook his head. "Nope. The prospector said it looked like they'd been taken there. Stabbed to death but almost no blood on the ground."

"So?" Spur couldn't shake the fuzz from his head.

Mayor Kincaid sighed, grabbed the ewer from the table, poured some water into the basin and motioned to Spur. "Come over here."

"Huh?" McCoy looked at him with one eye.

Kincaid gripped the Secret Service agent's shoulders, bent him at the waist and struck his face into the water. Spur bubbled and gasped but it did the trick. He forced his head from the basin and wiped his face.

"Better now?" Kincaid asked.

"Yeah. Thanks." Spur toweled himself off. "When're we going out to look at these bodies?"

The mayor threw Spur his gunbelt. "Right now."

Spur dressed. The horse that the mayor provided him with was fast, lean and eagerly responded to his commands. On their way out of town they rode down a familiar street.

"That's where I had that run-in last night," Spur said, pointing to the abandoned house. The bullet holes were plainly visible around its front door.

"Not many folks live in this part of town anymore," Kincaid said.

They rode west over harsh, dry land. It was still cool but the sun quickly built in strength. A half-hour later Kincaid slowed his mount.

"Has to be around here somewhere," the mayor said. "Right over there's Mick's claim."

"How about that? Looks suspicious." Spur pointed to a pile of dead bushes.

"Yeah."

They rode the fifteen feet and dismounted. The two dead men lay face up on the ground surrounded by dried sagebrush. Kincaid looked closer and Spur sighed.

"I'll be a sonofabitch!" he said.

"You know them?" Spur asked.

"Sure! Used to come into Ma's all the time. Loved

the women, those boys did. And never wanted me
to forgive them for their sins." He grunted.
"Haven't seen them around lately. I figured they'd
left town."

"I know them too," Spur said. "At least I think
I do. I only saw them for a second but I'd swear
those are the men from the hotel."

"The ones who were after Emma and Melissa?"

Spur nodded.

Kincaid stood back and crossed his arms. "So
they were after the only living witnesses to the
stagecoach robbery and now they're dead. Don't
make sense."

McCoy scratched his stubbly chin. "Unless they
were working for someone else."

Kincaid looked hard at him.

"They robbed the stage. They probably robbed
the post office, killed the Chinese man and the
young kid who happened along at the wrong times.
If they were working for someone else, that man
might have decided they'd outlived their usefulness
and put them out of business."

"Yeah, I follow you. But why dump them way out
here?" Kincaid pushed back his hat and wiped his
forehead. "Haven't been dead too long. Must've
happened last night or early this morning."

"The killer might have hoped that no one would
find them for a while. Might have thought it was
wiser not to stir up any more trouble in town."

"After all that shooting last night, I can imagine."

Spur studied the bodies. "Kincaid, who'd have the
most to gain from robbing Magnus' silver
shipments?"

The mayor laughed. "Every man, woman and

child in town. Times are hard since the mines closed."

"What about the men who work for Cleve Magnus? They must have some loot."

"Sure do. But they live out at the mine. Come into town once or twice a week and spend up a storm. They're what's keeping Oreville alive. He must have fifty men out there." Kincaid paused. "Folks are still packing up and leaving town. More than half the houses are empty. Stores are closing. I've even had to talk the blacksmith into staying so we'll have someone to make tools. Oreville's slowly dying."

"Sorry about that," Spur said. "How far away is this Magnus mine?"

Kincaid pointed to the range of rugged mountains which looked deceptively close. "About an hour's ride due east," he said.

Spur nodded and walked to his horse. "Think I'll head out there." He checked his canteen which the mayor had hung from his borrowed mount's saddle. It was full.

"Good luck, McCoy. I'll get these bodies into town."

"And thanks for the use of the horse." Spur stepped onto the brown mare.

"No problem. Just remember to bring her back in one piece."

Spur laughed and rode off toward the distant mine.

He let the cooperative mount walk the first few miles, but gradually urged her faster and faster over the rock-strewn, cactus-covered ground. The mountains gradually approached him but Spur soon realized that Kincaid had misjudged the amount of time it would take to get there.

The sun was an hour later in the sky by the time he stopped and took a drink. The mare snorted at the smell of water, so Spur poured some of the precious liquid into his hat and let her drink.

Refreshed from the stop, he rode again. A lighter colored area slashing across the shoulder of a huge mountain ahead showed where men had moved rocks and earth, exposing the underyling dirt that hadn't been covered with desert varnish. Must be Cleve Magnus' mine, he thought.

McCoy finally saw the trail leading up to the mine opening where the iron carts filled with ore were pushed to a sheer drop, dumped and hauled back inside. Large wooden buildings, bone white against the darker earth, probably housed the stamping and smelting operation. A trail emerged from the ground below him. The men seemed to ride into town quite a bit.

On the mountain range to either side of the Magnus' place were the battered remains of earlier mines, their buildings toppled, quiet in their isolated solitude.

Spur urged his horse on. Following the trail, he rode between low hills that had been thrust from the desert floor in prehistoric times.

He cleared the hillocks and headed over open ground less than a mile from the mine. A rifle blasted behind him. Spur struggled to control his spooked horse, ducking and wondering who the hell was shooting at him now.

# CHAPTER SEVEN

The rifle's explosion drifted away on a light desert breeze. Spur calmed his horse and slung up his Winchester, but the unseen gunmen's weapon fell silent. He must be behind one of the rocky hills.

"What are you doing out here?" a gruff voice yelled at him.

"Trying to keep my head in one piece!"

"Just a warning shot. If I'd wanted to kill you, you wouldn't be breathing now. State your business!"

An advance guard for Cleve Magnus? Sounded like it. "I'm here to see your boss. I'm with the government investigating the silver robberies. Mayor Kincaid from Oreville sent me here." And, Spur thought, hadn't told him about this little problem he might encounter.

Silence.

"Come on!" Spur said.

"Name?"

He sighed. "Spur McCoy. I sent Magnus a telegram saying I was arriving in Oreville yesterday and that I'd be out to see him."

"Okay. He tole me about you," the invisible gunman finally answered. "Now git before I change my mind!"

Spur rode on. He never saw the man.

A few minutes later her went through the whole procedure again. Warning shot. Challenge. Explanation. Hesitation. Permission to pass. Cleve Magnus wasn't taking any chances.

The mine came into sharp view as he started up the gentle slope toward it. It looked big enough to have fifty men working it. The operation was huge. Buildings were everywhere. Men streamed in and out of the mine and the large structures. A corral housed dozens of horses. Smoke rose from what must be the cookhouse. Hell, Magnus had his own blacksmith's shop.

As Spur rode into the camp, two men with rifles slung over their shoulders walked up and silently escorted McCoy to a hitching post.

"Tie her up," one of the men said, and spat a long brown stream of tobacco juice onto the sand. It sizzled.

They took him into the two-story building. Inside, it was bright and airy but the furnishings were minimal, no-nonsense. They went past a room full of tables and chairs and then up the stairs. The men deposited him before an opened door and walked away.

Spur went in. Cleve P. Magnus sat behind a plain pine desk reading a New York newspaper. He grumbled, realized that he had a visitor and stood.

For a man with that much firepower, Magnus was surprisingly short. Thin and balding, the big-jowled mine owner smiled broadly at Spur.

"Can't be too careful," he said, gruffly apologizing for his welcome. "Glad you could make it."

They shook hands.

"Have a seat, McCoy."

"Why so much protection for the mine?" Spur asked as he settled onto a hard, rail-backed chair.

Magnus fiddled with a pencil. "I'm convinced they'll try to rob me here, too. Get the goods before I can ship them anywhere. We smelt the damn stuff right here. Usual production is twenty pounds of silver a day. Yesterday, we did near to a hundred! Gave all the men a raise. As soon as news spreads in town those thieving bastards might get new ideas."

"I see."

Cleve shook his head. "All that silver ain't worth a damn if some bastard's gonna take it from me."

"Who's been robbing you? The post office? The stage coach? Who's behind all this, Magnus?"

He threw up his hands. "Damned if I know!"

"Got any enemies?"

Magnus shook his head. "Pay my men better than any other miner in Nevada." He grinned. "Shit, McCoy, I'm nice to old ladies. I only screw girls who wanna be screwed. Never touch whiskey or cards. Never stabbed a man in the back, always fight fair. I don't take what doesn't belong to me and I pump lots of money into Oreville." He shook his head. "It don't make sense!"

"Magnus, the two men who robbed your last coach shipment are dead. Found them in the desert this morning."

His eyes widened. "You sure about that? Did those two women identify them?"

"Not yet. But I did. Saw them try to murder Emma and Melissa Grieve yesterday. And they took some shots at me last night. Now they're dead."

Cleve Magnus rubbed his chin. "So it might be over? You mean I can get back to worrying about production and fights among my men and not these shitty robberies? Damn, that'd be nice!"

"Don't think so. From all appearances, the two were working for someone else. Your problems aren't over yet."

Magnus snapped the pencil. "Figures," he said, lowering his eyes. "I've never done anything to deserve this," he said. "Nothing!"

"You got lucky. Struck it rich. Some men think that's enough."

Magnus stood. "I'll be *damned* if I'm gonna let some unwashed thief take my silver!" he thundered, pounding his desk with his fist. "Damn him! Damn him!" Thump. Thwack. His lean face tightened.

"Magnus, I'm here to help you."

"Right. Sure! Can you guarantee that I won't lose another shipment? No. Shit, I don't know what to do!" Magnus walked to the window and stared out the dusty glass at his domain. "I'm putting four men inside the next eastern stage and another next to the driver. Every one of them are crack shots. *That* shipment won't be stolen unless an army attacks it."

"Yeah?"

"Yeah." He took a deep breath. "My men are spreading the word in town. That bastard'd have to be suicidal to go after the stage."

Spur nodded. "How much you shipping?"

Cleve Magnus rifled through the ink-splotched papers on his desk. "Here it is. A hundred pounds." He looked up at Spur. "You know how much pure silver I've stockpiled out here?"

McCoy shook his head.

"At least 2,000 pounds. More all the time. That's why I'm fearful that the idiot might try to get it directly from the source."

"Not likely."

"But there's a chance. There's always a chance!" Magnus yanked on his thinning hair. "It used to be so peaceful out here. Now I'm watching my back. Posting men in the desert as lookouts. Stockpiling the stuff when I should be shipping silver back east to my bank to be invested. Hell, McCoy; I'm going out of my goddamn bean!"

"Understandable, but calm down."

"Calm down?" he demanded.

"Yes. If you get any more spooked you might go crazy and shoot your own men." He had a thought. "They're loyal to you, right?"

Magnus vigoriously nodded. "Damn straight! Made sure of that. Weeded out the ones who weren't. And just in case some of them get a few big ideas, I keep the silver in ten different safes scattered all over this house. There's only one entrance. No one but me knows all the combinations. It'd take a third of my men to blow them all, if they had the time, the opportunity and the dynamite." He shrugged. "No, I don't see any problems along those lines, McCoy."

"Good. Sounds like you need all the friends you

can get."

"Yeah. Why are you here, McCoy? How come the U.S. Government sent you out to this Godforsaken place?"

"The Secret Service gets its nose bent out of shape when mail is stolen, like yours was. I also understand that next month you're making a large shipment directly to the Bureau of Engraving and Printing?"

Magnus grimaced. "That's a fact. Send them silver three times a year."

Spur smiled. "My boss also wants to make sure you can supply them with the materials needed to mint U.S. coins. That's why I'm here. I can—and will—stop this man."

"Yeah?" He smirked. "I'd be greatly obliged to you if you do. But you don't mind me guarding my own goods, do you?"

Spur shook his head.

"Good."

"I have a feeling your next shipment will be safe from at least two would-be thieves."

"Hope you're right."

Spur knew it was time to leave. He stood. "Keep looking over your left shoulder. I'll be back when I know more."

"I will, and you do that."

They shook hands again.

Magnus's lookouts allowed Spur to pass unchallenged on his way from the mine. He never saw them; they were well concealed. Still, McCoy waved as he passed the general areas where he'd been confronted.

Well over an hour later he rode up to the pile of

brush where he and Kincaid had seen the bodies. They were gone, the only signs that they'd ever been there were the brick-red stains on the sand. The mayor had cheated the buzzards out of supper that day.

He took a few swallows of water and offered some to his mare, who gratefully drank. As he stood in the wash, resting, getting his bearings, he heard a rider approach.

Spur covered the horse's wet muzzle with a hand to quiet her and led her into the deepest part of the wash. He stood motionless, watching the line of dust that marked the rider's passage speed from left to right over the ridge.

When it had fully passed Spur turned and looked. The man had to be going to the mine. Spur decided to wait. He found some jerky in a saddlebag and had a frugal lunch, slowly chewing the hard food. His horse found a scrubby bush and had its meal.

Afterward, Spur climbed a low ridge, shifted the brim of his hat to shade his eyes, and searched the landcape. The tiny figure of a rider moved in the distance directly toward Cleve Magnus's mine. He soon lost sight of it.

Spur took off his shirt and splashed some water onto his chest. He waited, drawing maps of the mine in the sand with a short stick. Taking the role of the thief, he imagined how he'd try to attack the mine itself.

Magnus's operation was guarded on one side by sheer walls of solid rock. They were impossible to climb. Only a frontal or side approach was possible. Maybe all three. He stared at the sketchy map, wondering if the desert sun had finally gotten to him.

Another hour passed. McCoy sat on the dirt and jabbed a stick at a furious scorpion, who lifted its tail and ran in circles to warn its attacker of an impending sting. He was soon bored and threw the stick at the scorpion. Unharmed, it trotted to a nearby rock and disappeared.

Spur bided his time.

In her office at the Motherlode Saloon, Julie Golden re-read the telegram that she'd received that morning. It was clear. She hadn't misunderstood the message that Lionel Kemp had hidden in the words. He'd decided to go ahead and have her do it.

She thought of the new man she'd met, a foreigner that her male employees said could be trusted. Julie had wasted no time after receiving Lionel's telegram in putting his plan into action. She wasn't merely satisfying his whim. The woman saw a shining possibility in his latest scheme.

A direct assault on the mine. Take the silver directly from it. No more grabbing a measly few pounds here and there.

A war.

She sighed, folded the telegram and stuffed it into the drawer where she kept the receipts of the girl's wages. If only this man worked out, Julie thought. If only he did what he was supposed to do and they were successful in their mission. If only Lionel Kemp didn't arrive back in Oreville until afterward. If only . . . .

She shook her head. "Julie Golden, stop thinking about it," she said out loud. The businesswoman cleared her desk, brushed off the ashes that one of her customers had unceremoniously dumped into its teak surface and straightened her hair.

She'd already talked to Burt, Harris and Pete about the possibility of finding several dozen gunmen. Her friends had been encouraging. All she was waiting for was—what was his name? Julie smiled at the memory of how her bartender had pointed him out to her downstairs.

She'd dragged him to her office. Once there, they'd talked and made love at the same time. He was uncertain but agreed to have a look at the place.

He was quite a man, she thought. She hoped Phillipas Telonia had good news on his arrival.

Julie sighed and pushed back her chair. Time to leave. He was to meet her at her house.

The rider finally returned. Spur got a glimpse of his face—dark and bearded. Whoever he was, he'd ridden out to Cleve Magnus's operation, hadn't been challenged and had left almost as soon as he'd arrived.

He probably didn't work there. Maybe he'd gone to survey the lay of the land. If he knew about the outposts he could circle away from them and still get a good look.

Spur shrugged. Maybe Magus was right. Perhaps the man behind the robberies was planning to hit the mine itself. But when?

And how?

# CHAPTER EIGHT

" 'Bout time you got back here!" Julie Golden said as the tall, bearded man brushed past her and walked into the kitchen. She closed and locked the door. "What'd you see at the mine?"

"Nothing good." The immigrant brushed caked dust from his coat and strode toward the bottle of whiskey that Julie kept on a shelf. Staring at the wall, he took a swallow.

"Phil! Phillipas!" Julie said, running to him. "Well?"

The frowning Greek wiped his lips. "Well what?"

She smiled. "Okay, you're tired. I understand. I'll have plenty of hot water for your bath in a few minutes."

He grunted. "Julie, we cannot do it."

"Why not?" she demanded.

Phillipas Telonia sighed and sat in a chair, staring down at the huge metal bathtub. "Perhaps if we had eighty men, maybe. But otherwise—"

"Don't talk," Julie said, shaking her head. "A lot of men can't think straight right after a hard ride. I know I can't," she quipped.

"No, no. It is not that." Phillipas shook his head again. "The mine, it is like a fortress. Guards everywhere. Magnus must have twenty or thirty men out there." He stroked the tips of his thick, black moustache. "Even with surprise on our side, we would need at least as many, maybe even forty men. Forty men might be enough."

"Don't talk." Julie smiled and walked to the stove, lifted the big copper pot and poured the last of the hot water into the tub. "You take off your clothes and get into that dang thing! I'll make you something to eat."

"Julie. Julie, look at me!" he demanded.

She did. He still took her breath away.

"I will not ride out to certain death for anyone. There is no way that you can do this."

"But—"

"No."

She sighed. So that was that. Or was it? "Here, let me help you undress." Julie knelt before him and took the booted foot that he stuck out toward her. She tugged. "Nothing's impossible, Phillipas. You got out of Greece before they caught you." Julie grimaced and pulled. "Now you're here just when I need you." The boot started to slip. "And together, there's nothing we can't do!"

"Except take off my boots?"

Julie smiled and yanked as hard as she could. It slid from his foot. "See? Nothing to it."

"Maybe." Phillipas flashed her a smile. "But

Julie, you cannot hire that many men."

"Why not?" The second boot easily came off. "There's plenty of them in this town who'd do it."

"You cannot trust them."

"Can't I?" Julie rose to her feet. "Phillipas, the men of Oreville haven't worked for months. They're desperate for money, even just to scrape up enough to leave. I'll find as many as you say we need."

He ripped off his woolen socks and scratched his left foot.

"But enough about that for now. Stand up, you big oaf!"

Phil grunted. "Feta cheese. I want some feta cheese!" He slammed a fist onto the table.

"There's no feta cheese in my kitchen. And you aren't eating until you get your bath!" She waved the air in front of her nose. "You need it."

"Okay, okay. But no food after. Just you and me." He ripped off his shirt and hauled down his pants.

"No underdrawers again, Phil?" Julie said, shaking her head as the naked man stepped into the tub.

"Too hot here."

Julie knelt beside him, dipped water in her hands and poured it over his head. The Greek spluttered.

"We can do it. I've done some checking. Three of my best employees say they can get all the men we need. Good shots, reliable, trustworthy."

He turned to her.

"Don't be surprised, Phillipas. This is my last chance of ever leaving Oreville and that—that *man* I told you about this morning. We can do it together." Julie picked up the cake of lye soap and a rough cloth. "Can't we?"

He sighed as she scrubbed his broad back. "You speak of war, my lady. War!"

She rubbed harder and bent her mouth to his ear. "Yes, General Telonia."

Spur McCoy's horse was foaming by the time he rode into Oreville. He tied the beast's reins to the hitching post, gave her a quick rub down and entered the Eastern Heights Hotel.

"Emma and Melissa in?" he asked the manager, who bent over the ledger.

"Huh? What?"

"The two women who were involved in the stagecoach robbery. You seen them?"

"Naw. Not since they walked out last night. Ain't been back, that's fer sure. Leastwise, not that Melissa. I'd remember her," the balding man said, and scratched his chin. "Ain't she a looker?"

"Yeah." He went to the stairs.

When Spur's urgent knock roused no one inside the womens' room, he opened the door with a skeleton key and went in. There were no signs of a struggle. Except for the shot-out wall, nothing looked unusual. Clothing had been placed in neat piles. The younger woman's underthings were laid out on the bed, ready to be worn. But the women weren't there.

The smell of Melissa's perfume hung in the air. Where were they?"

Spur went next door and knocked. A bleary-eyed, red-nosed cowboy nearly fell onto him as he opened the door. McCoy backed away from the liquor-laced breath.

"You know where the two women in the room next to yours went?"

The cowboy reeled, gripped the door frames and belched. "You got a dollar? I drunk up all my money and—and—"

Spur shrugged, retrieved a silver dollar from his pocket and held it out.

"Thanks, stranger. Sure. Melissa and that old bag headed out after supper last night."

"Where?"

He snatched the money and stormed past the Secret Service agent. "To Ma's. I saw 'em myself. Now I got me somethin' important to do."

Ma's? The woman who had the ugliest girls in town? The one the barber had told him about as he chopped off his hair? Spur watched the cowboy go, closed both doors and went down the stairs.

A woman like Emma Grieve didn't seem the type of lady who'd go into a saloon, but it was worth checking. The drunkard's thirst might have led him to say anything. Still, there were only two saloons in town that were still open after the boom years. He might as well visit them both.

Neither was named Ma's.

Stale smoke stung his eyes in the Placer, a dark, dusty, fly-buzzing saloon. The apron dozed, his left cheek plastered to the sticky bar. The stairs that led to the upper floor had been boarded up. One solitary drinker sat back in his chair, clutching a half-empty bottle with jealous hands.

Spur walked to the bartender and thumped his shoulder. The man stirred and opened his eyes.

"Yuh?"

"Is Ma here?"

"Hell no! And don't mention her. That hussy's stolen all my customers!"

Spur turned to leave as the apron's cheek hit the bar again.

Grunting, he walked across the street and down one block to the Motherlode. Inside, kerosene lamps shone. The floor was freshly swept. A huge mirror over the bar doubled the apparent size of the large, well-kept saloon. The bar itself was an oak and brass monstrosity, obviously brought there at great cost from back east.

This must be Ma's place, he thought. It had a softer edge than what most drinking men demanded. Green velvet curtains were bunched at the corners of the windows. The brass spittoons shone with regular polishing. Even the bartender looked as if he'd just been pressed with a sad iron.

Twenty men had assembled there to satisfy their guts and their groins. They drank and gambled, filling the air with curses and shouts and wild whoops as a plain-faced girl trudged down the stairs. Some of them must be Magnus's workers.

Two other girls worked the saloon. Spur watched them and ordered a whiskey. They weren't ugly, but certainly were nothing to write home about. Maybe the barber hadn't been as kind to them as he could have been.

"Damn her!"

Spur glanced to the left of him at the bar. The woman who'd just emerged from upstairs tugged at the bodice of her dress, readjusting her breasts. "Damn her to hell! That hussy thinks she can take all my men. Ha! Let me tell you something, mister; she won't last a week!"

"Something wrong, miss?"

The green-eyed wench laughed. "No. I mean yeah. But don't worry about it, sweetie." She patted Spur's butt. "Nothing I can't handle. My name's Squirrel Sue."

"McCoy."

The round-faced woman eyed him. "You're not here for a roll, are you? I can always tell."

"No. Truth is, I'm looking for Ma."

The whore rolled her eyes and sauntered off.

Just then an auburn haired young woman, conservatively dressed in a high necked gown of white silk, pushed through the batwing doors, glanced sternly at the bartender and rustled up the stairs.

Ma, Spur wondered? She certainly didn't fit the name, but the woman didn't look like a saloon girl and she definitely acted as if she owned the place.

As the woman hurried up, a sullen faced man stood at attention at the foot of the stairs, a rifle over his shoulder.

A guard?

Spur studied the saloon. The slick bartender was armed. He had pistols strapped to both legs. A rifle sat beside the huge cash register. McCoy easily spotted a second hired gunman. He casually stood beside the entrance to the saloon, constantly eyeing the crowd.

Why so much protection here, Spur wondered? He sighed and sipped the watered whiskey, thinking. Maybe Ma was a stickler for running a clean place. But then, how many female saloon owners were there?

Muffled screams echoed from the second floor. He'd heard the like a hundred times before. Some guy gets too excited with a poor working girl and she puts up a fight. It was a sad part of the business.

Hearing the screams, the guard next to the stairs stiffened and swung the rifle into his hands. A young, blonde girl stumbled down the stairs, dressed only in her chemise and petticoats. Her makeup plastered face cringed. She desperately hurried down the narrow steps.

"The show's startin' early, boys!" one man yelled.

A buck-naked man appeared from upstairs, hopped after her and easily caught the frightened young woman.

"Come on, honey! Goddamn! I paid fer you and you's gonna get it!"

"No!"

They wrestled. The guard broke it up, forced the girl's hands behind her back and marched her to the second floor while the saloon exploded with laughter at the unexpected scene.

The cowboy, suddenly aware of the man staring at him, smiled, waved and took the stairs three at a time to recapture his unwilling prize.

Spur heard a door slam. The guard took up his post again, cool but grinning. A piano creaked into off-key life under the bony fingers of a vested player.

"I have three aces!" someone yelled. A card player across the saloon overturned a table and drew his weapon.

"Damn you, Jackson! I have two, and I ain't the one who's cheating!"

"No fighting!" the bartender shouted.

As the gamblers faced off and the piano music droned on, Spur realized that he recognized the half-dressed blonde girl who'd run down the stairs.

It was Melissa, the witness to the stagecoach robbery.

# CHAPTER NINE

"You foolish girl!" Julie Golden stared at the cowering young woman. "Don't you want to get out of Oreville? Don't you want to see Philadelphia again, to get away from these robberies and guns?"

"And men?" Emma Grieve yelled over the saloon owner's shoulder.

Melissa hugged her shoulders and backed into the corner of her room. She raised her knees, unconsciously protecting the most private part of her body. The part that they wanted her to use. Tears ran down her cheeks. She shook. "How can you do this to me, grandmother?"

"It's all for the best, my dear," Emma Grieve reached out a hand but quickly retracted it. "It's the only way I can see that we'll ever leave this hell-hole. You know I don't have any savings. We're broke, Melissa." She softened her face. "Trust me, darling. It isn't so bad. I had some good times! Flat on my back, making money, meeting all sorts of interesting gentlemen. It was *fun!*"

Melissa sucked in her breath. "Grandmother!"

"Listen to her, child." Julie Golden smiled. "And wise up. You insulted my customer by running out of your room like that. I'll have to give him his money back and still send him to my best girl all because of you." Julie turned to the elderly woman. "Talk some sense into her, Emma. Will you?"

She set her lined face. "I'll try. Melissa, you're no virgin."

The girl turned from her.

"I know all about your shenanigans with the Miller boys, with Ted Pollard and David Seaton and—"

Melissa sighed and cut off her words. "Alright! What are you trying to say?"

Emma smiled. "At any rate, you're been with more than a few boys. And you're no more of a Christian woman than I am. That's why I don't understand you, girl. This nice lady's offering to pay you to do what you'd normally do for free! Why, if I was any younger and prettier, I might have a go at it myself."

Melissa lifted her head. "I like to chose my men. Besides, he smelled bad. And he wanted to do something to me that was so disgusting."

Julie hooted. "Hell, nothing's disgusting if they pay right. And he did. Ten dollars! You and Emma would've gotten half. Look what you've done!" She threw up her hands.

"I don't care. I'm leaving." Melissa rose and grabbed the dress that lay on the small bed.

"No you're not, young woman!" Julie advanced

on her. "You and your grandmother are staying here for your own protection. You can't be on the streets. It's not safe. And look what happened in your hotel room! Those robbers are still looking for you. So earn some money. I'll have some men escort you to the stagecoach when it's time. If you see ten men a day—"

*"Ten men!"* she shrieked.

"—you'll be out of here in no time." Julie went to the girl and took the dress from her hands. "There, there, Melissa. It's the only way. Your grandmother knows it, and so do you. Quit whining. Make yourself pretty. Get ready for your next customer. Okay?"

Melissa turned to her grandmother, but Emma Grieve crossed her bony arms and turned her face to the ceiling. The girl plopped onto the bed and brushed back her hair. She tried an unconvincing smile.

"What—what am I supposed to do?" Melissa asked her temporary employer.

"Don't worry. They'll tell you exactly what they want. One week," Julie Golden said. "In one week your troubles will be over."

She left the room and closed the door behind her. In the hall, Julie took a deep breath and straightened her back. That idiotic girl! Lionel Kemp would have Melissa and Emma killed if he heard they were still alive when he came back into town. But there was no way to tell them that.

She sighed and returned to her office. She had a business to run.


"I'm Alice. You want me?" She smiled, showing

a set of bad teeth, and pulled up a chair at Spur's table. The whore took a healthy swallow from his watered whiskey.

He thought it over. It would be difficult to get past the guard stationed at the stairs without causing a commotion. The girl was his ticket up there.

Spur McCoy looked her over. "You'll do."

Alice laughed and stood. "Honey, I'll do everything!"

She took his arm and dragged him to the stairs. The guard didn't look at the couple as they walked to the second floor. She turned to him once they'd reached the landing.

"The room at the end of the hall," she said, her face flushed at the prospect of money. "Tell Ma you're seeing Alice, her best girl. You pay her."

"Okay."

"A yellow feather means nothing special. Any other color means specialties, and I do 'em all!"

"Fine." Spur went to the door and knocked.

"Come in, sir."

Spur walked in, hat in his hand. The room smelled of roses. Jars of feathers littered the small desk. Behind it sat the young, attractive woman he'd seen striding into the Motherlode Saloon. Ma.

"What can I do for you?" Julie Golden set down her quill and smiled up at him.

"I guess Alice. Nothing special."

Julie smirked. "Fine. Five dollars."

"Ah, isn't that a little much?"

Julie jerked back in false indignation. "For my beautiful girls? No. Besides, that includes the free show that starts in two minutes."

Show? Spur finally remembered what the barber had told him just after he arrived in town. "Okay."

He placed a much folded fiver on Ma's desk.

"Let me make a note of this."

Spur thought as she bent over the ledger. She's a businesswoman all right, but he couldn't believe that Julie Golden was somehow connected with the silver robberies.

But he had seen Melissa in her saloon. And Melissa had been in the middle of one of the hold-ups.

"The show's in room 2. Be there on time, sir." She handed him a yellow plume. "This'll get you into it and into Alice's room right after."

He stalled. This was going much too fast. "I really didn't want Alice."

Ma lifted her eyebrows. "No?"

"No. What about that blonde girl I saw earlier?"

She shrugged. "Honey, half of them's blonde! Which one are you talking about? She might be busy now, but you could always wait."

Spur smoothed on a smile. "A wild one who ran down the stairs in her underthings a minute back."

Julie Golden smiled. "Heck, that's the new girl. She can't do anything—yet. I have to break her in. Come back in a week. She'll be ready for you then. Now git!"

"Yes, ma'am."

Spur smirked at her and walked out. He found Alice hurrying into room two, grabbed her arm and handed her the feather.

"Go right in and watch the show, but keep the damned thing or we'll both get into trouble. I have to get ready."

Drunken men brushed past him into the small room.

"I changed my mind. See you around."

"What? Come back here, stranger! Shit, you're the best lookin' man I've seen in years!"

McCoy laughed as he went down the stairs.

So Melissa was the new girl. She might be there by choice, but it sure hadn't looked like it. Julie Golden must be forcing her into working. But why?

Spur had to get her. And he couldn't do it alone. He needed help.

Mayor Kincaid wasn't in his office, but an adenoidal deputy said that he'd just gone to the telegraph office. Spur hurried there.

As he walked into the rickety building he saw Mayor Kincaid standing with his back to the door. The harried telegraph operator grabbed a pen.

"Just a second, mayor. Just a second! The sender has to repeat this message. I missed it the first time." He threw him an angry look.

"Alright. No problem," Kincaid said.

Standing in the door, Spur heard the familiar clack of the machine. He remembered when he'd posed as a telegraph man on an assignment years ago. He'd had to master Morse code. Did he still remember it?

The message began. Spur was surprised to find he could decode it as it came in over the wire:

"Oreville, Nevada
Julie. STOP. Had to halt here, STOP.

Silver-haired lady smiles at me, STOP.
Say she'll be mine tomorrow, STOP.
Lionel."

Spur puzzled over the strange message as the machine fell silent. He memorized it. Was it in code? Could be. But who was Julie?

"Okay, Boyd. I've waited long enough!" Kincaid said.

Another message started clicking into the room.

"Fer chrissakes! Never mind. I'll come back!" The mayor turned toward the door. "McCoy!"

"I was just coming to see you, mayor."

They walked outside.

"Ah, who's Julie?"

"Who's Julie? Just the owner of the best saloon in town. The Motherlode. Her name's Julie Golden, but everyone calls her Ma."

"Thanks."

"Have to be running." He turned to go.

"Wait, Kincaid!"

"Sorry, Duty calls. I've got to get to that damned church social, if you'll pardon the expression," Kincaid said.

Spur grabbed the back of his coat. "We have to talk!"

"Not now. See you about half-past." The mayor bolted down the street toward the distant chapel.

As the mayor trotted off, Spur thought. Someone had sent the telegram to Julie, to Ma. The message was so strange that he went over it again and again. Following an ingrained habit, he tossed out the unimportant words. Everything seemed to fall into place.

It was in code. He'd sent enough messages like it that he could spot one.

*Silver*-haired lady. *Mine. Tomorrow.*

The real message could read:

"Oreville, Nevada
Julie, STOP. Had to halt here, STOP.
Silver mine tomorrow, STOP.
Lionel."

Spur's face flushed. It seemed right. It felt right. A man named Lionel was letting Julie know that something was happening at the silver mine tomorrow.

But what? McCoy tried to convince himself that the hardened saloon keeper was involved in the silver robberies. The telegram almost convinced him.

Julie Golden had Melissa. The girl could be in danger, especially if this Julie was what he thought she was.

He stood. McCoy had to get her out of there.

# CHAPTER TEN

Phillipas Telonia passed Spur McCoy as he raced for the batwing doors. The Greek sidled up to the bar and raised a finger. Pete, the bartender, slapped a glass of whiskey in front of him.

"No ouzo?" he said, grunting.

Pete grinned. "Christ, you know what we have by now. Been hanging around here ever since you got into town." The clean-shaven bartender leaned toward him. "I told you when you hit Oreville to leave. There hasn't been any mining around here for months! Unless you call working for that Magnus mining!" He sent a circular wad of spit flying into the brass spittoon behind the bar.

"I know." Phillipas shifted the glass back and forth, staring into the amber liquid that it contained.

"Say, Telonia," Pete said. He lowered his voice. "What's with Ma? She's acting mighty peculiar."

He grunted.

"Bringing that new girl here. Leaving for home all the time and putting me in charge of her office!" He flared his nostrils. "Now she wants me to round up all these men who're handy with rifles. What is she up to?"

The Greek was silent.

"Hell, you can tell me!" Pete broadly smiled. "I'm her best employee. Worked for her since she bought the place. Never given her no trouble." The apron's voice dropped to a whisper. "Is she planning something big?"

Phillipas Telonia grinned. "Yes."

As he took a slow sip of the strange drink, he sighed and thought about Athens. His sweetheart who'd left him for the baker's son. His parents' graves overlooking the sea. The stone house where he used to live.

Then it had happened. He'd drunk too much ouzo, listened to too much Bouzouki music, smashed too many plates. The dancing, the dark-haired women, the heat of the Mediterranean night had gotten to him.

He hadn't planned to break the bottle and toss it into the air. He didn't aim, or tried to plant the jagged glass through the strange man's skull. But it had happened.

Phillipas remembered how he'd walked out, hired onto a fishing boat and ran from one port to another, from country to country, just a day ahead of the Greek police.

The mayor hadn't liked watching his father die that night.

And now, this goddess of a woman offered him

money to wage a personal war. It was hopeless, but he saw something in her eyes that reminded him of home.

So he'd do it. Phillipas drained the glass.

"So whiskey ain't too bad after all, is it?" Pete asked him.

What would happen at the mine? An attack? Impossible, Spur thought as he strode down Main Street. No woman could muster the number of men necessary to launch a successful assault on such a well guarded place. She didn't have the military experience to carry it off. Still, someone named Lionel had sent her the telegram. If he was behind all this, and it seemed that he was, he could hire the men for her.

Spur snarled and ran. He caught up with the mayor thirty feet from the church. "Kincaid, I don't care how many old ladies are waiting for you in there. We have to talk!"

The mayor shook his head. "You again, McCoy? If I don't show for the church social those fine ladies'll make damned sure I don't get reelected."

"Kincaid!" he bellowed. Spur felt the veins pop out on his forehead.

"Okay, okay. Jesus! What is it?"

"Know anyone named Lionel?"

The mayor scratched his chin. "Lionel. Sure! Lionel Stander farms dust on the trail heading west." Kincaid shrugged. "And there's Lionel Dreeson, Paul and Mary's son. Lionel Atwater, Lionel Curtis—"

"Okay. Okay!" Spur sighed. "Mayor, I need some help. Have to bust someone out of Ma's place."

The mayor threw back his head and laughed. "Hell, McCoy! Getting all moral on me or something? It'd take more manpower than we have in the whole town to force the men who go in there to leave against their will. Or most of the girls, for that matter."

"Not that! Kincaid, remember the women who were on the stage when it was robbed of Magnus's silver? The young girl and her grandmother?"

"Sure, Melissa and Emma Grieve. Why?"

"I just saw the girl in the Motherlode. Looked to me like she's being held there, forced into working for Ma."

"So?" He sniffed.

"Kincaid, we gotta get her out of there."

"Why? Stop talking nonsense, McCoy!" He spat. The thick saliva sizzled on the street. "Ma's no slave driver. Any of her girls could walk out of there whenever she wanted to. You've been drinking too much."

"I have some information that seems to link Julie Golden with the silver robberies."

The mayor whistled.

"Ma's hired extra security in her saloon—a guard at the stairs and one at the door. I don't know what all this is leading to, but we've got to get the girl to safety."

"Okay, okay, McCoy. Maybe you're right. But you've gotta help me explain to the church ladies after we clean up this mess."

"Forget about them! Come on. You can get me upstairs without causing too much trouble, right?"

"Well . . . ."

"Don't you know Julie Golden?"

"Sure. Yeah I know her!" he thundered. "And I'm not ashamed to say it!"

"Let's see her. Now!"

"You're some woman, Emma Grieve," Julie Golden said to the woman seated across her desk. "I never would have suspected that you used to earn an honest living like that."

Emma cracked a smile and crossed her legs. "I was young. It was fun and I made some money. That's why I can't understand why Melissa isn't taking to this." She shook her head, ruffling the black lace that fringed her bonnet. "The girl's lacking in plain sense, she is."

Ma's laughter filled her office. "I'm sure she'll do fine, Emma. After she gets used to it. They all do, you know. All the girls who came out west to be singers or dancers and ended up under my roof. Oh, they may fight it at first, but in the end they just lie back and let the men do what they want."

Emma set her gaze on the attractive young woman. "Julie, why are you doing this? What's in it for you?"

"What do you think? Money! Melissa is beautiful, young and inexperienced. Your granddaughter will be a welcome change for my steady customers. Some of these men have had every one of my girls ten times. She's just what I needed."

"I see." Emma lowered her eyes. "We're beholden to you, Julie. Me and Melissa. If she starts acting up again I'll—I'll whip her into doing it!"

"I'm sure that won't be necessary. She'll come around. And before you know it, I'll be seeing you off on the eastbound stage."

"That will be a fine day!" Emma rose on steady feet. "I should get some rest, I guess."

"Alright. Don't worry about Melissa, Emma."

"I'll try not to."

As the wizened old woman tottered from her office, Julie sighed and sank into her cushioned chair. It was necessary to keep the women there. Even though Lionel was out of town, he had plenty of men in Oreville who would shoot Melissa and Emma on sight if they'd been ordered to do so.

Julie hoped that he wouldn't return until after the stage had carted the Grieves from Oreville, far from the danger that lay all around them.

Ever the businesswoman, Julie brightened as the door opened.

"What are you doing in here, you little brat? You're twelve if you're a day old. Scram and come back in ten years!

"Telegram, Miss Golden." The freckled-faced boy awkwardly held out a folded piece of paper.

"Oh, sorry. Buy yourself a soda." Julie exchanged the note for a quarter and spread it on her desk.

Lionel's message pleased her. He'd given her the okay. She would attack the mine.

Drunken cardplayers shouted greetings to Kincaid as McCoy followed the mayor into the Motherlode Saloon. They casually walked through the boisterous bar. Justin Kincaid stopped at the foot of the stairs.

"Gotta see Ma about business, Harris," he said.

The guard grunted. "Go ahead. But your friend—"

"Goes with me! Come on!"

The politician who'd been cowed by a few old ladies vigorously strode up the stairs. McCoy was relieved to see the change of character.

They stopped on the landing. "Which room?" Spur asked in a whisper.

"I dunno. Alice is in 4, Marsha's in 3." As he rattled off the numbers and their occupants, the mayor's face brightened at the attendant memories. "Ah, let's see. As far as I know rooms 13 and 14 are empty. The two girls who used to live in them left town last month."

They walked down the hall. The liquid sounds of flesh banging together emanated from the rooms. The smell of perfume and sweat permeated the air. Ma's was busy, Spur thought as he stood before room 13.

"My lucky number," he said. McCoy glanced sharply at Kincaid. They both drew their weapons.

He opened the door. Melissa Grieve stared up at them in unconcealed horror. The girl's hair was mussed. Her bodice and petticoats were torn to ribbons.

"You can't make me stay here!" she hissed. "I know you work for Ma!"

"Quiet, girl!" Spur said. "We're here to help you." He threw her a blanket. "Wrap this around yourself!"

"Why?" she demanded.

"Just do it, Melissa!"

"McCoy, distract them!" The mayor jerked his head toward the hall.

"Right."

He holstered his weapon and quietly ran down the stairs. The guard stared up at him.

"Come quick," he said with feigned urgency. "And get the other guy! Ma wants you *now!*"

The muscular tough stood and turned his head toward the saloon's front door. "Burt, get yer ass upstairs!" he yelled.

Spur made it up in time to surprise Harris. He slammed the butt of his revolver into the guard's skull, digging it into the hard flesh and bone. Another sharp blow broke the skin. Harris grunted, spasmed and dropped.

Burt bounded up the stairs. Spur stepped out of sight.

"What the hell! You drunk or something, Harris? Get off yer fat butt!"

The guard bent over his downed friend. Mayor Kincaid and a blanket-wrapped Melisssa emerged from room 13.

"Hey!"

Spur cut off the man's word with a well-placed kick and a smashing blow to his head. Burt crumpled on top of Harris.

"Come on!" McCoy yelled to Kincaid.

The three of them hurried down the stairs. Spur surveyed the scene as they descended into the saloon. A few men who'd noticed the altercation looked up and went back to the business of serious drinking and poker.

"Hey!" a lean cowboy shouted, staring at the trio. "They're taking away the new girl!"

Spur found his group the center of attention. He firmed his grip on Melissa's arms.

"Stay out of my way, George!" the mayor yelled to a friend.

They slid between the scattered tables and chairs

toward the distant door. McCoy urged Justin Kincaid to move faster.

A sudden thought ripped through him. The bartender!

Spur crashed through two sodden men. He and Kincaid rushed toward the door, fighting through the snarl of angry drunks bent on keeping the new girl at their disposal. Fists flew. He took a solid punch on his chin.

"Damnit, people! This is serious!" the mayor yelled. "Get out of our way!"

"Like hell they will!"

Spur saw a knife slicing through the air toward them.

# CHAPTER ELEVEN

The deadly knife dug into the saloon wall inches from Spur's head, splintering the wood with a loud crack. A rifle blasted into life.

Melissa screamed and went limp in the two men's hands. Spur grimaced at Kincaid.

"You ain't leaving with that girl," the bartender yelled. He walked toward them, his eye to his rifle's sight. "Let her go and get the hell out of my saloon!"

Spur straightened his back. There were other ways to get out of a tight spot than firing. "What's wrong with you? You want this poor girl to bleed to death right here?"

"What?" The fancily dressed bartender squinted through his rifle sight.

Kincaid caught on. "That's right, Pete! Some bastard beat her up pretty bad. Me and McCoy here had just left Ma's office when we saw him. He knocked out Harris and Burt. Before we could stop him he jumped out the window!"

"You don't want this girl's death on your hands, do you?" Spur said. Melissa wavered on her feet, but McCoy knew she wasn't acting. She was overwhelmed by what was happening.

"Well—well—" the apron stammered.

Spur took a step toward the door behind him. "Lower your weapon, Pete. We're taking her out of here."

"Do it!" the mayor thundered.

The bartender's aim faltered. "But shit, Mayor Kincaid! Ma's told me to—"

"What's Ma told you to do?"

He froze at the woman's words. Pete lowered his rifle and wearily turned to face his employer. Julie Golden cleared the stairs, put her hands on her pretty hips and walked up to her employee.

Spur admired her coolness, the way she tilted her chin. The woman was in total control.

"Sam, if the girl's been injured she should be looked after. Isn't that right? What kind of a person do you think I am?" Julie shook her head.

The bartender gaped. "But, Ma!"

She brushed past him and fixed her gaze on Spur's. She smiled. "Go ahead. Take her. Quickly!"

"Thanks a lot, Ma. I'll pay double next time," the mayor said.

The two men helped Melissa through the batwing doors. Once they were in the sunlight she straightened up, fresh as can be.

"Who *are* you people?" the girl asked, looking from one to the other.

"No time for that now. Kincaid, where's the safest place to drop her?"

He snapped his fingers. "Post office! It's guarded day and night."

"Fine."

"Wait!" Melissa stepped toward the doors. "My grandmother's still in there!"

"In the saloon?"

She vigorously nodded, flinging yellow hair around her head. "We can't leave her in there with that woman!"

Emma Grieve burst through the batwings. "Land sakes, child! What's happened?"

Spur snorted. "No time to explain, granny. We're taking you somewhere safe."

"From whom?" she demanded. "We have to get Melissa to a doctor!"

"She's fine."

"I am, grandmother. Really!" The girl smiled and grabbed the elderly woman's hand.

Kincaid and McCoy escorted the pair to the post office. Spur kept an eye on the rear but no one followed them. Ma must have changed her plans.

"You were being kept there against your will, right?" he asked the suddenly vivacious girl.

"Yes! That horrid woman forced me to do the most disgusting things!"

"No, dear," Emma said. "She was helping us!"

Melissa wrung her hand from her grandmother's. "She was not!"

Incapable of figuring it out, Spur sighed and ushered them into the post office.

"We're just closing," the armed guard said as the mayor stepped in.

"Fine. These two women are in danger. Protect them around the clock with your very lives!"

"Yes, sir!" The ex-soldier braced.

"I don't understand!" Emma said as McCoy and Kincaid walked back to the door. "Why are you doing this? Miss Golden was helping us to leave Oreville!"

"I'm not sure. I don't know!" Spur threw up his hands. "It's possible that Ma's involved in the silver robberies, like the one that happened to that stage you were taking? Those might have been her men shooting at you in your hotel room."

Emma shivered. "I don't believe you," she yelled. "That' woman's a saint!"

"Maybe. Or maybe she wanted to make you both saints." Spur sighed.

"You can trust him, ladies!" Kincaid said. "Spur McCoy's a government agent. He's been sent down here to find the men who've been stealing the silver!"

"I'm not going to make you stay, Melissa," McCoy said to the girl as she fiddled with a stack of envelopes. "You're free to come and go as you like. But if you step past that door I can't be responsible for your safety. Understand?"

She nodded. "Yes. Perfectly. And I'll see to it that grandmother stays here too."

He kissed her forehead.

"Well!" Emma Grieve said.

The men walked out.

"They'll be safe enough there," Kincaid said. "I'll have food and water sent into them, and the guards'll keep them company."

Spur took off his hat and slicked the wet hair from his neck. "When's the next stagecoach headed east?"

"Not until next week."

"Great. Then we'll have to find somewhere else to put them. It's been an interesting day, mayor." He sighed. "What do you think about this assault on Cleve Magnus's mine?"

"I don't know. I don't see it happening." Kincaid thoughtfully scratched his chin. "Get a good night's sleep, McCoy." He peered at him. "Looks like you could use it."

"Okay."

Spur walked to the Eastern Heights Hotel, his mind a blur of thoughts and unanswered questions.

Lionel Kemp slammed a fist into his thigh as he rode the gelding through the gathering dusk. He'd been a fool to think that Julie could handle the whole thing herself. It wasn't wise to trust a mere woman to oversee such an important mission.

So he'd changed his plans, sent her a telegram, hired a horse and started back toward Oreville. No sense in warning the bitch of his return, Kemp thought.

The sky deepened into a blue that quickly faded to black. Stars poked from the sky above his bobbing head. Lionel Kemp sighed at the forgotten feeling of a saddle under him and the world stretching out before his eyes.

It had been a long time since he'd been on the range, trying to earn a few bucks by rustling cattle. That had been so successful that he'd saved enough money to go into business in Oreville.

Back then, money was just starting to pour into the town. The mines were hitting such rich veins that he'd bought up virtually all the surrounding property. Kemp quickly quadrupled his money by selling off lots to the merchants who set up shop, hoping to cash in on the miner's luck.

Nothing held him back. Though he never staked a claim, lifted a pick axe or bought a mine, Lionel Kemp was soon the richest man in town. He saw to it that his hand-picked politicians got elected. Dozens of pretty women lined up to share his bed for the night. He owned half the men in town. The law couldn't touch him, no matter what he did. He owned that, too.

He'd lived a high life for over a year, opening his own saloons and equipment stores to soak money from the pockets of the rich men who settled in Oreville. His bank accounts swelled.

Then the nightmare had begun. The gold and silver crazed miners exhausted the earth's riches. Huge operations shut down overnight. Hundreds of people pulled up their stakes and left town. Within a week, word had spread across the country, halting the flow of fresh manpower into Oreville. Two weeks after that it was a virtual ghost town. His once valuable property wasn't worth two bits.

Lionel had gotten by. He'd lived off his earnings for as long as he could. When he'd squeezed his assets as far as they'd go, Kemp realized that he was in trouble. Unwilling to give up his comfortable lifestyle, he'd sold his last successful business—the Motherlode saloon—and looked around for something else to do.

Then it came to him. One night he woke with the perfect plan. The victim? The wealthy widow who'd bought his saloon.

Julie Golden had been easy to fool. He'd hired a savage man to kill an eighteen year old boy by bashing in his skull for $5. While the murder was happening, Kemp was busy at the woman's house, getting her falling-down drunk and taking her to bed.

After the gunman had dragged the body into her house downstairs, Kemp knocked her out and deposited the unconscious woman besides the dead boy. An empty wine bottle in her hand completed the scene. Kemp went home to let Julie come to her own conclusions.

Now that he had something on her, Lionel hatched his scheme of stealing Magnus's silver. It wasn't a good living but it was better than nothing. Then the bastard had gotten too careful, guarding his shipments. And Kemp was dangerously low on money, no more than two month's worth. He had to clean out the mine of its stored riches and head out of town forever.

An owl flapped past the moon. Lionel Kemp laughed as he thought of Julie Golden waking beside the murdered youth.

Julie squeezed her Greek lover's hand as fifty men assembled in the valley five miles out of town. Lit only by thin moonlight, she couldn't see their faces. But she had to trust them. It was the only way.

"Talk to them, Phillipas," she urged him.

The immigrant grunted and kissed her cheek.

As he addressed her army, Julie smiled and stood behind him, head bowed, as if she didn't understand what he was talking about. But the man's enflamed words, his call for the citizens of Oreville to take what was rightfully theirs and to bring renewed life to the town, even stirred her.

Julie studied his sharp gestures and self-assured posture. He was perfect, she thought. The kind of man others would follow. Phillipas had been born to it.

He promised them $100 each—more if they recovered a huge store of silver. The men cheered and thrust their rifles into the inky desert sky.

Julie closed her eyes. As soon as all this was over, she and Phillipas would ride into the desert with the silver, slowly making their way to California. It would be dangerous, of course. When Lionel realized that she'd betrayed him he'd stop at nothing to find her.

But Julie blocked out the dark thoughts and dreamed of a happy life as Phillipas Telonia whipped the crowd into a frenzy with his accented words.

Lionel Kemp, she thought, you've finally met your match.

Spur answered the knock on his door. He'd gotten out of bed at sunrise, shaved and dressed in clean clothing, so he greeted Mayor Kincaid with a hearty smile.

"McCoy, you may be right."

"Good morning to you, too. About what?"

"About the mine being attacked." Kincaid looked around the room. "I've heard rumors that several men left town last night. Dozens of them, all riding west. They could have been going to a meeting."

"I see." Spur frowned. "Possibly. Things like this have happened before. Angry men band together to take care of business. But I don't remember hearing about an all-out assault on any mine, especially a silver mine."

"Me neither, but I thought you should know. Keep me informed, McCoy."

"Thanks."

Spur thought hard as he closed the door. It didn't sound good. It didn't sound good at all. He considered questioning the men in town, but that wouldn't do much. Even if one of them admitted that there had been a meeting, and that the group was planning to take the mine, it wouldn't stop the battle.

McCoy had to warn Magnus. He had to be there just in case.

That morning, Julie heard her kitchen door bang open. She stifled a cry of surprise as Lionel Kemp stormed into the parlor. The beautiful woman rose from the settee, glanced down at Phillipas and ran to the dusty man.

"You're back early!" she said, smiling at him.

"No shit." Kemp growled and threw off his coat and hat. "Who the hell's he?"

"Ah, Lionel Kemp, meet Phillipas Telonia."

The immigrant rose and stretched out a hand, but Kemp turned to Julie.

"I'm her—"

"General!" she said, breaking off his words. "We organized everything last night—well, Phil did. I've got the men and he got them fired up. We're ready, Lionel!"

Kemp studied her face. "Really?"

"Yes." She forced a laugh. "Lionel, I knew I couldn't do it alone. Since I thought you'd be gone—after I received your telegram—I figured I had to have some help. That's when I met Phillipas." She smiled. "Pete introduced us. He's the best man for the job."

But as Kemp switched his gaze from the woman to the man, Julie felt herself dying inside. Lionel had come back. She'd have to stay home while they rode out to attack the mine. She wouldn't be able to leave with Phillipas. All her plans had crumbled to dust the moment Lionel had walked through her door. She'd never be rid of him.

"I'll make coffee." Julie walked into the sun-brightened kitchen. She made no move toward the coffee pot and didn't go outside to the well.

Make the best of it, she thought. Anything could happen before tomorrow night. Lionel might decide to leave after he had the silver. He might ride out before everything happened. Or she could have Phillipas kill him.

Kill him!

The thought unnerved her. Julie glanced around the spotless room. She remembered that night when she woke up with a headache beside the dead man. She'd always felt that Lionel had done it—one of his cruel tricks on her. But he'd almost been successful in convincing her otherwise.

He deserved to die for what he'd made her do.

Julie grabbed the coffee pot and slammed through the door. She furiously worked the pump handle, filled the metal container and returned to the kitchen.

After stoking the flames in the firebox she set the water on it to heat. Julie Golden sighed and walked into the parlor.

"Good. You've planned well, Telonia," Lionel was saying. "Almost as well as I would have done it."

"Thank you, Kemp." The Greek basked in the man's praise.

"But we'll have to cut the men's pay. I can't afford to give them each a hundred dollars—that'd be five thousand!" Lionel shook his head. "We'll cut it to fifty and not tell them until it's over."

Phillipas shifted on the settee. "That would be dangerous, Kemp. The men may turn against me—against you!"

Lionel laughed. "Leave it to me. I'll handle it."

Kemp rose from the settee, grabbed the bottle of whiskey from the table near the window and drank.

Julie nervously looked at Phillipas. Could she ask him to kill Lionel? And if so, would he do it? Of course he would, she told herself. She didn't know much about him, but he seemed so angry and lonely. Desperate. Haunted.

She fingered the curtains. Phillipas turned to her. His face was flushed with excitement. The Greek immigrant winked.

He'd do it if she told him that Lionel was lying to him, Julie thought. He'd kill the man if she told him that he was going to keep all the silver for himself.

When to ask him. Tonight? She couldn't risk it. If

Phillipas failed her she'd be in Lionel's power again, and that was something she couldn't face.

Not tonight!

# CHAPTER TWELVE

"It's me, Mayor Kincaid!" Justin shouted as a rifle exploded not far from the riders. "Me and McCoy have to see Magnus! Let us pass!"

"Alright," the unseen guard said.

Spur grunted as they rode toward the mine. "You've got a hot state here, Kincaid," he said as heat shimmered from the sand below them.

The mayor took off his hat and slicked the sweat from his forehead with the back of his hand. "Hell. This is nothing. You're missing the really sizzling weather. Come back in two months, McCoy."

"No, thanks." He fixed his eyes on a dark slash on the mountain that marked the mine.

"You figure he'll believe us?" Kincaid asked.

"I don't know. He's so worried about guarding his silver that he'll probably act as if the threat is real. That's the kind of man he seems to be."

Kincaid guffawed. "Come on, McCoy. You only

met him once. How'd you know that?"

Spur squinted into the sun. "I know men like him. Lots of them. But I wish I knew who Lionel was— the man who sent that telegram to Julie Golden that started this whole thing."

"Back to Lionel again? Hmm. I was figuring it was a first name. But maybe not." Justin Kincaid bit his lip. "Then again there's Lionel Kemp."

McCoy looked at him. "Who's that?"

"Used to be the biggest landowner in Oreville. Owned the fanciest saloons. After the mines started closing he lost a shitload of money. Abandoned a lot of his property, withdrew every dime he had from the banks and sold most of his businesses." Mayor Kincaid met Spur's gaze. His left eye twitched.

"What is it?"

"Lionel Kemp sold the Motherlode Saloon. To Julie Golden."

Spur took in the words. "What happened to him?"

"Hell, I don't know. He sorta dropped out of sight. Haven't seen him around town. Rumor says that he's pretty close to Julie, but he moved out of his house."

Their mounts picked their way carefully over the rocky ground. Spur wished he had a cheroot. "A man who's lost that much money might be pushed to desperate acts."

"Agreed," Kincaid said. "Maybe you're right, McCoy. Maybe Lionel's been using Julie as some kind of organizer to handle the silver robberies. I doubt if she's actually done any of them, but she could be involved in other ways."

"Doing Kemp's dirty work for him." Spur shook his head. "Willingly?"

"Who knows? Let's just get out to the mine. If you're right about the telegram, Magnus might lose more than one shipment of silver tonight!"

They kicked their horses' flanks, urging the protesting beasts into a trot as soon as the ground smoothed into sand broken by scrub and short dunes. As they rode, Spur tried to picture the beautiful woman sending out men with orders to steal and to kill. If she was responsible, this Kemp must have been forcing her to do it. But how?

"Come on, Isabella," Kincaid said. "You got a new shoe, and we'll water you as soon as we get to the mine. Don't let me down, girl!"

Spur grinned at the mayor." Shit, Justin; you talk to that thing as if she was human."

Kincaid looked at him with a curious smile.

A half hour later they'd rubbed down their horses and followed their escort to Cleve Magnus.

"What brings you two out here?" he asked.

"Trouble, Magnus." Spur paced. "I don't know how to tell you this, but there's every possibility that an army will assault your mine."

"What?" The big jowled man pulled on a glass of whiskey, coughed and sighed.

"Tonight. This guy who's been taking your silver isn't satisfied with a shipment or two. He wants to clean you out and he's hired himself a lot of men to do it."

The mine owner poured himself another drink, carefully placed the top on the decanter and pushed it away. He downed the liquor in one gulp. "Okay."

Kincaid glanced at Spur and then looked at

Magnus. "Okay? Just okay? Cleve, didn't you hear what the man said?"

"Sure I heard him!" Magnus snorted. "I've been thinking something like this would happen. The men in Oreville are so broke they're losing their minds." He stared hard at McCoy. "How sure are you of this?"

"As sure as I can be. Information's sketchy. I've put it together from what I have."

Magnus nodded. "I can't ignore the threat. Okay, I'll take steps. No one would be so stupid to attack during the day, so it'll have to be at night. I'll cancel the evening shifts and alert everyone, station extra guards around this building. Since this is where I store the smelted silver, they'll head here first. I'll have every man armed and on the alert by dusk."

"Might be a good idea to stock up on extra ammunition," Spur said. "You'll need it."

"Good idea. I'll have a few men ride into town."

"Tell them to act casually, not to attract any attention. If we can make the thieves think they're surprising us, it'll be to our advantage."

"Right!" Magnus stood and rubbed his palms together.

"Hell, Cleve. Are you looking forward to this? An all-out war?"

"In a way. By tomorrow it'll all be over. I won't have to worry about any of this. Either way, win or lose, it's history."

"We're not sure anything's going to happen," Spur added, "but you're doing the right thing."

Magnus pounded on his desk. "Frankie!" he bellowed.

A fresh-faced youth instantly appeared in the doorway. "Yes, boss?"

"Come with me. We've got work to do!" He turned to his visitors. "You boys sticking around?"

"Thought we might, if you don't mind. I've got some ideas on how to defend this place."

"Defend the mine?" Frankie rolled his eyes. "Shit, boss; what's happening?"

"Either the end of the world, or the light at the end of the tunnel. Come on!"

"It's time."

Julie started at Lionel's words. She watched, helplessly, as he and Phillipas checked their gear— ammo bags, rifles, revolvers.

"Is there anything I can do?" Julie asked.

"Yes." Phillipas turned to her, "Pray for us."

She bit her thumb. "You two be careful out there, you hear me?"

Kemp laughed. "Don't worry your pretty little head about me. We'll be back before you know it."

They walked out the door and mounted up. She watched from the window until they were lost in the evening's darkness.

Julie slumped onto the settee. She nearly dissolved into tears. Lionel hadn't left her for a second since he'd arrived. He and Phillipas spent the whole day planning the attack. They even went together to relieve themselves. She hadn't had a single chance to talk privately with Phillipas.

So he wouldn't kill Lionel. They'd attack the mine, get the silver, and come back. Kemp would send Phillipas away and she'd live in bondage for the rest of her life.

Julie wrung her hands. This wasn't what she'd planned.

The door burst open. The woman caught her breath as Phillipas stepped in. Julie ran to him and groaned as he wrapped his arms around her.

"I forgot my kerchief," he said, kissing her neck.

"Phillipas, I—"

"I have to leave, Julie."

"I know. I know! But Phillipas!"

He held her at arm's length. "What?"

Looking into his eyes, she shook her head. "You be careful out there."

"I will. Goodbye."

He was gone again.

She hadn't been able to do it. Her resolve had disappeared as soon as she saw his expression. As much as Julie Golden hated Lionel Kemp, she wasn't a savage. She couldn't order the man's murder.

The woman sat by the window, determined to stay there until she saw the two men in her life riding back with their prize.

Dusk. Spur was satisfied with Magnus' preparations. He'd been careful not to make any obvious changes. To the untrained eye, it looked as if it was business as usual at the mine. A few men were stationed at each end of the rusty iron track that led from the mouth of the shaft's entrance to the smelting plant. They pushed a car back and forth, up and down. It was impossible to see that it was empty from a distance.

No more kerosene lamps than usual flickered from the trees and buildings scattered around the place. Smoke rose from the bunkhouse, the cookhouse and the other major structures, while it belched from the spiraled chimneys rising from the building that housed the smelting operation.

Looking over the desert, Cleve Magnus, Justin Kincaid and Spur McCoy had one last discussion before their final meeting with the men.

"The attack could come at any time," Spur said. "We may be warned by shots from the desert, either from the perimeter guards or into them. Or they may bypass the guards. Either way, they have to approach from the desert. The hills are too steep to mount a successful attack from the rear."

He turned to look at the shoulder of the mountain on which the mine—and they were situated.

"We've agreed that it would be best to have one-third of the men to the southwest, stationed behind bushes and rocks. To the right, the northeastern side, another eighteen men will wait. The rest'll stay in the camp itself to guard it, out of sight but at the ready. Is everything clear?" Spur asked.

The men grunted affirmatively.

"Great. Magnus, go talk to your men. Have them in position in five minutes!"

"Will do."

As the short man trotted off, Kincaid turned to Spur. "You know, we may be doing all this for nothing."

"I know." He grabbed a cheroot from the mayor's coat pocket and lit it with a lucifer. "But this is my job."

Cleve Magnus had 53 men at the mine. Kemp was counting on having surprise on his side. Spur hoped that foreknowledge would be in their favor.

If anything happened . . . .

They waited.

Magnus huffed back to them. The three men crouched behind the line of water barrels that rimmed the porch of the main house. Eight armed men were at the ready inside. Every other man was at his station, but an eyeball check told Spur that they had been well hidden.

"Good work, Magnus."

The man grunted. "What'd you expect? This ain't poker, for Chrissakes!"

Three hours later they were still waiting. Their talk had ceased. McCoy felt the men's edginess, the tension that rippled the air behind the barrels where they squatted.

Spur kicked out a cramp that had flared in his leg, maintaining his continuous scan of the desert floor below them.

A rifle boomed in the distance. The explosion split open the night silence. McCoy peered into the darkness as the sound echoed off the sheer cliffs behind them.

"The first guard?" Kincaid asked beside him.

"Maybe."

"Do you think—?" Magnus began.

Spur shook his head. He checked his Winchester for the thousandth time as Cleve and Justin squirmed beside him.

Another rifle blast shook the area. Closer this time. Much closer.

Straining his ears, Spur heard unmistakable

sounds of a mass of horses approaching the mine. He couldn't see them but they sure were out there.

He'd been right. Somehow, he'd been right!

Spur grinned at the wary Kincaid and Justin. "You boys ready for a fight?"

"Yeah. Let me at the bastards!" Cleve said.

"Then let's give them an old fashioned welcome."

Spur twisted to his side. One of Magnus's men ducked out of sight behind a pile of wooden crates.

Everything was ready.

The first shots had been fired.

# CHAPTER THIRTEEN

A thin, high cloud passed before the first quarter moon. Spur hunkered down behind the rain barrels and fruitlessly surveyed the desert floor that lay beyond the mining operation. As his eyes adjusted to the darkness he began to make out shapes against the light ground—clumps of rocks, stunted juniper trees. Two minutes after he'd heard the rifle blasts nothing had happened.

McCoy turned to Cleve Magnus. "You told your men not to show themselves too early, right? They'll hold off shooting until they're right here?"

"Yes, damnit!" the miner said. "Hell, isn't this thing ever going to start?"

"It already has. Listen, Magnus! The horses are getting closer."

Two-hundred hooves pounded the sand. Spur finally saw the moving bulk that approached the hillside mine. They were much less than a mile away.

"That's them," Mayor Kincaid said. "Damn if you weren't right, McCoy!"

He softly grunted. "Like I told you, that's my job. Get set, men."

By the sparkling light of the moon, Spur watched as the mass of riders parted in the middle. "They're breaking up into two groups," he said, wondering what Kemp had promised them for the night's work.

"I know, I know; I got eyes!" Magnus said. "Jeeeezus!"

"Shut up!" Kincaid's voice was low.

It began all at once. A front of ten riders stormed up the hill and launched an all-out attack on the mine. A second wave of ten more men charged onto Magnus's operation. After the first of their rounds had slammed into the house, Magnus's men fired on them from around the camp, blasting deadly messengers into the oncomers.

Spur slammed a slug into a townsman as he rode toward the house. He blasted away with a cursing Kincaid and a jubilant Magnus. The air filled with the sharp scent of gunpowder. Blinding explosions easily revealed the positions of Magnus's men.

But Spur wasn't surprised that the army began to scatter. The undertrained men obviously hadn't been prepared for this. Lack of discipline killed their united strength, breaking it into pockets of offense.

Pain-wracked men died as they slid from their horses. Spur spent two minutes firing and reloading his Winchester, bobbing above the triple-thick line of barrels that Magnus had had filled with sand, ducking back to safety; endlessly repeating the routine.

"Shit! They mean business!" Kincaid said.

"So do we!" McCoy said. "Come on, mayor! Where's your backbone?"

"Trying real hard to stay in one place!"

The front line of barrels splintered before them. Spur picked off as many of the attackers as he could, but the dim light and the horses' frenzied reaction to the battle blazing around them made accuracy difficult at best.

The second group of townsmen had split again. Some distance away, Spur heard the two other groups clashing with the men Magnus had planted on either side of the mine to stave off any entrance from those sides.

"Yeah!" McCoy said as five riderless horses ran from the area, trampling the dead men that lay littered on the ground. Of the twenty men who'd stormed them, Spur counted seven still on horseback and one dashing madly back into the desert. He let him go; he was harmless.

As McCoy expertly broke open his Winchester and reloaded, an attacker pumped out two shots as he streaked past them. Cleve Magnus howled and dropped his weapon.

"Damn shit!"

Spur grimaced. Leaving the safety of the barrier, he dashed along the right side of the house and pounded up toward the rear. He'd aimed even before the rider who'd plugged Magnus flashed by.

The deadly bullet slammed into the man's chest as he rode past, instantly killing him.

Spur trotted back to the others. The fighting was less violent. "Where'd you get hit, Magnus?"

"Hell, McCoy. It's only my arm." The miner grabbed his rifle. "I'm gonna get those bastards!"

"You can still handle that thing?" Spur asked as he fired at a mounted attacker. He missed.

"Sure as I'm Cleve P. Magnus!"

The level of gunfire quickly fell off. The three remaining attackers surveyed the scene and rode hell-bent away from the mine. Spur blasted a parting shot at them for good measure.

"What's the 'P' stand for?" Justin asked.

Shouts and victorious cheers from the men stationed around the camp drowned out the mine owner's answer. Fighting on the two flanks eased off as well.

"What did you say, Cleve?" the mayor asked.

"Holy shit! No time for talk, boys!"

A wave of eight fresh riders, probably funneled from the secondary positions, exploded around them. Spur, Kincaid and a barely functional Magnus managed to pick off two of them, while their compatriots routed five more. But the agonized screams issuing from various parts of the camp meant that Magnus was losing men, too.

The riders soon tired of their exposed positions. They dismounted and scattered to prepare for an all-out fight. At least one of them was surprised by one of Magnus's men who killed him as he dropped from his saddle behind a pile of broken ore.

"Persistent little devils, aren't they?" Kincaid said.

"Yeah."

Spur blasted a waist-high boulder behind one of the attackers. The lead ricocheted and slammed into a townsman as he ducked behind an overturned wagon.

"Lucky shot," Magnus said, groaning from his wound.

"Luck? Hell, I planned that!"

Three separate battles turned the sky into a series of brilliant explosions. Smoke hung thickly throughout the camp. Kincaid blasted two of the three men to hell as Spur finished off the other one.

In the distance, he noted several riders rapidly departing, heading for Oreville in defeat.

"That's it for them," McCoy said.

Magnus let out a piercing whistle.

"What's that for?" Spur asked.

"You'll see."

Two of the man's workers—"Crack shots," Magnus proudly said—emerged from their hiding places and approached the bodies. They quickly removed weapons and checked for signs of life.

Their battle was over. Spur rose to his feet with Kincaid and Magnus. He turned to gaze at the war still raging to the southeast. Two men on horseback charged up to the main area of the camp.

"Shit! Haven't they had enough? Those boys just won't quit!" Magnus said, rubbing his arm.

Seeing the men standing around the building, they turned north toward the face of the mountain. Spur cursed as they dashed behind the cookhouse out of the line of fire.

"They can't go far," he said, and bolted.

Spur pounded the dirt with his boots. He'd just

reloaded so he had two easy shots before he had to get busy again. As he passed the cookhouse Spur picked off one of the fleeing men. He plummeted to the ground and rolled to a stop.

The other rider kicked his mount's flanks, urging him on. Huffing, Spur raced up the mountain beside the iron tracks. He ducked as the attacker took a wild shot behind him. The riderless horse sped past.

He could have only one destination. In. Into the mine.

Spur lateralled across the rough road as the attacker flew into the wooden supported mine entrance. Too far away for a good shot, he lowered his aim.

It was only a matter of time, he thought. Just one entrance to the mine—Magnus had briefed him on that. He had to wait.

The camp was quiet below him. Spur filled the empty chamber and tapped his boot heel. The fighting had ended. Standing out of direct fire, he wasn't surprised to hear the kerosene lamps inside blast into darkness with the gunman's ammunition.

Spur was suddenly weary. "Come on out, asshole! I hold all the cards. It's time we all went home."

Silence.

McCoy dislodged a gnarled juniper bush from the bone dry dirt. Hefting it in his hand, he threw it before the narrow mine opening.

Two explosions echoed from inside. Light flashed along the steel car railings as the tree fell to the ground.

"Damn!"

Spur smiled at the man's voice. "Out of ammunition? Get your ass out here, man! I won't kill you in cold blood. You'll get a fair trial."

Again, nothing. He was betting that the attacker had used up his ammo but couldn't depend on that. And McCoy had the feeling that he wouldn't be able to talk the man out.

What to do?

Spur produced a lucifer from his coat pocket. He picked up a small rock and held the tip of the match at its rough surface. He waited.

The horse moved inside the mine. The sound of its hooves grew louder. A second before it emerged from the mine, Spur struck the match and threw it onto the dead juniper. The oil-rich bush burst into an inferno. Suddenly faced with the whirling tower of fire, the advancing horse reared back in terror, sending its rider hurling to the dust.

Spur grabbed the man before he could get up. He locked his hands around the attacker's arms behind his back.

"Walk!" he bellowed.

"Damn you!"

He was thin but strong. With an effort, Spur pushed him down the mountain as the old juniper crackled and roared behind them. It was too easy, Spur thought as he forced the man into the camp. He hadn't even tried to get free. Of course, he was probably just a simple townsman who'd been trying to earn a few dollars. The guy was probably scared stiff.

"You got one of them?" Kincaid asked as he ran up, rifle dangling from his right hand.

"Yep."

"Who is that?" The mayor grabbed the gunman's chin and jerked it up. "Shit!" he said, moving closer. "I'll be. It's Lionel Kemp!"

Spur automatically tightened his grip. "The ringleader, eh? You didn't plan this party very well, Kemp. But we tried to make you feel welcome. Come on!"

McCoy ran the man into the camp, the mayor taking up the rear.

Cleve P. Magnus met them. "Jesus, McCoy! Twenty of my good, loyal men are dead!"

"You've got Kemp here to thank for that. Get me some rope!" he barked.

One of Magnus's hired hands threw him a coil. Spur slipped one end under Lionel's wrists and quickly knotted a firm knot. The man sullenly refused to talk as he was trussed up.

"That should hold him," Spur said.

"Yeah. Now we gotta find a good tree for the lynching." Cleve surveyed the bare ground around the buildings. "Shit! No trees out here in the desert!"

Spur grunted. "There's not going to be any lynching."

"No? Then I'm gonna blast his guts out!" Cleve Magnus swung up his rifle.

"Drop your weapon, Magnus! Hasn't there been enough killing?"

"Not quite!" He laughed.

Kincaid grabbed the wounded man's good shoulder. "You're not thinking straight. Hell, you've got a hole in your left arm for Godsakes! Cleve, you do this and you'll hang for murder."

"Who's gonna convict me? You? Let me go!"

Lionel looked up at the man and spat in his face. Magnus blubbered, his short body shaking with unmitigated rage.

"Damn you all!" he said.

"Take this," McCoy said, thrusting the loose end of the rope that bound Kemp's hands toward the mayor. Spur kicked the Spencer from Magnus's hands and landed a clean punch to the mine owner's chin. Cleve spun and slowly sank to the ground.

"Just what he needed," Spur said.

"You can't blame him, McCoy. I'd probably do the same thing." He drew the rope taut. "I don't like this animal you've given me. Here, you take him!"

Spur caught the rope. Lionel stared at the ground.

"Gotta get him back to town. You going with me?" Spur asked.

"Ah, well, I guess so. But there's a lot to be done here." He looked around the camp.

"Someone should send for the barber. He'll be happy as a pig in shit to have some work to do." Spur looked at the row of eight sitting, wounded men, and the bodies that lay sprawled around the camp.

"Yeah. Okay. Just a minute." The mayor grabbed a bucket and poured it onto Magnus's face.

He exploded into consciousness, blowing the liquid from his lips, shaking his head and shoulders. The mine owner slowly rose to his feet. "Jesus," he said, rubbing his chin. "What happened to me?"

"You ran into a fist," Spur said.

"And a bullet," Kincaid added.

"You lost your head, Magnus. Me and the mayor

are taking Kemp back into town. Give us any more trouble and you'll pay for it."

"Uh, yeah. God, I need a drink!" The mine owner turned toward his wounded men.

After placing the bound man on a horse, Spur and Kincaid mounted up and led him from the camp.

The first few miles were slow, but aquamarine eventually tinted the eastern sky. They quickened their horses' pace as dawn broke over the desert.

"What's Julie Golden to you?" Spur asked the sullen Lionel Kemp. When no answer issued from the man, Spur asked again.

Kemp sighed and shrugged. "She's a girl, a pretty girl who robbed that bastard's silver for me for quite a while. I underestimated her," he said.

"Yeah. But she was working for you. She didn't do anything directly?"

Lionel glanced at McCoy. "She sucked my dick—that was about all."

Spur quieted Kincaid's instant guffaw with a sharp look. "This war was your plan, then."

"Yeah. It was all mine." He jerked his head. "How the hell did you know about it?"

"I've got my ways, Kemp. When a rat's planning to raid the pantry, you can smell the stink. No, it wasn't one of your men. I don't know how you conned them into doing your dirty work, but I'm happy to report as many as ten of them wised up and rode back into town."

"Yeah. They were a big help."

"Say, McCoy; we might meet up with some of them on the way." The mayor tapped the butt of the rifle he'd slung over his shoulder.

"It's possible. But I don't think it'll be us they're shooting at."

Lionel grunted.

They rode on.

A half hour later they were following a trail of blood. The liquid had created reddish-brown stains on the sand. As they increased their distance from the camp the droplets enlarged. Soon McCoy and Kincaid saw the dead body.

"You happy, Kemp?"

"Shut up!"

"It's one thing to steal some silver here and there. It's another thing to have an eighth of the town's men killed for your petty appetite for money."

"I don't have to listen to this!" he shouted, wrestling on his mount.

"Like hell you don't," Spur said. "We're gonna fill your ears until we get back to Oreville. It could be worse; we could have let Magnus fill you with lead."

"That might have been better."

Spur smiled. "Kincaid!"

The mayor glanced at him through the increasing daylight. "I was just wondering what that damn 'P' stands for in Magnus's name. But what is it?" The mayor shook his head.

"You know a shorter way back to town than this Godforsaken chicken scratch?" Spur asked.

The mayor scratched his chin. "Yep. The old Indian trail. Isn't used much, kinda dangerous in places."

"Let's take it. The sooner we get this man locked up, the better!"

"Okay."

Spur followed the mayor's lead, turning west. "We'll dump him in the post office. That means we really have to find some place to move Melissa and Emma, but that shouldn't be too much of a problem anymore."

"Yeah. What about Julie Golden?"

McCoy hesitated. The bound man riding in front of him slightly turned his head at the woman's name. "I don't know. I'll have to question her. Kemp here's admitted to doing everything."

"She hired her own men to steal Magnus's silver," Lionel said. "I just put her up to it. I never pulled one single robbery."

"But you received the goods," Spur suggested.

He snorted.

"I don't know, Kincaid," McCoy said to the mayor. "I'll figure it out when I have to."

"Fair enough."

Fifteen minutes later, their mounts entered rocky terrain. The once smooth desert floor broke up into jutting hills, yawning cracks and huge piles of boulders. It was rougher riding but Spur was satisfied that he'd taken the correct course. He wanted Kemp off his hands as soon as possible.

"I warned you," the mayor said as they passed a difficult stretch of land. "This ain't the way to a church picnic. Which reminds me about the ladies' social I missed."

At that instant, Lionel Kemp stabbed his mount's flanks with his heels. The beast launched into a run, racing for the edge of a hill ten yards away.

"Damn!"

Spur unslung his rifle. Before he could get a bead on him, the man had dropped out of sight. Angry at himself, McCoy urged his horse to a run.

"No. Wait! The Merrone!" Kincaid yelled.

Ignoring the man's cry, he quickly cleared the land.

Spur couldn't halt his horse in time. He flew from the animal's back as he fell ten feet and plunged into a white water river. The world tumbled and bubbled around him. He couldn't breathe.

# CHAPTER FOURTEEN

Spur spun in the surprisingly strong current of the Merrone River. It's icy water drilled into his skin like a Chinatown doctor's needles, prickling him all over. Holding his breath, he clawed for the bank and searched for a foothold, not knowing which way was up as the water tossed his body in all directions.

McCoy saw his frightened horse's legs paddle by. Furious at this unexpected turn of events, he righted himself and broke through the surface of the churning water.

Air blasted from his mouth and nose. He panted, wiped the Nevada liquid from his eyes and blinked at the sight of the retreating figure riding the water away from him. Lionel Kemp shot down the Merrone.

Spur cursed and reached for his rifle. It was gone, of course. The impact of his body falling into the river had knocked it from where he had slung it over his shoulder. It could be halfway to Oreville by now.

Weaponless, McCoy lunged into the current. He struggled to force his chilled limbs to move. Dusting off his ancient swimming skills, slicing with his hands, Spur rode with the river, keeping just his eyes above the water to watch Lionel's escape.

The man was clever, Spur admitted to himself. He heard Kemp's laughter over the rush of the water. The bursts of wild, crazed guffaws infuriated him.

The riverbed slammed against his feet. He stumbled on the slippery rocks, splashed and tore his way toward the criminal, half-swimming, half-walking.

The rock walls that the river had cut into the desert floor drew closer together on both sides. Spur struggled through the speeding water. Kemp's head dipped out of sight several times. Faster, McCoy told himself. Faster!

A quick look at the edge of the cliff to his left showed nothing but the barren ridge of earth. Mayor Kincaid must be following him up there somewhere, but Spur couldn't rely on him. Besides, he wouldn't need any help if he could just get his hands around Kemp's scrawny little neck.

Spur held his breath as a wall of water slapped into his face. He blew it out and dragged himself through the Merrone. His clothes had turned to lead. Even though the Secret Service agent was moving with the current, the extra weight hindered his progress. Spur shrugged off the sodden jacket and ripped his shirt from his torso.

Lionel Kemp rose and dropped from sight sixty feet in front of him. Worn rocks pierced the boiling water's surface ahead. Beyond that, he couldn't see the river. A small fall, Spur wondered? He'd find out soon enough.

The Merrone pulled him along with incredible strength. McCoy held his breath and slid head-first over a smooth boulder. He felt his body shoot into the air and violently plummet into a deep pool.

The dive sent him to the bottom. Spur slammed his hands against the slimy rocks to prevent a broken nose, jacknifed and pushed off them. He surfaced and blew out his breath.

Rattled but unharmed, he wiped his eyes. Fifteen feet away he saw the wet bootprints that marked Lionel's escape from the river. They led onto a sandbar that jutted into a bend in the water flowing from the pool and disappeared into a thicket of cottonwoods.

Great!

Spur swam to the bank, walked up its gently sloped surface and strode into the trees. He slapped water from his pants, shivering.

"Give it up, Kemp!" he yelled.

"Not on your life!"

Spur heard the man's thrashings through the underbrush and saplings that sucked water from the earth bordering the river. McCoy brushed back short trees on either side, set his jaw and huffed as the light from the rising sun slowly filtered through the leaves, warming his body.

He worked through his exhaustion, finding additional stores of energy. After all, this wasn't the first time he'd gone without sleep.

The accumulation of hundreds of years of dead leaves and fallen branches slowed his steps. Every three feet he repeated the painstaking process of pushing one boot into the unstable mulch and retreating his other foot from the hole he'd plowed into it behind him.

It was slowing Kemp's movements too, Spur thought as a stiff twig scraped his bare chest. He barely noticed the pain of dry wood entering his toughened skin.

"You're making me mad, Kemp!" he bellowed.

Lionel returned nothing but the crashes of his frantic escape.

Spur grimaced and continued his slow progress. The trees grew more thickly. Their trunks crowded each other and inumerable saplings strained to grow in the thin light. Spur saw hints of bare sand through their trunks on either side. The cotton-woods must be following an underground stream, he thought. Kemp would use the trees for cover as long as he could. Unarmed, without a horse, the man would never be so stupid as to run into the featureless desert.

No. He was going to make this as hard as possible.

A sharpened spear of wood shot through the air from the forest ahead. With no time to react, Spur gasped as it grazed his left shoulder.

"Damn!" he yelled. The man must have been whittling as he moved.

Two more deadly spears plowed into trees inches from his naked torso. Furious, Spur dug them out and hurled the pointed sticks back into the forest ahead. "I've had it with you, Lionel Kemp!"

Spur redoubled his efforts, crashing faster and faster through the undergrowth and leathery leaves. No more spears showed themselves. He instinctively stopped after five more yards.

The forest was silent save for the sound of an early morning breeze which stirred the cottonwoods' leaves into gentle motion. Kemp wasn't moving.

Where was he?

Spur searched the woods. The ground seemed clearer, as if a devil wind had swept through the trees from the desert floor, scouring it of some of the dead leaves. A spangled trail of water still stretched before him, clearly marking Kemp's joyous passage, but it was thinner, less visible. They were both drying off.

Had the man set a trap?

McCoy weighed his options. He would walk into whatever Kemp had waiting for him, hoping his wits would save his hide. He could break out into the desert, circle ahead and try to surprise him.

Or he could stand there and wait.

Rage shot through his veins. Spur trudged forward, pivoting his head with every step, searching the trees with his trained eyes. Color flashed through the trees ten feet ahead. Lionel had been wearing a red checkered shirt. Must be him.

McCoy warily approached, moving as slowly and quietly as he could through the aggravating leaves. Though there were fewer of them they crunched with every step.

He glanced at a dead tree trunk that lay across the ground. The fallen tree had created a wedge in the mulch. It might be a good foothold. It led somewhat toward that place where he'd seen the shirt, which had now vanished.

Fixing his eyes onto the spot so that he didn't lose it in the tangled confusion of luxuriant growth, Spur stepped onto the log. It didn't shift, so he inched along it. A color alien to the natural vegetation showed itself again.

Closer. Spur broadened his pace. Perfectly balanced on the four-inch thick trunk, he slipped to its end and pushed through the trees.

McCoy almost laughed as he saw Kemp's shirt hanging above his head. The bastard had slipped the buckle end of his belt around an overhead branch and attached his shirt to the other end. The wind had created the illusion of movement.

It took Spur one second to sum up the situation. Instantly alert, he searched the surrounding trees and saw nothing.

Kemp wasn't there. He'd set up the diversion and it had worked. Cursing the day he'd ever heard of Oreville, Spur blindly stumbled through the trees. The fallen leaves were so jumbled that they showed no trail. Kemp could be anywhere.

But he hadn't heard the man move. True, Lionel enjoyed a short lead. But still . . . .

Spur stopped. A rustling ten feet from him quickly halted. Kemp was walking with him to cover the sound of his escape. He was crafty, McCoy thought. But not crafty enough.

Spur pinpointed the location of the sound and raced toward it. He moved faster, surer. He finally had his first clear view of Lionel Kemp as the man ran like hell.

Increasing amounts of light filtered through the

trees. As they neared the open desert, Spur gained on the man but couldn't get within arm's reach.

The two men burst into the desert. McCoy gave it full steam. He easily overtook the man, slammed his hands around Kemp's torso and flung him onto the dirt like a sack of flour.

Lionel scrambled to his feet with a groan and assumed a boxer's stance.

"Come on. Put 'em up!" he jeered.

Unprepared for the boot that Spur drove into his jaw, Kemp reeled back and fell.

McCoy jumped onto his chest, grabbed Lionel's head with his left hand and pounded the man's face until his knuckles drew blood. The feeling of his fist smashing into Kemp's kisser was so satisfying after all the trouble the man had caused him.

Lionel's lips split. He struggled against Spur's blows as his eyes puffed and his chin cracked beneath one of McCoy's better placed punches. Kemp quieted and lay still beneath him. McCoy finally released the bloodied man's head. It dropped onto the sand.

Spur wearily rose from the unconscious man's chest and stood. A howl of pure pleasure ripped from his throat. After his quick celebration he knelt and grabbed Kemp's wrist. The man was still alive. His pulse was regular. He'd simply gone into shock and passed out.

Satisfied that he hadn't killed him, McCoy stuck his fist on his hips and looked at the desert. He didn't have a clue where he was, how far he'd ridden the Merrone or the location of the trail back to Oreville.

A turkey vulture, alerted by the smell of fresh

blood, wound through the sky overhead in a lazy downward spiral.

Now what?

"McCoy!"

The word crept on him from a distance. He saw a rider approaching. It called his name again and waved a kerchief wagging hand.

Spur smiled. Kincaid.

The faint sight of a second rider behind the mayor surprised and pleased him. They'd need more than one horse to get the three of them out of there.

McCoy squatted beside Kemp. He watched scarlet drops of blood slide from the man's face, fall onto the sand and sizzle in the sun.

Justin Kincaid rode up a minute later. "I'll be damned," the mayor said. "I thought I'd lost you!"

"Never underestimate the Secret Service," Spur smiled.

Kincaid stared down at Kemp's torn face from his mount. "Hoowhee! Must've been some furious fight. But you look pretty good. Not too busted up."

"Let's just say it was one-sided."

Kincaid humorously grunted.

"Who's that I saw riding behind you?" Spur asked.

"What?" The mayor twisted. "I don't know. I came here alone!"

The rider halted ten feet from them.

"Magnus!" Spur shouted as the dust settled onto the ground. "What in hell are you doing out here?"

The sweating miner pumped death into Kemp's chest with his rifle. The sound of the explosions rattled through the desert.

Kincaid stiffened. "Cleve, I warned you that—"

Spur grabbed the mayor's arm. "Forget it, Justin."

"But—but—"

"I killed him," he whispered. "He was already dead."

Kincaid nodded at McCoy as Magnus dismounted and trotted up to them.

"He's dead, ain't he?" the miner said, standing beside the body.

"Yeah. You won't be losing any more of your hard earned silver to that bastard."

Magnus sighed and kicked Lionel Kemp's lifeless body. "Look what you made me do!" he yelled. "Your money-hungry greed turned me into a savage! Made me kill you! Christ, it's just what I always promised myself I wouldn't do. Even though I lived out here with gunmen and lawlessness, I always tried to live a fairly clean life."

Spur cleared his throat. "Ah, Magnus, I don't think—"

"He's dead. It's over." The miner turned to the mayor. "Okay, Justin. Lock me up. Just like you said. I'm ready to face the consequences of my actions."

The mayor glanced at McCoy and slapped Magnus's back. "Forget it, Cleve," he said.

"What're you trying to do to me? McCoy, you got jurisdiction here. Order him to arrest me!"

"He won't do it. Look, Magnus. I'll let you go scot-free. But there's one condition," Justin said.

Spur stood back, crossed his arms and scratched the annoying wound in his chest.

"What's that?"

Kincaid grinned. "That you tell me what the

damn 'P' in your name stands for!"

"Well jeez, Justin!" Magnus threw off his hat, ground it into the dust and thought. "What the hell. I guess it was my right to shoot down the bastard, after what he did to me. After all those men he killed, all that silver he stole from me. Right?"

Spur nodded. "I suppose so."

"Then what the hell." He smiled and pushed his face toward the mayor's. "Okay, okay. Phineas."

The mayor jerked back. "What'd you call me?"

"No, no. Phineas. The 'P' stands for Phineas!"

Spur guffawed along with Kincaid. "Phineas?" he said. "Your parents must have hated you."

Magnus shook his head. "Come on. Let's get the hell out of here. I still need that drink!"

"Not so fast, Magnus. Who gets to take Kemp's body on his horse?" Spur asked.

The miner looked at it. "Can't we just leave him here? Hell, the buzzards'll be out in force in no time. By tomorrow morning he'll be picked clean."

Spur looked at the dead man. "No. The law's the law," he said, as sunlight glinted off the two red pools on Lionel Kemp's chest.

# CHAPTER FIFTEEN

"Sorry, no haircuts today," Blair yelled as he heard the door to his barbershop bang open. "Come back next year!"

"I don't want a cut after the lousy job you did last time." Spur dropped the body that had been Lionel Kemp onto the crowded floor.

The sweating man turned and groaned. "Hell! Put that thing somewhere else! You hear me!" Blair kicked the lifeless form toward the door. "Can't you see I'm up to my ass in bodies, both living and dead?"

He was. His barber shop/surgery/undertaker's operation was overflowing with customers. Spur acknowledged a few of the wounded men that he recognized as Magnus's workers.

"Hell, it's not a rush job," McCoy said. "He won't be going anywhere."

"And neither will I. Chrissakes. How can I

possibly finish all this work? Cleaning, cutting, stitching—and that's just on the ones that's still breathing." The barber squatted beside a man, splashed whiskey into his chest wound and dug for the bullet. The patient's face turned white. "I don't even wanna think about all the bodies they're bringing by wagon from the silver mine. Shit! Why wasn't I a bartender? You know, a clean job?"

"No adventure."

The barbership smelled of the effects of violence —sweat, alcohol and blood.

"You get him fit for burial, you hear? As a government agent, I'm ordering you to do your duty."

"Then you better rustle up some help for me. I don't have the time to make any more plain coffins. Now git!"

Spur turned from the scene of carnage and walked into the sun.

Mayor Justin Kincaid hurried toward him. "I just checked, McCoy," he said, out of breath. "Seems one of the first of Kemp's men who returned to town last night spread the word on what was happening out at the mine. A citizens' committee was formed. They nabbed the rascals as they rode in with their tails between their legs. Got seven of 'em locked up in the post office."

Spur grunted.

"There's still one we haven't found. A Greek fella. He was a general or something."

"Hmm. What about Melissa and Emma Grieve? They're not in there with all those—"

Kincaid smiled. "Naw. They're back in their hotel room at the Eastern Heights, now that they're out of danger."

McCoy lifted his left eyebrow. "And Julie Golden? What about her?"

"Damn! Didn't think about Ma. I don't know where she is. Maybe you better—"

"Yeah." Spur walked to the Motherlode.

Julie found herself suffocating. She pushed against the heavy, sweating flesh that pinned her to the bed and gently skidded to one side on the cool sheet.

He was so handsome, she thought, listening to Phillipas Telonia's rhythmic snores. Julie threw off the covers and rested her head on his chest. His strong, regular heartbeat was soothing.

She'd waited beside the window last night for hours. After chastising herself for sitting and doing nothing, Julie had walked into the cool air and yanked weeds from her kitchen garden by moonlight.

Every five minutes or so, she'd turned toward the east and searched the sky for any signs of the war that raged there. Though she saw nothing, Julie had felt as if she were there in the middle of it.

In truth, she was. Why hadn't she left town? After Lionel had gone the first time she could have taken the stage, leaving everything behind but what she could carry with her. But then she'd met Phillipas and everything had changed.

Julie had screamed as her kitchen door banged open at midnight. Her general had thrown off his hat and held out his arms, but she'd hesitated.

"Where's Lionel?"

The Greek man had shaken his head. "I do not know, Julie. We were losing so bad that I came back. We have been defeated. No silver."

"At least you're still in one piece," Julie had said, and giggled as Phillipas swept her from the floor. The sharp stench of gunpowder intoxicated her. She had found herself unable to resist his exploring mouth, his battle-induced lust.

In spite of the danger of Lionel Kemp walking in, they'd made love again and again until exhaustion quieted the fire of their loins. They'd fallen asleep while their bodies were still joined.

Now, as she blinked and studied the rippling curtain that blocked out the world, Julie Golden sighed and ran her fingers through the curly black hairs that festooned Phillapas' chest. She slowly realized something: Lionel hadn't come back.

He couldn't have. Whether it was in victory or defeat, Lionel wouldn't respect their privacy. He would have barged in to gloat if he'd gotten the silver. If not, he would have punished them both.

Could he be—

A warm hand clasped her breasts. Julie's general grunted in his sleep.

Lionel Kemp was dead. The thought seemed to brighten the room. She bent and kissed the man's mouth.

He quickly woke, grabbed her ears and returned the sloppy kiss. It was long and thrashing, but Julie didn't give in to the surge of heat that spread through her body. She broke it.

"Phillipas, Lionel didn't come back last night."

"So?" he pecked her chin.

"Do you think he was killed?"

He sighed and nodded. "Most probably. They knew we were coming, Julie. Magnus knew.

Somehow, they had prepared. We must have lost half our men. I came back to you as soon as I saw that we had no chance of winning. It was no good."

She nodded.

Phillipas sat up. "You are not upset?"

"Not really. Lionel Kemp—" Julie bit her tongue.

The Greek laughed. "I know all about him, what he did to you."

She stared disbelievingly at him.

"He told me on the way to the mine last night. Kemp said that after we had the silver, he would leave Oreville, so it did not matter. He boasted of how he had that young man murdered and tricked you into believing you had done it. He was not good, Julie."

She flushed at the revelation. She knew she hadn't done it! "But you are, Phillipas. You're a very good man!"

"Let us make love again."

Julie sat beside him. "No. Phillipas, we have to get out of here."

"Now?"

"Yes. Now! Get dressed, dear. We're leaving!" She sprang from the bed and tore through her closet.

"But Julie, there are no stagecoaches . . ."

"We'll ride. I haven't been riding for years, but I have done it before." She smiled as she struggled into her bodice. "Don't you see? If they even suspect we were involved they'll come after us."

He grimly nodded. "Okay, Julie. Okay!"

"I have money, Phillipas. When I thought—I mean, just before the attack I drew out my savings. Over $2,000. Lionel would have spent it if he'd known about it, but I never let him know. We can get to some other town and leave all this behind us."

"Yes."

The immigrant stood and collected his clothing from the floor.

"You know, Phillipas? Everything will turn out fine!"

Spur asked at the saloon, but the wary barkeep said that Ma hadn't been in that morning yet—even though it was nine-thirty. Frustrated, he asked Pete to tell him where the woman lived.

"Nothing doing!" he barked. "If you want a girl, I'm the man to see. Tell me which one." Pete blushed, reached under the bar and banged a glass of feathers onto its polished surface. "Well? Which one gets you hard?"

"Never mind."

As he walked to the door he heard glass shatter behind him.

"I ain't doing it no more!" Pete yelled. "I just plumb ain't! Not seemly for a man! No, sir!"

Spur inquired of a well dressed man, who pointed out Julie Golden's house—a large structure on the outskirts of town.

The front door was open. He walked in and checked every room. The place was empty. The stove was cold. The kerosene lamps blazed away in the morning light. There was no sign of Julie Golden.

Back outside, Spur saw fresh hoof prints leading from the house.

If she'd left town she was a smart woman, Spur thought. True, it seemed that everything she'd done had been controlled and instigated by Lionel Kemp, but that would be hard to prove now that he was dead.

At any rate, the silver robberies wouldn't continue.

He closed the door, sighed and walked to Mayor Kincaid's house.

"You have to think about your future, young woman!" Emma Grieve crossed her bony arms. "Only a rich man will give you all the things that this cruel world will stubbornly refuse to hand you on a silver platter. Until you meet the right one you'll have to earn your living. We'll simply have to find you a good position somewhere."

"Really, grandmother!" Melissa smoothed her skirt over her legs as they sat on the porch bench in front of the Eastern Heights Hotel. "Just because you did it, doesn't mean that I have to!"

The elderly woman shook her head. "Did what?"

"You know very well, you old biddy! What Ma made me do!" Melissa's cheeks colored.

Emma Grieve held her breath and chuckled. "Melissa, your mind's a train that always pulls into the same station. Young lady, I'm not talking about that. I can tell it doesn't suit you. But what about the stage?"

Melissa looked away from her. "It doesn't leave until next week."

"Child, listen to me! You have a fine voice. You can dance. Why don't you become an entertainer? You could tour the west, giving shows in saloons, earning good money. The men in lots of these towns are starving for something to look at, to listen to, to dream about. Oh, I know what they say back east about female entertainers. They call them tramps. That may be, but singing and dancing's a might easier to do than earning a living on your back."

Melissa grabbed her grandmother's arm and shushed her. A man in a clerical collar stopped in shock before the women, blanched and hurried off.

"I know," the girl said. "Maybe you're right. It might be fun, dressing up and putting on shows like I used to do every Christmas." She rubbed her palms together.

"You think about it, girl." Emma patted her shoulder. "You could be a big star someday, even go back East, open your own place and settle down there—with or without a fat, rich husband."

Melissa smiled.

"I'm sorry, Mr. McCoy. My father's out doing something or other." Kelly Kincaid licked her lips as she stood in the doorway. "But he thought you might be stopping by, so he left you this note. Please come in."

Spur walked in and took the piece of paper.

"McCoy, stay put until I get back. I'm sure my daughter can entertain you.

Kincaid."

He looked up at Kelly. The eighteen year old girl stepped past him and closed the door. She turned her eyes to his and simply stared.

After a heated visual exchange, Kelly smiled. "Will you accept my father's hospitality, Mr. McCoy?"

"Ah, sure! I wouldn't want to offend him." The tension between the man and the young woman grew. It was stifling hot. "After all, he was a great help last night."

"I'm sure he was." Kelly rubbed her thighs. "Well! Let's not waste any time. My father told me to take good care of you."

He chuckled. "You don't mean—"

"That's precisely what I mean, Spur McCoy. And I always obey my father."

McCoy put out his arms. "So start entertaining!"

# CHAPTER SIXTEEN

She was young, willing and beautiful. But this wasn't the right time, not here in her father's house. The girl's overture was so explicit that Spur cautiously backed from her.

"You don't mean that. Your father would never consent to you and me—"

"You read the letter to you," Kelly Kincaid pointed out. She ripped the mayor's note from Spur's hand. "Please! I really need it! Besides, my father's no ungrateful idiot. He wanted to thank you for all you've done for him, and I suggested something like this."

"Thank me? *You* suggested this?"

"Yes." She advanced on him like a panther after her prey. Kelly licked her lips and tossed her blonde hair.

Spur thought it over for two seconds, slipped off his coat and unbuttoned his shirt.

"What the hell!"

Kelly giggled, her blue eyes flashing. "You know I can be very *entertaining*. Last time was just a rehearsal for the performance I'm about to give you."

"This is going to get you into trouble some day, young lady!"

She struggled out of her green silk dress. "I keep hoping, Spur. But let's not think about that now."

Spur yanked off his boots and socks, straightened and shoved down his trousers, marvelling at the ferocity of the girl's undressing. She tore at her chemise until it split in half and ripped at the three petticoats that hid the lower half of her delicious anatomy.

"Kelly Kincaid! You'd think you've been without a man for years!"

"Heck, Spur." She smiled as she finally unbuttoned the first petticoat. "A few days is like a year."

She was just as beautiful as he'd remembered, McCoy thought as the woman removed the last two petticoats and stood naked before him. Her skin was as white as eggshell, her hips and breasts curved out in all the right directions. Her body was far more developed and mature than those of many other eighteen year old girls. He reached for her.

"Nothing doing," Kelly said, backing from him until she leaned her nude form against the stair railing. "Get outta your drawers! I wanna see him!"

"Hope you want to do more than see him." Spur smirked and kicked off his underwear. His manhood sprung up between his legs, throbbing and ready for work.

"Yes. Oh, yes!"

Kelly jiggled her shoulders back and forth, pressing her lips together and sat on the third step of the stairs. "Come here, you gorgeous hunk of man!"

Spur forgot the dangerous position the girl had put him in and walked to her. "Kelly, I—"

"Shut up. Don't talk. Just put it in my mouth." She licked her lips.

"What the hell."

Her pretty head was just at the right level. Spur sighed as his toes hit the bottom step. Kelly grabbed his hips and impaled herself on his erection. He gasped at the warm liquidity of her mouth, at the fury of her licking tongue, at the girl's willingness to do this to him.

"Mmmmm."

He fell forward, gripped the newel post and slammed a hand against the wall as she pumped her head between his legs. Spur shivered. His penis slid in and out of her mouth. She was so good, he thought. His body tightened. McCoy stifled a gasp. She was almost too good. His elbows buckled.

"Ah, Kelly!" He regained his balance and lightly gripped her head, guiding her erotic movements, gently thrusting into her accommodating mouth. The silky sensations fanned the heat that pulsed in his body.

She should be choking by now, Spur thought. But she wasn't. She wanted more, more. He slid down her throat.

"Jesus, Kelly!" McCoy snapped out of it. "Come on, little girl. We have to stop. Your father could walk in that door and see us!"

She groaned and took him until his testicles pooled on her cute chin.

"Shit! Kelly, you're too damned good. I'm ready to shoot off in your mouth!"

Kelly still wouldn't stop, so Spur forcibly pulled out of her and stood back. He gasped as his penis spasmed and throbbed, staring in disbelief at the seemingly innocent but gloriously naked young woman.

"Just when it was getting so fine." She pouted and delicately wiped her lips.

"Look, Kelly. Maybe we better go upstairs. To your bedroom. You know? Most people do it in beds."

"Really?"

"Kelly!"

"Ah, don't spoil my fun!"

The lithe young woman spun around, planted her hands on the third step and stuck her beautiful bottom into the air. "Whatever you say, Spur. Let's go right up."

He grunted, appreciating Kelly's round backside. His control broke.

"Come on! Climb onto my back and we'll go to my bedroom. If that's what you really want." Her voice was sexy-husky. "Do you, Spur?"

He laughed. "Okay, little lady. You win." He rubbed his organ against her wet lips. The warmth of her body enflamed him. "You win the grand prize."

"And it sure is grand! Stick it in, Spur! Slam me with your sausage!"

Rubbing her cheeks, he sheathed himself, pushing into her slick opening, unable to stop until he'd drilled as far as he could go. The incredible tight wetness shocked him. Kelly groaned and came alive, bucking, writhing, as raw sensation exploded in her body.

"Yes. Oh, yes!"

Spur reared back and smoothly plowed into her. They were perfect for each other—two people needing the same thing, the same hot pleasures that woman and man have shared since the beginning of time.

Her buttocks bounced as he pumped in and out, slamming himself full-length, enjoying her body. Kelly groaned and flung her head back in time with each of the man's deep, penetrating thrusts.

Spur broke out in sweat. The room heated with the sun and the intensity of their actions. Kelly turned a lust-crazed face toward him and gasped.

"Ram me!"

She worked his penis with her internal muscles. He rode her so hard that his plunging set off her pleasure. The young woman spasmed and screamed as pure electricity exploded through her body. She shook like a wet dog and howled.

As she rocked through her orgasm Spur hunched over her, slapping his hairy chest to her back. He took her hanging breasts in his hands and squeezed her nipples, intensifying the young woman's experience. Feeling those luscious orbs sent him over the edge.

Somewhere far behind him the door opened, but Spur forgot it. His body jerked. Every muscle in his lean frame tightened as he poured his seed into Kelly, blasting his lust into the lovely lady, cursing and gasping and hugging her as he shook through his ultimate pleasure.

It was too soon but he didn't care. Spur ecstatically roared. He slowed his spastic pumps, edging away from the moment until they were firmly connected and their drenched bodies were plastered together.

"Ah, um, I'll leave you two alone."

Dazed from the sex, Spur turned a weary head behind him. Mayor Justin Kincaid shot him a funny smile.

"May—Kin—I mean!" One last tremor rippled through him. "I can—"

He laughed. "McCoy, you better get some rest. Looks like you need it." Justin Kincaid left his house.

"Kelly, ah, Kelly!" McCoy said. He started to pull out of her but the woman slammed back against his thighs.

"What?"

"Your father—"

"Don't—don't worry about him." She gasped and pleasurably groaned. "I told you. He's used to seeing me like this. Besides, he said I could."

Spur nodded, though she couldn't see it. The young woman slowly lifted her body onto the third step. McCoy moved with her, maintaining their pulsating contact until he was curled up behind her. They lay on the cool wood until their heartbeats levelled and their breathing returned to normal.

"Your father's almost as remarkable as you," he said.

"Thanks!" Kelly sighed and twisted her head around. "Spur McCoy, that was absolutely exhausting." She quickly pressed her full lips to his.

"Agreed," he said, kissing the girl's nose.

"And I think we should do it again."

He groaned.

Two hours after he'd first walked into Justin Kincaid's house, Spur let the mayor's daughter bathe him. He dressed and finally managed to leave the still unsatisfied girl.

A woman like that could be dangerous to a man, he thought as he walked to the telegraph office. In more ways than one.

McCoy sent a telegram to General Halleck. In it he detailed the things he'd accomplished in Oreville. The robberies were permanently stopped. He'd prevented the success of a major attack against Cleve Magnus's mine. The one man responsible was unavoidably dead. Spur said that he was ready for his next assignment.

He had no qualms about letting Cleve Magnus kill Lionel Kemp early that morning. It may not have been right, but Spur couldn't have stopped it. Besides, in the miner's mind, the battle that had raged last night was still going on.

As he walked from the telegraph office into the blazing desert sunshine, Spur reseated his newly bought hat (to replace the one he'd lost track of during his swim in the Merrone River) and headed for the Eastern Heights Hotel.

Three days until the next stage out of town. He could buy a horse and leave, but he deserved a short holiday. It would give him time to ride out to see Magnus again.

The man saved him a trip out to the mine. Cleve rode up to the hotel and dismounted just as Spur was walking in.

"McCoy! Just wanted to thank you," the short miner said as he tied up his horse at the hitching post.

Spur smiled. "No thanks necessary. You know that I was just doing my job."

"Yeah, sure. Lots of men could have ridden into my camp and saved my butt the way you did!" He snorted. "You know exactly what you were guarding? You want to know how much smelted silver I had in the house?"

"Tell me."

"I just finished counting it before I rode into town. Five-thousand pounds."

Spur whistled. "I guess there'll be no problem in you supplying the Bureau of Engraving and Printing with the silver they need."

"Nope."

"How many men did you lose?"

Magnus grabbed his hat. "Too many. Twenty. I'll never be able to repay the bastard who had them killed."

"You, ah, already did." Spur looked up at the sky and whistled.

"Come on, McCoy! Kincaid told me that he was already dead when I shot him out there!"

"I lied. To get you off the hook. Hope it lets you get some sleep at night." He slapped the miner's shoulder and laughed. "Phineas."

The miner's face reddened. "So? Yeah? What's your first name, McCoy? You didn't get that moniker while you was a little sucking baby! They didn't call you Spur then!"

He turned and walked into the hotel. "True," he

said, "but they sure as hell didn't call me Phineas!"

Twenty miles from Oreville, Julie Golden broke twigs between her hands and made kindling. Phillipas dumped an armload of wood in front of her.

He produced some matches, expertly laid the wood and touched a flaming lucifer to the stack. The fire crackled into life. Phillipas drove a forked stick into the ground beside it and hooked on the coffee pot.

At midday, the sun burned directly overhead. The heat from the fire made Julie move away from it. A bird twittered as it flew overhead.

"You ever get used to those stupid saddles? I'm rubbed raw down there!" she said, soothing the inside of her thighs.

The Greek laughed. "Yes, in time."

"I'll believe you because it's less painful than the alternative." She fixed her green eyes on his. "Where should we go?"

He shrugged. "I do not know. You're the boss."

"Stop saying that, Phillipas!" Julie tossed her head and stood. The pain intensified. "Hell, if I had my way we'd stay here. I never want to see another horse again!"

Her mount whinneyed.

"I think that would be fine with her."

"You—you!"

Julie fell onto him, knocking the sturdy man to the sand. She chewed on his moustache and peppered his face with kisses.

"Julie, my Julie."

Satisfied at her revenge, she slipped to the ground

and nuzzled his neck. "You know who told Magnus about us? About our attack?"

"No," he said, biting her ear.

"Ouch! Whoever it was, I guess I owe him a favor." She sighed at the feeling of Phillipas' tongue and teeth.

"Why? He ruined everything! We didn't get one ounce of silver!"

"Quite true, my Greek friend. But I got the best thing of all. You."

He laughed and kicked the coffeepot onto the fire. Phillipas pushed Julie onto the dirt as the flames sputtered and went out.

 **DIRK FLETCHER**

**The pistol-hot Western series filled with more brawls and beauties than a frontier saloon on a Saturday night!**

*Spur #40: Texas Tramp.* When a band of bloodthirsty Comanches kidnaps the sultry daughter of a state senator, the sheriff of Sweet Springs call on Spur McCoy to rescue the tempting Penny Wallington. Once McCoy chops the Indians' totem poles down to size, he will have Penny for his thoughts—and a whole lot of woman in his hands.
__3523-5                     $3.99 US/$4.99 CAN

*Spur #39: Minetown Mistress.* While tracking down a missing colonel in Idaho Territory, Spur runs into a luscious blonde and a randy redhead who appoint themselves his personal greeters. He'll waste no time finding the lost man—because only then can he take a ride with the fillies who drive his private welcome wagon.
__3448-4                     $3.99 US/$4.99 CAN

*Spur #38: Free Press Filly.* Sent to investigate the murder of a small-town newspaper editor, McCoy is surprised to discover his contact is Gypsy, the man's busty daughter, who believes in a free press and free love. Gun's blazing, lust raging, McCoy has to kill the killer so he can put the story—and Gypsy—to bed.
__3394-1                     $3.99 US/$4.99 CAN

**LEISURE BOOKS**
**ATTN: Order Department**
**276 5th Avenue, New York, NY 10001**

Please add $1.50 for shipping and handling for the first book and $.35 for each book thereafter. PA., N.Y.S. and N.Y.C. residents, please add appropriate sales tax. No cash, stamps, or C.O.D.s. All orders shipped within 6 weeks via postal service book rate. Canadian orders require $2.00 extra postage and must be paid in U.S. dollars through a U.S. banking facility.

Name _____
Address _____
City _____ State _____ Zip _____
I have enclosed $_____ in payment for the checked book(s).
Payment <u>must</u> accompany all orders.☐ Please send a free catalog.

# BUCKSKIN GIANT
# SPECIAL EDITIONS
## Kit Dalton

*The hard-riding, hard-bitten Adult Western series
that's hotter'n a blazing pistol and as tough as
the men and women who tamed the frontier!*

*Muzzle Blast.* A vicious little hellcat with a heavenly body,
Molly Niles is the kind of trouble Buckskin Lee Morgan
likes, especially when she makes him a deal he can't refuse.
If he drives her horses from Niles City to Fort Buell, the
hot-blooded beauty will pay him cold cash. Lee takes the
offer, and things heat up quick—on the trail and in the
bedroll. It is a tough job, but Morgan has grit enough to guide
the ponies, and spunk enough to tame a wild filly like Molly.
_3564-2                              $4.99 US/$5.99 CAN

*Six-gun Shootout.* The Old West is full of towns ruled by
brute force and lawless greed, but Rock Springs, Wyoming
Territory, is the worst. It takes a man with a taste for lead
to survive there—a man like Buckskin Lee Morgan. When
an old girlfriend calls on Morgan to find the gutless murderer
who ambushed her husband, he is more than ready to act
as judge, jury and executioner. For Morgan lives by one law:
anyone who messes with his women is a dead man!
_3383-6                              $4.50 US/$5.50 CAN